D0553789

"What is this?" he asked slowly. His gaze swept briefly over her face. The frown line between his eyes sharpened.

Her face burned so hot that she doubted she needed the rouge on her cheekbones. "We purchased some makeup at the East Market yesterday."

Fei Long's lip curled. "You look ridiculous."

Her heart squeezed tight. Then it plummeted, like a crushed and ruined butterfly.

In so few words he had scattered all her confidence, all her hopes. There was no pleasing Fei Long. Not looking at him, she scrubbed at the tint until her lips were raw. She wanted it off—all of it. The powders, the perfume and all pretense that she could be a lady worth any notice.

"Yan Ling."

He rose from his desk to move toward her. She tried to slip past.

In the next moment she caught a glimpse of Fei Long's face, of his dark and tortured eyes. A muscle tensed along his jaw before he lowered his head....

* * *

My Fair Concubine
Harlequin® Historical #1094—June 2012

Author Note

This story was a bit of a departure from the high drama of my previous works. The Tang Dynasty was a golden age of Chinese culture, and I wanted to explore the vast capital city of Changan with its infamous entertainment district and teeming marketplaces. *My Fair Concubine* allowed me to play a little with a beloved classic theme while adding a Tang Dynasty twist of my own.

For history buffs, the practice of *heqin,* or peace marriage, was a very important diplomatic practise, which the Tang rulers used more than in any other era to keep the peace with neighboring kingdoms such as Tibet and Khitai. The alliance brides ranged from daughters or nieces of the emperor to palace women to daughters of court officials. A substantial body of poetry and writing exists about and by the *heqin* brides, and they achieved a certain legendary status. A famous poem by Princess Xijun lamenting her marriage "to the other side of heaven" is referenced in the book.

The collection of characters in this tale allowed me to explore people from more humble origins, and their actions unfolded before me like the scenes of a play. There is not much detailed writing on the lives of servants, tea house girls or actors, so I took liberties to fill out the players with my imagination. I hope you enjoy the journey through tea houses and city parks, as well as an adventurous jaunt to the bawdy, seedier side of the imperial capital.

I love hearing from readers. For more information about my stories, or to contact me, I can be found online at www.jeannielin.com.

My Fair Concubine

JEANNIE LIN

™ **Harlequin**®

TORONTO NEW YORK LONDON
AMSTERDAM PARIS SYDNEY HAMBURG
STOCKHOLM ATHENS TOKYO MILAN MADRID
PRAGUE WARSAW BUDAPEST AUCKLAND

Recycling programs
for this product may
not exist in your area.

ISBN-13: 978-0-373-29694-1

MY FAIR CONCUBINE

Copyright © 2012 by Chi Nguyen-Rettig

Printed in U.S.A.

Available from Harlequin® Historical and
JEANNIE LIN

Butterfly Swords #1014
The Dragon and the Pearl #1062
My Fair Concubine #1094

and in Harlequin Historical *Undone!* ebooks

The Taming of Mei Lin
The Lady's Scandalous Night
Capturing the Silken Thief

Dedication

As always, I have to thank my editor, Anna Boatman,
and my agent, Gail Fortune, for their continued insight
and support, no matter where my writing takes me.
This story owes a lot to the Tuesday critique group: Amanda Berry,
Shawntelle Madison, Kristi Lea and Dawn Blankenship.
Thank you for all the feedback, brainstorming and gossip sessions.
To my last line of defence: Little Sis, Inez Kelly and
Bria Quinlan—I don't know how I'd be able to ever let a story
out of my hands without you. Finally, a special thanks to
Inez's husband, Ryan, and Louise Harrison
for their help in the archery scenes.

Praise for
Jeannie Lin

THE DRAGON AND THE PEARL
"Beautifully written, deliciously sensual and rich with
Tang Dynasty historical and political detail, this exquisitely
crafted, danger-filled and intriguing story redeems the ruthless
villain from Lin's *Butterfly Swords* (a remarkable feat in itself),
pairs him with a smart, resourceful heroine and lets them play
cat and mouse for much of the book before joining forces
for a well-deserved romantic ending. Exceptional."
—*Library Journal*

BUTTERFLY SWORDS
"Chang Ai Li flees her wedding and her enraged bridegroom
in Lin's exciting debut, an adventure tale set in turbulent
eighth-century China. Especially vibrant writing describing
the culture, clothes and countryside."
—*Publishers Weekly,* starred review

"If *Crouching Tiger, Hidden Dragon* merged with
A Knight's Tale, you'd have the power and romance of
Lin's dynamic debut. The action never stops, the love story
is strong and the historical backdrop is fascinating."
—*RT Book Reviews*

Chapter One

China, Tang Dynasty—AD 824

Fei Long faced the last room at the end of the narrow hallway, unsheathed his sword and kicked the door open.

A feminine shriek pierced the air along with the frantic shuffle of feet as he strode through the entrance. The boarding room was a small one set above the teahouse below. The inhabitants, a man and a woman, flung themselves into the corner with nowhere to hide.

His gaze fixed on to the woman first. His sister's hair was unbound and her eyes wide with fear. Pearl had their mother's thoughtful features: the high forehead and the sharp angles that had softened since the last time he'd seen her. She was dressed only in pale linen underclothes. The man who was with her had enough daring to step in between them.

Fei Long glanced once to the single wooden bed against one wall, the covers strewn wide, and his vision blurred with anger. He gripped the sword until his knuckles nearly cracked with the strain.

'Bastard,' he gritted out through his teeth.

He knew this man he'd come to kill. This *boy*. At least Han had been a boy when Fei Long had last seen him. And Pearl had been a mere girl. Now she was a grown woman, staring at him as if he were a demon risen from the underworld.

'Fei Long.' Pearl's fingers curled tight over her lover's arm. 'So *now* you've come.'

The soft bitterness of the accusation cut through him. Pearl had begged for him to come back a year earlier when her marriage had first been arranged, but he'd dismissed her letters as childish ramblings. If he had listened, she might not have thrown herself into ruin and their father's spirit wouldn't be floating restlessly between heaven and earth.

The young man stretched himself before Fei Long, though he failed to match him in stature. 'Not in front of Pearl,' he implored.

Though he trembled, the boy fought to keep his voice steady as Pearl clung to him, hiding just behind his shoulder. At least the dog managed to summon some courage. If Han had cowered or begged for his life, he would already be dead.

'Step away, Little Sister,' Fei Long commanded.

'No.'

'Pearl.'

'I'd rather die here with Han than go to Khitan.'

She'd changed in the five years since he'd seen her. The Pearl he remembered had been obedient, sweet-tempered and pleasant in all things. Fei Long had ridden hard from Chang-an to this remote province, expecting to find the son of a dog who had stolen her away.

Now that she stood before him with quiet defiance, he knew she hadn't been seduced or deceived. Zheng Xie Han's family lived within their ward in the capital city. Though lower in standing, the Zheng family had always maintained a good reputation. His sister had turned to Han because she'd had no one else.

The tension drained out of Fei Long, stealing away his rage. His throat pulled tight as he forced out the next word. 'Go.'

The two of them stared at him in disbelief.

'Go,' he repeated roughly.

Fei Long lowered his weapon and turned away while they dressed themselves. Shoving his sword back into its sheath, he faced the bare wall. He could hear the shuffle of movement behind him as the couple gathered their belongings.

The bleakness of the last few weeks settled into his gut like a stone. When he'd left for his assignment to the north-western garrison, Fei Long had believed his home to be a harmonious place. Upon news of his father's sudden death, he'd returned to find his sister gone and debt collectors circling the front gates like vultures.

His father's presence had been an elaborate screen, hiding the decay beneath the lacquered surface of their lives. Fei Long now saw Pearl's arranged marriage for what it was: a desperate ploy to restore the family honour—or rather to prolong the illusion of respectability.

When he turned again, Pearl and Han stood watching him tentatively. Each of them had a pack slung around their shoulder. Off to face the horizon with all their belongings stowed in two small bags.

Han bowed once. 'Elder Brother.'

The young man risked Fei Long's temper to deliver the honorific. Fei Long couldn't bring himself to return the bow. Pearl met his eyes as they started for the door. The heaviness of her expression struck him like a physical blow.

This was the last time he would ever see his sister.

Fei Long took his money pouch from his belt and held it out. The handful of coppers rattled inside. 'Here.'

Han didn't look at him as he took it.

'Thank you, Fei Long,' Pearl whispered.

They didn't embrace. The two of them had been apart for

so long that they wouldn't have known how. Fei Long watched their backs as they retreated down the stairway; gone like everything else he had once known to be true.

'Jilted lover,' the cook guessed.

Yan Ling's eyes grew wide. The stranger had stormed up the staircase only moments earlier with a sword strapped to his side and the glint of murder in his deep-set eyes. She'd leapt out of the path of his charge, just managing to hold on to her pot of tea without spilling a drop.

She stood at the edge of the main room, head cocked to listen for sounds of mayhem upstairs. Her heart raced as she gripped the handle of the teapot. Such violence and scandal were unthinkable in their quiet town.

'Should someone stop him?' she asked.

'What? You saw how he was dressed.' Old Cook had his feet in the kitchen, but the rest of him strained as far into the dining area as possible. 'A man like that can do whatever he wants.'

'Get back to work,' the proprietor barked.

Yan Ling jumped and the cook ducked his head back through the beaded curtain that separated the main room from the kitchen.

'Worthless girl,' her master muttered as she rushed the pot of tea to its intended table. She pressed her fingers against the ceramic to check the temperature of the pot before setting it down. Cooler than ideal, but still hot enough to not get any complaints.

It was late in the morning and the patrons had thinned, but that was never an excuse to move any slower. Lately it seemed nothing she did was fast or efficient enough. She'd never known any life but the teahouse. The story was she'd been abandoned as an infant in the room upstairs, likely the very same one where a new scandal was now unfolding.

She paused to stack empty cups onto a tray. At that moment, the young woman and her companion hurried down the stairs, leaving not even a farewell behind as they swept out the door. Yan Ling expected the sword-carrying nobleman to come chasing after them, but only an uncomfortable silence followed their exit.

The patrons began to whisper among themselves. Her master should be happy. This incident would have the townsfolk lingering over more than a few extra teapots worth of gossip.

When he finally emerged, the gentleman appeared surprisingly calm. He descended the stairs with a steady, powerful stride and his expression was as still as the surface of the moon. Instead of leaving, he marched directly over to the proprietor and flashed an official-looking jade seal. At that point, even the proprietor's wife flocked over to welcome him. They ushered him to an empty table at the centre of the room, nearly breaking their backs bowing with such enthusiasm. Her master shot Yan Ling a sharp look, which she understood immediately. Bring tea and fast. She rushed to the kitchen.

'Is there a lot of blood?' the kitchen boy asked as she pushed through the curtain.

'Shush.'

She poured hot water over a fresh pot of leaves and flew back out with her hand around the bamboo handle. Back out in the main room, the stranger didn't even spare her a glance as she poured the first cup for him.

His robe was of fine woven silk and richly dyed in a dark blue. He wore his thick hair long, the front of it pulled back into a knot in the style of aristocracy. She was stricken by the strength of his features: the hard line of his cheekbones and the broad shape of his face, which narrowed slightly at the chin.

With a cursory bow, she set the pot down and moved away. There were other tables to tend to and most patrons wanted to drink their tea in peace. Yet her attention kept on wandering back to the stranger.

Hours later, he was still seated in the same spot. He wasn't even drinking his tea any more. Instead, he had taken to staring into his cup.

Government official, they guessed in the back room, though he travelled without any escort and had a sullen expression that continued to sink lower as the day slipped by. Her guess was that he needed something stronger than tea.

By the end of the day, Yan Ling moved from table to empty table in a restless circle, wash rag in hand, as she wiped away at wooden surfaces rubbed bare from use. The teahouse crowd had long returned to their homes. Only the nobleman remained, still hoarding his cold tea.

As long as he stayed there, she was supposed to attend to him. Her master had made that very clear while he sat comfortably in the corner, tallying up the cash. The wooden beads of his abacus clicked together, signalling that the day should be done.

Her feet ached and no matter how much she wriggled her toes in her slippers, the feeling wouldn't quite return to them. The clang from the kitchen meant that the cook and his boy were cleaning their pots. A mountain of cups and bowls and little plates would be waiting for her.

Cook tried to get her to pry information from the man, but of course she wouldn't do such a thing. He'd suffered enough public scrutiny that day to deserve some privacy. She guessed him to be twenty-five years, with a slight crease between his eyes that she imagined came more from deep contemplation than age.

Gingerly, she approached the table. 'Does the honoured guest need anything?'

She reached for the clay teapot, only to have him wave her back with an irritated scowl. For a gentleman, he was uncommonly rude, but she supposed wearing silk and jade gave him that privilege. He propped his elbows onto the table, shoulders hunched, to return to his vigil. From the emptiness of his stare, the young woman had to have been someone close to him. His wife? But no man would let his wife escape with a lover after catching them together.

Yan Ling turned to wipe down her already-cleaned table once more when the stranger spoke.

'I need a woman,' he mumbled. 'Any woman would do.'

Her stomach dropped. She swung around, her mouth open in shock. The stranger raised his head. For the first time, his eyes focused on her, looking her up and down.

'Perhaps even you.'

Any sympathy she might have had for him withered away. If his tone had been leering, or his look more appraising, it might have been less offensive. But the coldly pensive way he'd said it along with the addition of 'perhaps', as if to plunge her worth even further—Yan Ling grabbed the teapot and flung the contents at the scoundrel.

The stranger shot to his feet with a curse. With a choked cry, her master jumped up from his table and his wife soared like a windstorm from the kitchen, apologising profusely. Even the cook and his boy were gawking through the curtained doorway.

'Get out!' the master's wife shrieked at Yan Ling before turning to fuss at their precious patron. The front of his expensive robe was stained dark with a splatter of tea.

'We are so sorry, my lord,' she crooned. 'So sorry.'

Yan Ling clutched the teapot between both her hands while she stared.

The nobleman swiped the tea leaves away in one angry motion while his eyes remained fixed on her. He had lost that distant, brooding expression he'd worn all day. The look he gave her was possibly worse than the one she'd seen as he'd charged up the stairs. Heat rose up her neck as she stumbled back.

What had she done?

'That know-nothing, good-for-nothing girl,' her master railed.

Her ears rang as she ducked into the kitchen through the beaded curtain. Steam enclosed her, but the clang of the pots couldn't block the sounds of her master and his wife apologising profusely to the nobleman.

It wasn't as if she hadn't been taunted before, but over the last years the teasing had taken on a different tone as her bone-thin figure had curved its way into womanhood. She'd learned to deafen her ears and stare ahead, never meeting any of the not-so-subtle glances thrown her way. Yet to suffer such insult from someone who appeared so refined—it was unbearable.

Ignoring the curious stares from cook and the kitchen boy, she slipped through the back door. Her palms were damp and she wiped them restlessly against the sides of her grey tunic. Fear set her heart skittering.

The teahouse was where she'd lived all her life, but it was not home. The proprietor and his wife were not her father and mother. This had always been clear to her and she'd had to earn her bed, this roof and every meal with service and obedience.

One moment of hot-headedness. She'd lashed out at a well-dressed nobleman, of all people. She wasn't even a servant when it came to this man. She was the humble servant of humble servants. Who was she to be outraged?

She would certainly be scolded by both master and mistress, each separately and then together. Yan Ling could hear them already. She had become too much of a burden to feed, to clothe. She wasn't even pretty enough to bring in more customers. They might even be angry enough to take a bamboo switch to her.

A beating was all she'd have to suffer, if she was lucky.

Fei Long rose after no more than three hours of sleep in the very same sparse boarding room where he'd found Pearl, above the cursed teahouse. There weren't any other lodgings in this small town. To add to his shame, he'd needed to leave a promissory note with the proprietor affixed with his family seal in return for his stay. All of his money had gone with his sister.

The morning sun streaming through the shutters didn't bring any more clarity. Brooding over the situation hadn't given him any solutions either. Once he returned to the capital, he'd have to face the consequences of letting Pearl go. He tied back his hair and dressed himself, attaching his sword at his belt. The robe had dried from the tea that the she-demon had thrown at him. It was a minor mishap in an epic tale of disaster. The tragic tale had started with the unexpected news of his father's death and would likely end with him throwing himself on the imperial court's mercy.

A stretch of dirt road separated the inn from the town centre, which was a cluster of wooden buildings overlooking the market area. Beyond this road, the cities would shrink to the tiny villages and settlements barely known to the heart of the empire.

Pearl's future was left to the open road and to fate now. Perhaps it was a better situation than his. His sister was free without the weight of the family name bearing down on her. As eldest son, as only son, preserving their honour was his burden.

An attendant brought his horse from the stable. As he headed toward the animal, a small, grey figure shot out into the street.

'My lord!'

A quick glance revealed the teahouse girl scurrying in his direction. He turned his back on her as he took the reins from the attendant.

'My lord, please wait.' She sounded harried and out of breath behind him. He didn't answer as he faced the horse to the street, leading him by the bridle.

'I must beg your pardon,' she continued, her footsteps trailing behind his.

So, none of the impudence she'd shown the previous night. He could be generous. It was a small insult considering, and not worth the trouble.

'Granted.'

He braced his foot in the stirrup to prepare to mount, when a tug at his sleeve stopped him.

The young woman recoiled as he turned to her. 'Please. Forgive my intrusion, honourable sir. My lord…'

The list of courtesies made him impatient. He frowned as he waited for her to finish. She clasped her hands together nervously and spoke faster.

'I've been thrown out by the teahouse owner!'

Her bottom lip trembled and she looked away, trying to hide the unsightly outburst of emotion. Her hair was tied in a simple fashion and allowed to sweep down over one shoulder. For the first time, he noticed that her eyes were red and slightly swollen.

'That was not my intention,' he replied gravely.

Once again, he tried to mount. Again, she reached for him. This time, he stopped before she needed to tug at him. She took two steps away instead of one when he swung around. Did propriety mean nothing to her?

'I am truly sorry for ruining your robe. I'll wash it myself,' she promised. 'If you can just speak to the proprietor and his wife.'

The horse tossed his head, agitated with the delay. Fei Long felt the same agitation growing within him.

'This matter is not my concern.'

'I'm being punished—'

'As you should be,' he replied simply.

There was no cruelty in his words. Despite being attacked

without provocation, he hadn't demanded retribution. She was fortunate he didn't believe in beating servants.

'But I've apologised.' She blocked his path now, this willow-thin girl who was all eyes and hair. 'Sincerely, humbly, with all my soul, apologised. Please take pity. Won't you help me?'

He made a scoffing noise at the back of his throat, which seemed to startle her. She frowned at him.

'These are your amends to make, not mine, young miss. Go humble yourself before your master and mistress and make your plea with them.' He started to lead the horse forwards, trying to put some distance between them to show that the matter was closed. 'Besides, you are not sorry at all.'

For a second, her eyes flashed. Her mouth hardened much like it had back in the teahouse before he found himself drenched in cold tea. If she'd had anything in hand to throw, he would have prepared to duck.

Less than a breath later, her expression grew plaintive and accommodating. 'But I am sorry, my lord.' She padded beside him, taking two steps for each of his one. 'I've worked for the teahouse since I was a child. There's nowhere else I can go. A girl like me out in the streets…'

Her voice trailed away in defeat and Fei Long halted. He was reminded of Pearl, though there was no reason for it. The girl looked nothing like his sister. Unlike Pearl, she was thin, hard-headed and she had a mouth on her.

He'd spared Pearl from the political marriage that their father had arranged, but now she was left to wander without a home. He would always wonder if his actions had truly been a kindness. Unlike Pearl, this tea girl didn't have anyone by her side.

'How old are you?' he asked.

She was taken aback by the question. 'Nineteen years.'

A little older than Pearl, but that might be a benefit. He already had a sense that this teahouse girl was much shrewder than his sheltered younger sister.

'Can you read and write?'

'Only numbers.'

A wispy cloud of an idea had begun to form while he was wallowing at the teahouse last night. A thin spark of light, before it had been effectively doused by a cascade of cold tea flung in his face. The plan came back now as he stared at the same culprit who'd snapped him out of those musings.

'Smile,' he said.

She blinked at him warily, then forced her mouth upwards in what ended up looking more like a grimace. He looked down at her feet next. They shrank back from his scrutiny, as she curled her toes back within the slippers.

His gaze returned to her face and he kept his open perusal for assessment purposes only: dark eyes set against smooth skin. Fair enough to pass for a lady's. The set of her jaw was too hard and her face was on the thin side, though her features were not unpleasant to look at if she didn't scowl so. Softened a bit she could even be…pretty. Not that beauty was required for what he had in mind.

'You are more peculiar than I thought,' she muttered, backing away.

With her head lifted and shoulders raised, as they were right now, she took on a semblance of righteousness and pride that might just be suitable for the part.

He let go of the reins. 'I have a proposal for you.'

'I know exactly what sort of proposal you mean.' She shook an accusing finger at him. 'I don't care how rich you are, I was right to pour that tea on you.'

Now it was his turn to pursue her. And it took some effort. She was walking fast down the street.

'Young miss, let me explain.'

Her step quickened. 'Leave me alone. I may not be learned

or wear expensive clothes like you, but I'm a respectable girl. I won't do…do *that*.'

'*That* wasn't what I meant.'

The townsfolk paused in their morning stroll through the marketplace. Their discussion was starting to gather attention.

Fei Long angled himself in front of her, cutting off her escape. He dropped his tone. 'What I'm proposing is very respectable. A matter of imperial duty, in fact.'

She snorted. He was suddenly convinced that before him was the answer to his dilemma. The teahouse girl had nowhere to go and he needed someone to replace Pearl. Khitan was a rough, untamed land compared to the empire. This she-demon was bold enough to carry off such a deception. She was delicate in appearance at least, and not so hardened that she couldn't be schooled. There was little elegance about her now, but that could be changed.

There was much work to do before she could pass as a daughter from a good family. They didn't have much time, but he was convinced it could be done. It had to be done.

'My family name is Chang, personal name Fei Long,' he began. 'My father was an official within the Ministry of Works and our family lives in the capital city. Have you ever been to Changan?'

She looked over one shoulder, then the other, as if reassuring herself that they were indeed in a crowded public area and she was safe from his clutches. 'No,' she answered finally.

'What's your name, young miss?' he asked.

If he could get past this polite exchange, then he had a chance of convincing her. Two strangers who exchanged names were, of course, no longer strangers. Even peasants would understand those rules of courtesy.

She took her time assessing him, taking in the height and breadth of him, and staring at the sword in his belt. The girl would duck and bow when necessary, but this was no shy and sheltered nightingale. She had a boldness within her that Pearl lacked. He waited anxiously for her reply. For the first time in weeks, hope burned inside him, embodied in this tiny reed of a girl.

'I don't know of my family name,' she replied, still hesitant. 'But I'm called Yan Ling.'

'It's called *heqin*,' he explained.

The nobleman looked to her for acknowledgement and she had to shake her head. Fei Long led his horse down the street while she walked beside him, falling a few paces behind in deference.

'An arranged peace marriage,' he continued. 'My sister was selected to go to the land of Khitan to be married to a foreign lord.'

So the young woman had been his sister. 'Where is Khitan?'

'North of the Taiyuan prefecture.'

She nodded. They continued for a few steps.

'Where is Taiyuan?'

He paused and her face grew hot as he regarded her, but there was no need to be ashamed. Of course he knew more than she did about foreign lands. She'd only left town a few times to accompany her master to major festivals. The thought of leaving town now with Fei Long frightened her, but the thought of being left to the streets frightened her more.

'I can show you a map some time,' he said, in a tone that was not unkind.

She wasn't entirely convinced of his mad tale. And if she did believe him, was it even possible for her to pose as his sister? Everything she said or did felt awkward next to Chang Fei Long. Anyone could see they weren't from the same breed.

'You said they were expecting a princess. I'm no princess.'

'Neither was my sister, Pearl.'

He slowed his stride to match hers and Yan Ling felt especially small, more from the authority in his bearing than from his actual size.

'A past emperor gave one of his favourite daughters away in an alliance marriage to a barbarian chieftain,' he explained. 'The story has since become quite famous. Have you heard of it?'

He paused to look at her and again she shook her head. They didn't speak of the comings and goings of the imperial family in their little teahouse.

'The princess wept and begged for her father to reconsider, composing verses of poetry lamenting what she considered her exile from her beloved empire,' he recounted. 'But the Son of Heaven couldn't rescind the agreement to his ally. When the princess left for foreign lands, the Emperor was heartbroken. When another neighbouring kingdom petitioned for a Tang princess, the Emperor chose one of his concubines and bestowed the title of princess upon her. The newly appointed princess went to fulfil the alliance rather than the Emperor's true blood.'

'So now our Emperor wants to send an imposter instead?' she asked.

'It's not uncommon. The alliance brides may be nieces or distant members of the imperial family. Occasionally even daughters of high-ranking court officials might be chosen. It was a great honour to our family when my sister, Pearl, was elevated to the rank of princess.'

Yan Ling stared at him, trying to sort out the strangeness of such whimsical decrees. 'Wouldn't that make you a prince?'

'Not quite—however, the decree does bestow imperial favour and duties upon our family.' He looked uncomfortable. 'Duties that cannot be refused.'

She supposed the divine Emperor could do whatever he wished. 'But what if the barbarians find out they don't have a real princess?'

'It doesn't matter. The political arrangement itself is the important part. The marriage seals the agreement and the title is just a formality showing the Emperor's commitment.'

She didn't like the thought of being a peace offering, travelling to this faraway place along with bolts of silk and a fleet of horses. Hadn't Fei Long practically looked her over as if she were a horse? Checking her teeth, checking her feet to see that they were small enough to belong to a high-born lady.

'Tang princesses are highly valued in the barbarian lands,' he insisted. 'You'll have every need taken care of.'

A ripple of pleasure ran through her, lazy and warm with promise. She would never need to worry about being cold or hungry again. Her back wouldn't ache from serving customers from the first light of day to deep in the night.

'I couldn't even imagine this if it were a dream. You're just telling stories,' she accused.

'It's true.'

'Then why did your precious sister run away? If I were Miss Pearl, I would never give up such an opportunity.'

He tensed. Only the twitch of a muscle along his jaw revealed any emotion. 'She was young with...romantic notions. Not thinking of reason or duty.' He met her eyes, his gaze scrutinising. 'You seem much more practical.'

'I am very practical,' she agreed. The teahouse had always been about survival and keeping a roof over her head.

They stopped before the town's civil office. Without a word, the nobleman handed her the reins and strode through the front gate, completely assured in her compliance. The horse paced a few restless steps while she clutched at the reins with a life-and-death grip.

'Stop,' she commanded in a fierce whisper. 'Hear me? Stay still, *you*.'

She prayed the horse wouldn't run off. If it decided to, she'd be dragged along with it. She didn't know how to tame a horse.

In truth, she didn't know how to do much more than serve customers in a teahouse. So she stood with the reins wrapped twice around her hand and considered her situation.

To be a princess, even a false one, would be like being re-born into the next life. Perhaps the stars of her birth weren't as dim as she'd always thought. She wanted very much to believe Fei Long, but there were plenty of stories about tricksters travelling the countryside, collecting young women in order to sell them off to brothels. Fei Long could very well be one of those scoundrels, though he struck her as honest. Maybe too much so. If anything, he seemed lost in this fancy scheme of his.

At times, he intimidated her with his proper manners and knowledge. At other times, she considered smacking him across that thick skull of his—which had been the start of all her troubles.

Fei Long emerged from the gates and came towards her, holding a pouch in his hand.

She gave up the reins with relief. 'What is that?'

'I have to settle with the teahouse. An honourable man repays all his debts.'

From the heft and size of the pouch, it must have held more coins than a month's take at the teahouse. She chuckled.

'What do you find so funny?'

'They just gave that to you?'

'Yes,' Fei Long said, puzzled.

She laughed outright. She couldn't help herself. For some reason, this was the funniest thing she'd ever seen. She recalled the jade seal that he had shown at the teahouse, which practically had her master kow-towing.

'They just give you money…' she caught her breath between gasps '…for nothing!'

She shook her head and grabbed at her sides. They ached from laughing so hard. When she looked up, Chang Fei Long was glaring at her.

'Our family name is good as a guarantee of payment,' he said stiffly.

She sucked in a breath and tried to compose herself. Of course it wasn't funny to him that someone like her would never touch money of her own, no matter how hard she laboured. Lord Chang simply had to walk into a municipal office. Yet she was the beggar, he the nobleman.

Money from air. All things were possible—even a peasant posing as a princess in a foreign land.

'Yes,' she said, in a long-delayed answer to his proposal. 'Yes, I'll go with you, my lord.'

They headed back towards the teahouse then. Her former master would see that she was leaving town with the same gentleman they'd thrown her out over. The thought had her doubling over in laughter once more.

Chapter Two

The journey was a quiet one, with Yan Ling plodding onwards in her slippers while the nobleman rode alongside on his horse. She'd been full of questions at first. How far away was the imperial city and what was his home there like? Fei Long, or Lord Chang, as she was coming to think of him, had a tendency toward short answers. The silence and the ache in her feet slowly drained away her initial sense of adventure.

She stole glances at Chang Fei Long, trying to work out what sort of man she'd tied herself to. It was odd to have such a young master. He was confident in the saddle and the sword at his side seemed like a natural part of him. Everything about him spoke of nobility, from the upward tilt of his chin to the way his shoulders were always pulled back. She tried to imitate his stance when he wasn't looking and her back grew stiff after a few minutes of it.

He must have been wealthy to live in the capital, though he travelled without any attendants. From what little she'd ascertained, he hadn't carefully planned this trip to the provinces.

'Are you tired?' he asked when they stopped for a rest.

'No, my lord.'

He'd taken care of watering and feeding the horse, while she stood watching and wondering what her new duties were. The thin slippers she wore were not fit for travel, but she didn't dare complain even though her feet throbbed with a constant ache. Fei Long was frowning at her so she made sure to remain as quiet as possible.

'We need to make better time,' he grumbled.

Maybe she was wrong about him being young. He certainly had the temperament of a grumpy old man at times.

She bit into the steamed bun he'd bought from a street vendor that morning before they'd left town. The pork filling was cold, but she appreciated the savoury sweetness of it. The journey had left her drained. Keeping her mouth full also ensured she couldn't misspeak. The nobleman might still decide he didn't need the extra trouble of bringing her along. Surely there were more suitable young women in the imperial city. If he abandoned her out on the open road, she'd have nowhere to go.

A sense of helplessness hovered over her as she finished the meal. She didn't know Chang Fei Long's moods yet and it was her duty as a servant to learn those things. He said so little, unlike her former master and mistress who'd had no issues about complaining long and loud.

When he swung himself onto his horse without a word, Yan Ling was certain he'd decided she wasn't worth the trouble. She started preparing her plea, but instead he extended his hand.

'Come,' he said, when she didn't move. 'You barely weigh a *tan*. The horse can carry us both.'

His broad fingers engulfed her slender ones. He tightened his hold to tug her upwards as she braced her foot over his in the stirrup. It was miserable beyond description. She felt like a rag doll, hefted onto the back of the saddle. They were higher off the ground than she had anticipated and she wobbled, clutching on to Fei Long's robe. Fortunately he held on to her and finally got her settled in behind him.

She was pressed against him, closer than she'd ever been to

any man. The expanse of his back and shoulders stretched out before her and her first thought was—how was she supposed to hold on? The warmth of him lingered even after he let go.

Yan Ling had never clung to a man like this, the intimacy all the worse for being forced. She'd never ridden a horse before either and was certain she'd fall and break a bone. The horse gave a snort and shifted forwards. In a panic, she grabbed on to Fei Long's waist, hugging him too tightly. He tossed an irritated glance over his shoulder and she loosened her grip. She shifted on the saddle, trying to find her balance. Eventually she settled on holding on to his shoulders.

'Ready?' he asked.

She nodded, then realised he couldn't see her with his back to her like that. 'Yes, my lord.'

He urged the horse forwards with a slight movement of his heels. Yan Ling tried her best not to touch him too much as she swayed upon the saddle.

The sky was beginning to darken when they reached a walled city. The guards stepped aside to let them pass and Fei Long quickly located an inn along the main avenue. They left the horse to an attendant and headed to a brightly lit restaurant. The double doors were thrown open in welcome. Kitchen smells of garlic and cooking fat wafted out into the streets.

Yan Ling fell into step behind Fei Long as he entered the dining area. The day before, he'd entered their little teahouse with the same assured grace. The host spotted them across the crowded dining room, or rather he noticed Fei Long in his fine robe, and hurried over to greet a valued patron. They were directed to a table at the back and she stood awkwardly while Fei Long seated himself and spoke to the host.

She took to looking about the room. The place was twice the size of their teahouse and nearly every table was full. Her fingers ached just looking at the number of bowls and plates out on the tables. It would take hours to wash all the dishes in a place like this.

A young attendant came by carrying tea. Yan Ling shot forwards to intercept him and there was a brief struggle as she gripped the edges of the lacquered tray.

'Hand it over,' she scolded, managing to take possession of the tea without spilling a drop. The boy gave her a confused look before wandering off.

She placed the tray onto the table and arranged the porcelain cup neatly in front of Fei Long. At least this was something she knew how to do. The nobleman watched her with that penetrating gaze of his as she poured. When the cup was full, she set the pot down and stepped back with immense relief. This was harder than she'd ever imagined and they were only one day into the trip. What would be expected of her once they reached the great city of Changan?

'Yan Ling.' Her name sounded strange coming from his lips. So proper and enunciated. It was almost too elegant to be hers. He gestured to the chair opposite him. 'Sit down.'

She complied, folding her hands in her lap nervously as she waited. Steam rose from the pot beside her. Fei Long reached for the handle and poured her a cup. She took it from his hands obligingly, but refrained from drinking since he hadn't yet touched his tea.

He watched her with eyes that were dark and thoughtful. 'You're not my servant.'

'I'm…I'm not?'

He shook his head, looking a bit uncomfortable with the situation himself. 'You're not required to attend to me. You are here to learn and I am here to teach you.'

She nodded fervently, though she still didn't understand. This situation was growing even worse. The uncertainty of it left her bewildered and anxious. In the teahouse she knew exactly what was supposed to be done from the moment she woke up.

'What am I to learn?' she asked.

'Manners. Etiquette. How to write, how to speak. Every-thing that would be expected of a *heqin* bride.'

Everything? 'When was your sister supposed to leave for Khitan?'

'In three months.'

Her stomach sickened. Lord Chang didn't look happy either. Or maybe he always frowned like that. She'd seen that look more on his face than any other. He lifted his cup and she mirrored his movement. The tea was a bit hot so she blew over it gently.

'You shouldn't do that.'

She flinched at the reprimand. Hot liquid splashed over her fingers.

'Wait for the tea to cool and sip slowly.' He demonstrated while she stared at him incredulously. She did the same, not daring to do much more than touch her lips to the rim.

'And when you took the cup from me, you did it with one hand.'

Had she?

'Two hands,' he went on. 'With a slight bow of your head as you accept the cup.'

Heaven and earth, she didn't even know how to drink tea properly! She, who had grown up in a teahouse. But she'd never had the opportunity to accept a cup of tea from anyone. She poured her own tea and drank it in the kitchen with the rest of the servants.

'Two hands. Slight bow,' she recited under her breath.

The next minutes were excruciating. They sat and sipped tea as if it was a sacred ritual, and apparently it was. Fei Long told her about entire classical texts written about tea. She glanced at him over the rim of her cup while she drank. With every moment, she waited for the next arrow to fly: sit straight, head up. No, head too high.

'Are you a general in the imperial army?' she blurted out.

'No. Why?'

He did carry a sword and seemed to like giving commands. 'I was just wondering,' she said, glowering.

'I serve as a squad captain in the north-western garrison,' he answered stiffly. 'But I had to leave to attend to my father's affairs.'

She nodded. Her neck was tired from nodding. 'That's a very powerful position, then?'

He stared at her. She realised she was staring back and lowered her gaze.

'No,' he replied after a pause, regarding her intently, as if she'd said something highly improper, and took a methodical sip of tea. 'It is a very worthy post.'

'Yes, my lord.' She squirmed beneath his scrutiny. 'I'm certain it must be.'

She didn't know a thing about military rankings or the exalted history of tea. Every day would have to be like this if she was going to learn what she needed to know.

Yan Ling was exhausted by the time the food came, but she was grateful to have something besides the nobleman's discerning stare to occupy herself. Her mouth watered at the dishes placed before her. The journey had worked up her appetite and she piled slices of pork along with sautéed bamboo shoots and greens onto her rice. The flavours were rich with a blend of garlic and chilli. Indeed, a meal for a princess.

Not two bites in, the arrows started again.

'Slowly,' he reprimanded in a low voice.

Weariness had beaten down her defences. She narrowed her eyes and shot him a poisoned look of her own. It missed the mark, though. Fei Long was looking downwards, concentrating on the motion of his balanced chopsticks as he ate with perfect moderation.

Fei Long had occasionally travelled with servants. They rarely needed instruction, always knew their place and moved about unnoticed and unseen. He didn't know what to do with someone who was untrained and without a predetermined role and function. This became painfully obvious when he went to his room at the inn and found that Yan Ling had followed him dutifully into the chamber.

She blinked at him, awaiting some instruction undoubtedly. When none came, she turned and headed to the door. He let out a breath of relief, but it was short-lived. Yan Ling closed the door and once again faced him, hands folded. Waiting.

The family's servants and hired hands always disappeared *somewhere* once they settled down for the night. He didn't know where. He didn't care where.

'Yan Ling.'

'My lord?'

He preferred not to think of her as a female as they travelled together, but it was hard not to once they were alone like this. He considered calling for the innkeeper and asking for some other place for her, but that was impossible. Where would they put a lone young woman? He had proposed this scheme and taken her along with him, which meant her well being and safety was now his responsibility. And nothing was more important to Fei Long than his responsibilities.

The low platform of the bed lay against one wall. He gathered the bamboo mat that had been laid over the top of it.

He deposited the rolled mat in Yan Ling's arms. 'Take any spot you wish. Sleep well.'

She looked left and right. The situation was clearly as uncomfortable for her as it was for him. Quickly, quietly, she moved to the furthest corner from the bed. He averted his eyes and prepared himself for sleep, striving to ignore whatever was happening in the corner.

First he removed his sword and then started to undo his outer robe. He paused with his hand over his belt and glanced over his shoulder.

Yan Ling had arranged the mat in the corner. She was lying

upon it with her back to him. Her slippers were arranged neatly beside the mat and she'd untied her hair. He stared at the black curtain that fell down her back. An unbidden thought came to him and he wished it hadn't.

'Miss Yan Ling.'

She lay very still. Too still to be asleep. 'Yes?'

Her voice sounded muffled and she didn't face him, an act for which he was grateful. His throat grew dry with embarrassment, but he had to know.

'Your virtue—' The miserable words lodged in his throat. He coughed. 'Is it…intact?'

She gasped and spun into motion, twisting around to push herself up to sitting position. 'What are you suggesting? I told you I'm a good girl.'

'Nothing,' he said in a rush. 'I'm not suggesting anything.'

He took a step forwards, which launched her backwards. Her back collided against the wall.

'You stay right there!' She shook a finger at him.

'I didn't bring you with me to claim you for myself, I've been honest with my reasons from the first. You need to be pure to be married to Khitan.' Heavens above, his face was on fire.

'Well, I know what happens when men and women are together alone.'

'I don't think of you in that way,' he insisted.

Irresistibly Fei Long was plagued by a flicker of an image of the two of them, his arms around her bamboo-thin form, which he immediately tried to banish. Damn it all. It was only because she was insinuating it.

'Intentions can change quickly.' Yan Ling's gaze narrowed on him as she reached for her slippers. 'Male, female, there's no logic to it in the heat of things. I'm sleeping outside.'

He moved to block the door before she could rise. Now he was starting to get irritated. 'My intentions won't change. Do you want me to swear it?'

She stared at him wide-eyed, one hand clasped to the neck

of her tunic. Her skin was pale against the grey fabric and her hair fell over her eyes. 'How can you be assured you won't act differently in a…in a storm of passion?' she forced out.

He almost laughed at her then, and at himself as well. There was an easy solution to this that they had both forgotten.

'There will be no "storm of passion". I know who I am,' he said calmly. 'And I know who you are.'

She regarded him warily. 'So?'

'We're from very different classes in society.'

'Yin and yang know no class,' she retorted.

'But I do and I won't forget,' he promised. 'Ever. I swear I won't touch you. It's in neither of our best interests.'

She pulled away from the wall, but remained crouched and defensive. 'Because I'm of a lower standing than you, you'd never touch me?'

'Yes.'

Her shoulders remained tense. She seemed to be struggling with his logic, but finally she came to some resolution. 'I suppose, my lord, that I should find that a comfort,' she muttered.

He was left trying to decipher the sudden bite in her tone as she returned the slippers to the edge of the mat. She lowered herself to the ground, keeping her eyes directed away from him.

'Yes, my virtue is intact,' she said. 'And I trust it will remain so.'

She curled up again and turned to the wall. Carefully, he returned to other side of the room and sat down on the bed. There were ten or so more nights of this madness between here and Changan. *Ten more nights.*

He would need to be sure to have a place secured for her wherever they stayed to avoid this mishap in the future. There was a reason for rules and codes of conduct in society. Everyone knew his place in the scheme of family, home and country. As long as every man served his purpose, no one was led astray. They hadn't even reached Changan or started playing the game yet, but the shift in their statuses was already causing disorder and strife.

Fei Long watched the small figure in the corner. It wasn't long before the tension eased away from Yan Ling and her breathing grew soft and deep. The journey had been a long one that day and she wasn't accustomed to riding. He remembered the first time he'd spent most of the day in the saddle in the early part of his military training. Every muscle had ached and he'd fallen asleep before hitting the pallet.

He extinguished the lantern and pulled the quilt over himself as he lay back on the wooden platform. Yan Ling had pushed on that day with little complaint and tried her best to learn. Those qualities showed both strength and determination. This common tea girl was more than she appeared.

Think only of success, Sun-Tzu had taught. Fei Long would think only of success and he had ten days to lay out a plan.

For tonight, he decided not to remove his outer robe while he slept.

Chapter Three

Yan Ling gradually stirred to the chill of the air. The sharpness of it made her curl up into a tight ball. Instinctively, she tucked her chin to her chest and folded her feet close to her body to conserve warmth. Maybe she could coax a few more minutes of sleep out of the morning before the clanging in the kitchen woke her up.

Suddenly a soft weight fell over her, cutting off the chill. A hand settled gently over her shoulder and she jolted awake. Her arm shot out, her knuckles colliding against something solid.

'The death of me—!'

The startled cry chased the last of the sleep from her. This was not her pallet. She was no longer in the teahouse. She sat up and found herself clutching a woven blanket. Fei Long was crouched at the edge of the mat, one hand pressed over his left eye.

'What are you doing here?' she demanded.

'You looked cold,' he growled.

She stared at the blanket that had mysteriously appeared around her. Fei Long lowered his hand from his face, though he still winced from the blow. In the morning light she could make out every line of displeasure over his well-defined features.

'Forgive me,' she squeaked out.

'If I had known you could hit like that, I wouldn't have worried about your virtue.'

Was he…was he teasing her? Nothing else about his manner said so. His dark hair fell loose about his shoulders, giving him an untamed look that shocked her to her toes. The haze of the morning and his disarray made the moment uncomfortably intimate, though he was blinking at her with more ire than usual. She clutched the blanket tighter around herself.

Fei Long pulled himself to his feet and removed himself to the other side of the chamber. A knock on the door provided a momentary distraction. She went to open the door and the attendant presented her with a wash basin. Dutifully, she carried it to the table beside the bed and set it down.

The nobleman had his back to her. He ran his hands over his hair and then tied it into a topknot with a strip of cloth. In a coordinated dance, she returned to her corner to fold the blanket and roll up the mat while he moved to use the wash basin. She was accustomed to such rituals growing up in the cramped quarters of the teahouse kitchen. This was how people living in the same small space without doors or screens allowed each other some privacy.

In a breach of such politeness, she watched out of the corner of her eye as Fei Long rolled his sleeves back in two crisp tugs at each arm. Dipping his hands into the basin, he splashed water over his face. It slid down over his chiselled jaw and throat and she didn't realise she was staring until he caught her. A sharp line formed over his eyes.

'My lord,' she intoned by way of apology. Her face burned as she rushed over to hand him a wash cloth.

He took the cloth from her without a word while blood rushed to her face. In many ways, looking at him so boldly was a worse transgression than dousing him with tea in anger. She held her breath and waited to be reprimanded.

'The water is still warm,' came his brusque reply. He pressed the cloth to his face and took his sword from the bedside before leaving the room.

She had to remember that Chang Fei Long was well-born and well-mannered. Everything had to be done with care. More so when they reached the capital and she began to train to be an alliance bride.

Blessedly alone, Yan Ling used the water to quickly wash. One of the few belongings she'd taken from the teahouse was a wooden comb. She untangled her hair and concentrated on braiding it back out of her face. She had to at least look presentable now that she was attending a nobleman. Fei Long returned just as she tied the end.

'We have some things to do before leaving the city,' he said.

Unlike the day before, he had plenty to say while they took their morning tea and meal. He needed supplies, she needed clothes. She hadn't considered how ragged she must look beside him. Her grey tunic was over a year old and had been patched at the elbows.

By the time they rode out, she was outfitted in a leaf-green robe made of light cotton. She ran her hands wondrously over the sleeves. The weave of it was finer than anything she'd ever worn. What would the townsfolk think of him buying her such fancy clothing as if she were a—she blushed to even think of it—a pampered concubine?

Fei Long was intent on using every moment of the day now for education. He recited a classic titled *The Three Obediences and Four Virtues* to her while they rode, asking her at intervals to repeat back what she'd just learned.

'You have a good memory,' he said at one point.

It might have been the very first compliment he'd ever paid her. Perhaps it would make up for her rough, provincial manners.

Ten days passed quicker than Fei Long had anticipated. Changan, the imperial capital, stood a day away. They only had a few months before Pearl was supposed to take her place as princess. Fortunately, Yan Ling was a quick learner. He had drilled her on etiquette and her dialect had shifted slightly to mimic the patterns of speech of the capital.

'We'll be in the city by late in the afternoon,' he told her.

Their morning tea had become the staging point for the day's goals. Yan Ling listened intently as she did every day.

'The mourning period over my father's death provides us some privacy,' he continued.

'When did you lose your father?'

'Over a month now.'

'Such a loss.' She quieted and bowed her head reverently before speaking again. 'Your family must be saddened by the loss.'

'That's a private matter.'

'Oh. Sorry.' She bit her bottom lip.

'Don't do that.'

'Do what?' In her nervousness, she bit down even harder.

For now, he decided to let it go. Yan Ling needed to learn that she was no longer in the common room of a teahouse with its hum of chatter and gossip.

'His death was unexpected,' he said.

Fortunately, she took his cold tone to mean there would be no more questions. Of course there was sadness. His father, the man who had given him life and raised him, was gone. But Fei Long didn't have time to grieve. As soon as he'd returned, everyone had surrounded him, asking him, 'What now?' Pearl was nowhere to be found. He'd let the household mourn in his stead. There were too many new responsibilities as eldest son and the new head of the household.

'You'll be carried in a palanquin into the city.'

'What's a palanquin?'

'A litter. You'll sit inside while we enter. It wouldn't do for you to be seen. Too many questions.'

Her lips moved in a silent conversation with herself as she

recited his instructions. He found the habit endearing and took a sip while he watched her.

'Once you're installed in our family residence, there will be a whole new set of lessons,' he continued. 'You'll need to learn how to read and write. We'll also need to practise court etiquette—entirely different than private etiquette.'

Her lips pouted and she blew out an exasperated breath. This part he didn't find quite as endearing.

'You'll need to practise controlling your expressions,' he reminded her. 'And not make such faces all the time.'

'I wasn't making a face, my lord.'

'You were.'

'What does it matter when it's just the two of us?' she demanded.

They hadn't had many arguments during their journey, but this was a recurring one.

'Practise these habits all the time and they'll come naturally,' he said, forcing patience. 'Remember, you were not accustomed to being heard or seen as a servant. Others will be watching you now. At times you'll be the centre of attention, such as when you're presented to the Khagan.'

'Surely I have better manners than a foreign barbarian,' she scoffed.

His lips twitched. 'That is a matter for debate.'

She opened her mouth to argue, but the carriers had arrived with the palanquin.

'Come, it's time.'

He led her out to the street, noting that her back was held straighter, her head an inch higher. The carriers afforded her a slight bow as she approached. His chest swelled with pride. This was going to work.

Of course, it was hard to dismiss his dishonesty. He was deliberately deceiving the imperial court. Two courts, if he counted the kingdom of Khitan. But all parties were getting what they wanted. Khitan received an alliance and a princess and the Tang Empire didn't have to worry about barbarian attacks from the north at least for a few years. Yan Ling would be taken care of. His family name and honour would be preserved for ancestors and heirs alike. So many good deeds had to balance out one black one.

He stepped forwards to pull aside the curtain on the sedan himself, Yan Ling paused as she was about to duck inside.

'Wait—should I call you "Elder Brother"? Will you call me Pearl?'

'There's no need for that. You'll be safely inside the family residence.'

'What about the other servants? Will they know?'

Her voice was pitched higher now. The prospect of going to Changan was making them both anxious. Fei Long pressed a hand to the small of her back and gave her a slight push into the compartment.

'We'll work everything out later.' He drew the curtain over the opening to cut off her protest.

As he made his way towards his horse, the side curtain flew open. Yan Ling peered out, framed by the window. Her eyes appeared wide and curious in her delicate face.

'What if someone asks me who I am? What will I tell them?'

He strode back to the litter with purpose. 'You won't have to say a thing. Why would anyone even talk to you? Such nonsense.'

With that, he dragged the curtain closed and went to lift himself onto the saddle.

Think only of success.

The morning went by without event. A nagging silence surrounded him without Yan Ling behind him on the saddle. Every flutter of the curtain drew his eye. More than once, he wanted to ride up alongside the transport to speak to her. Not that he had anything to say. He had the urge to see her, if only to make sure that she was secure. So much depended on Yan Ling.

The earthen walls of Changan appeared over the horizon when they were deep into the afternoon. Soon the expanse of the city filled the view. Imperial banners flew from the battlements and the arches of the East Gate opened before them.

He tapped against the litter. 'We're here.'

Two fingers peeked through the curtain to pull it open just a slit. 'Heaven and earth,' Yan Ling breathed. 'So magnificent.'

Whenever he returned from the outer provinces, the vastness of Changan always struck him with renewed awe. The exterior wall stretched on for several *li*. Within the main gates, the city was divided into further compartments, each ward a small community with shops and neighbourhoods. Throughout the city, there were numerous parks and lakes and canals. Changan could swallow entire cities within its depths.

A squad of city guards was stationed at the East Gate. They allowed them in after a cursory inspection of his seal. Inside, the city opened up to the familiar grid pattern of criss-crossing avenues. The family mansion was within the residential area just beyond the East Market.

A muted call came from inside the sedan. 'My lord…Lord Chang. *Elder Brother.*'

He turned his head to see a slight part in the curtain, enough to reveal the curve of Yan Ling's cheek and one brightly inquisitive eye.

'Are those pears in the trees?' she whispered in delight.

The avenue was lined on either side with fruit trees, planted years ago under imperial order. With a hand on the reins, he directed his horse toward the round yellow fruit. The branch shook as he twisted one free before returning to the palanquin to pass it through the window. Then he gestured towards the curtain, making an abrupt, horizontal motion. She flashed him a quick smile, with only the corner of her mouth visible, before disappearing back inside.

The palanquin joined the heavy traffic along one of the main avenues. Even though they were within the city, it would be at least another hour before they reached the mansion. At that time he'd have to sneak Yan Ling into the household and enlist the help of the servants. Discretion and loyalty were key to the plan. A single whisper of gossip could travel a hundred *li* and have them all in chains.

If Yan Ling had been asked to describe in one word how the imperial capital differed from her home town, she would have said it was the colours. She'd grown up in a muted world of greys and browns. Their clothing was of the plainest cotton, without the indulgence of special dyes. The buildings were erected from stone and wood. Even the river was murky as it wound through the forest green.

Now that she was in the capital, wealth didn't look like the gleam of gold and silver. Wealth was in the red banners cascading from the balconies of the wine-houses and restaurants of Changan. The rainbow bolts of silk in the marketplace. Even the fruit piled in the stalls sparkled like jewels: rosy peaches and startling pink dragonfruit with green-tipped scales.

The buildings were all ornamented and painted. The structures climbed ostentatiously upwards, reaching towards heaven. The citizens themselves walked side by side in luxurious brocades. Their sleeves hung to the ground, enough material for an entire new garment, yet used for mere adornment.

The pear in her hands had been kissed warm by the sun. Fei Long's fingers had brushed inadvertently against hers when he had handed it to her. For all his rigid manners, he was good at heart and kind in the most unexpected ways. She bit into the pear, enjoying the crisp sweetness as she wondered what other surprises the city would bring.

She wouldn't live here for long, Yan Ling reminded herself. After the spring and before summer was done, a caravan would take her north to the frontier of Khitan, but this one look alone at the imperial capital was worth it.

* * *

A long time passed, made longer by the confinement. Restlessness took over and then boredom. She wanted to burst out of the sedan and take in the city, but Fei Long had warned her about staying hidden. Finally the transport halted and she was lowered to the ground.

They were here. She fixated on the curtain in front of her. Her palms began sweating and she swallowed past the dryness in her throat. What would await her on the other side? Fei Long had spoken very little about his household. There was Pearl who had run away and the elder Lord Chang who was no longer with them.

The curtain opened and Fei Long was there. He met her eyes and a silent flicker disrupted his expression before it settled like the surface of a pond. He extended his hand and she took it. His was firm and steady while hers trembled. She stepped outside and peered around the corner like a mouse avoiding a cat's paw.

'That's not Pearl!'

They had stopped in an alleyway, away from the main street. A young woman dressed in a light blue robe stood before a side gate. Her clothing marked her as a servant and her tone marked her as a long-time one.

'I'll explain later.' Fei Long placed a hand to Yan Ling's back to propel her forwards. The gesture was not at all reassuring. 'Dao, take Miss Yan Ling to Pearl's room.'

Dao appeared close to her in age. The girl threw her an assessing look before bowing dutifully and opening the gate. Yan Ling looked to Fei Long for one last sign of reassurance, but he was tending to the business of paying the porters.

The gateway led into a spacious courtyard surrounded by rooms on all sides. A well-tended garden filled the space, complete with manicured trees, rock sculptures and a wooden pavilion at the centre. Through the portal at the far end, she could see a front courtyard as well. Fei Long's home truly was a mansion.

The pathway winding through the courtyard was covered with smooth river stones. Yan Ling halted in the middle of it and turned in a full circle to take in the sight of the buildings surrounding the garden. Covered walkways lined each side. A hum of voices and activity came from within the chambers.

'Please come with me, miss. The private chambers are in the back of the house.'

Dao was watching her carefully. The servant girl had a soft, peach-shaped face and elegant almond eyes that were narrowed with scrutiny, though her expression remained tranquil. Her hair was parted in the middle and tied in two long tails that framed either side of her face.

Yan Ling gave the garden one last glance before following Dao into an interior corridor. The bedchamber itself was cool and quiet. A stream of light filtered in through a window that faced the courtyard. A painted screen divided the room in two with a sitting area near the door and a more private sleeping area arranged in back.

Dao bowed as she prepared to take her leave. Yan Ling thanked her and bowed in return. That caused some confusion. The servant paused, blinked at her, then bowed one more time before retreating and closing the door.

Once she was alone, Yan Ling took a turn about the chamber, unable to resist running her fingers over the polished finish of the furniture in the sitting area. The chair cushions were embroidered with a peony pattern and the wood was nearly black with a reddish tint. It would be a shame to sit on such pretty chairs. Her legs were still stiff from sitting in the sedan for most of the day anyway.

She imagined the precious Pearl would have sat before the low table to take her morning tea and do whatever else it was that high-born women did to fill their days. Fei Long hadn't said much about that. Perhaps he didn't know either. He seemed to rely on the *Four Virtues* for his knowledge of the practices of women, which led her to believe there would be courtesy and harmonising—with what, she wasn't quite sure—and perhaps some needlework.

The bed was another adventure. The padded bedding was placed within an alcove that receded into the wall. Yan Ling took off her slippers and crawled inside on her hands and knees, feeling like she was exploring a cave.

At the teahouse, her bed had been a thin mat within the storeroom, warmed with residual heat from the stove in the kitchen. Here she could roll over several times and still be in bed. She lay down and tried exactly that. She rolled over once towards the wall and then again, giggling to herself. All this room for one little teahouse girl.

She stood and inserted her feet back into her slippers. Back in the sitting area, she chose a chair and seated herself, making extra effort to keep her spine straight and her shoulders back. Chang Fei Long had been both kind and generous to give her this chance. She would work her hardest to repay him.

The chamber door opened again. At first she thought that the servant girl Dao had returned, but it was evident from the flowing robes and the glitter of jewels around her neck that this was a lady of the house.

'Oh! You're not Pearl,' the woman said as she glided into the room in a cloud of amber silk. Her hair was coiled elegantly and pinned high over her crown. A pearl dangled from a hair ornament fixed into one side of the arrangement. It was accompanied by smaller baubles fashioned in the shape of flowers.

Yan Ling stood, struggling for a suitable greeting. 'Pearl isn't here, my lady.'

This woman stepped forwards with a familiarity that had Yan Ling retreating behind the chair.

'Well, good girl! She must have succeeded then. But who are you?'

'I…I came here with Fei Long—I mean, Lord Chang.'

The lady titled her head in puzzlement, causing the pearl ornament to swing in an entrancing fashion, but then she appeared to accept without any further question. 'I'm Min, Lord Chang's concubine.'

Concubine? Fei Long hadn't mentioned he had a concubine.

'No, the *elder* Lord Chang,' the woman corrected, smiling at her confusion.

Now that Lady Min had come into the light, Yan Ling could see she was actually plain in appearance, but a youthful energy radiated from her. Her beauty was expressed in the carefree exuberance of her movements rather than her features.

'Maybe you can help me,' Lady Min began cheerfully. 'I had the most wonderful revelation while paying my respects at the temple to the elder Lord Chang.' She pulled out a bundle of cloth hidden in the billowing folds of her sleeve. 'I was coming to see if Pearl wanted to come with me, but she's away with her true love, so all the better.'

Lady Min set the bundle down on the low table and straightened regally. She raised her hands to smooth out her hair. It occurred to Yan Ling that she should be studying and copying her movements, but Min flitted about like a dragonfly on gossamer wings, impossible to envision in stillness.

The lady began to pull the pins from her hair and handed them over to Yan Ling one by one. 'I don't know why it took me so long to think of it, really. And then today in front of the temple altar, with all that smoky incense everywhere, it just came to me.'

She shook her hair loose and Yan Ling couldn't help but be a bit envious. The thick mane flowed down to her waist. Min reached down to unroll the cloth bundle, revealing a pair of scissors among other implements.

'What is your name?' the lady asked.

'Yan Ling, my lady.'

'Help me with this here, Yan Ling. I can't see the back very well even in my mirror.' The lady pressed the scissors into her hands and turned around, running her hands once more over her hair.

The scissors lay like a leaden weight against her palm. Yan Ling was feeling a bit ambushed. 'I'm afraid I don't have much experience cutting hair. What if I ruin it?'

'Oh, there's nothing to worry about. It's all coming off.' Lady Min was uncustomarily excited about the prospect.

Yan Ling swallowed. 'All?'

'Yes. We'll use the scissors first and then the razor. I'm going to join the nuns at the Temple of the Peaceful Lotus.'

The lady turned around, waiting expectantly. What else was she to do? Yan Ling raised the scissors and opened them around a lock of lustrous black hair. She closed her eyes and made the first snip. The blades sheared through the lock with a definitive snick.

'I've been very lucky,' Lady Min said. 'The last few years have been happy here. The elder Lord Chang was a kind man. No matter what they say, he had a joyfulness about him. Always in good humour. I laughed every day, you should know.'

'That's good to hear.' Yan Ling picked up another lock and cut it away, placing it beside the first one on top of the cloth. It seemed such a crime to sacrifice all that beautiful hair. 'But I'm surprised. The younger Lord Chang is so serious all the time.'

She could also say humourless, stiff, didn't know his way around a proper smile.

'He gets that from his mother,' Min replied. 'Lady Chang was also a good woman. I was her attendant, you know.' Her tone became wistful. 'She was practical and ran the household admirably.'

'Lady Chang is gone as well then?' More locks fell away. Yan Ling was getting bolder with the scissors as well as her questions.

'Several years ago. Right before her son passed his military exams. I don't think the elder Lord Chang ever forgot her. All the carousing, drinking, extravagance—' she had to take a breath before continuing '—dice and women aside.'

Yan Ling frowned at the description. 'Wasn't Lord Chang a government official?'

'Lord Chang was a department head in the Ministry of Works. And well loved, too. Everywhere he went, men would call out his name, wanting to be the first to greet him. His death was such a shame.' Lady Min's voice grew distant. 'He slipped coming home late one night along the canal. Hit his head and drowned, the city guards said. Poor man... Are you nearly finished? My head feels so much lighter.'

It was one thing to die at a venerable old age, but to go so unexpectedly. Her heart went out to Fei Long and his family. 'I think it's done.'

Only jagged tufts remained where there had been a beautiful head of hair only minutes earlier, but Lady Min wasn't yet satisfied. The lady picked up a porcelain jar and poured some oil from it into her hand. Then she ran her palms over her head, massaging the ointment in circles. She handed Yan Ling the razor and sat down in one of the chairs.

By that time, Yan Ling had accepted the strangeness of the situation. With great care, she scraped the blade gently along Lady Min's scalp. The blade was sharp and the hair fell away easily.

'If you'll forgive me for asking, you sound content with your life here. Why leave?' Yan Ling asked.

'It seems the right thing to do to repay the elder lord's kindness. I'd be nothing but a burden here. And it's not such a sacrifice. The temple gardens are tranquil. The nuns spend their day in prayer. A simple life.'

Over the next half-hour, Yan Ling finished shaving the rest of the lady's head. She found a mirror within Pearl's dresser in the private area of the room and brought it out.

'Waa... Look at me!' Min turned her head this way and that as she peered at her reflection in the polished bronze.

She rubbed her hand over the newly smooth surface with an expression of amused curiosity. 'I look like a newborn baby.'

'When will you go to the temple?'

'Tomorrow.' She grinned. 'I'm already prepared.'

Min began gathering up the locks of hair and the other supplies. 'I better return these to Old Man Liang before he realises they're missing.' She paused as she picked up the jewelled hairpins. 'Well, I don't have any use for these any more.'

They laughed together. With the laughter, some of the apprehension Yan Ling had harboured throughout the journey uncoiled within her. She grew pleasantly warm in their small intimate circle. Yet at the same time, she was stricken with a pang of sadness. She would be alone in a house of strangers once more when the lady left.

'You should take them.' Min held the pins out to her. 'And thank you.'

Without warning, the lady swept her up in an embrace. Yan Ling returned it with not as much grace as she would have liked, but Lady Min didn't seem to notice. When they moved apart, the lady ceremoniously placed the hairpins across Yan Ling's palm.

'Fei Long must not be so different from his father after all, bringing you here. He's not completely blind to a young and pretty woman.'

'Oh, no.' Yan Ling's face grew hot and she shook her head vehemently. 'That's not why I'm here at all.'

She quickly explained her role in replacing Pearl as the alliance bride, though there was no way to escape the questionable nature of their journey, alone together when they were neither family nor husband and wife, sleeping in the same chamber. Yan Ling flushed with embarrassment. Maybe this was why Fei Long needed someone with no reputation to lose. If she had any sort of family name to call her own, it would be ruined already.

'Well.' Min blew out a breath after the explanation was done. 'As I said, not so different from his father as I thought.'

'What do you mean by that?'

'Fei Long wasn't always so morose. There's still some life in him.' Min embraced her again. 'Just remember. The elder Lord Chang was a good man. No matter what you may hear.'

The lady stole away in a swirl of silk. After a moment, Yan Ling sank onto the chair, wondering what had just happened. And why, when Min had been so overwhelmingly cheerful, did her parting words sound like a dire warning?

Chapter Four

Yan Ling had never heard Fei Long shout during their journey together. He rarely raised his voice above the stern and steady tone that she'd come to know so well. That morning, she learned that he could shake the rooftops if he chose to.

The yelling brought her out of her room and sent her running into the central courtyard. Maybe there was a fire. Surely someone was dying.

Dao nearly collided with her on the pebbled walkway. 'Lady Min,' Dao pronounced, looking to the front of the house. 'She's done something crazy again.'

The pieces fell into place quickly between the male and female voices raised in argument followed by the sight of Min running through the courtyard, sobbing loudly. Her bare head gleamed in the morning sun while her opulent robe fluttered behind her. Dao stared after the lady with eyes wide and mouth open as Min disappeared into the back of the house.

'What is this place?' Fei Long was shouting. 'This isn't my home. This is a den of wild animals.'

'Will he calm down if we just wait?' Yan Ling looked to Dao, whose only answer was to shake her head helplessly.

'Bald as a Shaolin monk,' he ranted. 'I must already be dead. This must already be the afterlife because *no one alive could be so stupid.*'

Several servants from the kitchen and surrounding chambers peeked into the courtyard, only to duck away when Fei Long continued his tirade. Min's sobbing had receded into the house, but it grew louder once again. She came back into the first courtyard with eyes swollen red and a travel pack slung over her shoulder.

'On my mother,' Dao swore under her breath. 'The scandal.'

'Stop her before she leaves the house,' Yan Ling directed, her pulse skipping. 'I'll go speak to Lord Chang.' Maybe it wasn't her place to be giving orders, but she felt responsible for helping Lady Min.

The servant girl ran in one direction while Yan Ling hurried in the other. She slipped into the front part of the house and wove her way through the hallway. It wasn't hard to find Fei Long. He had taken to swearing a river of oaths behind a closed door.

'My lord.' The door loomed before her. She pressed a hand to her stomach to try to calm it. 'Are you all right?'

The stomping inside ceased. 'Miss Yan Ling, this is a private matter. Please return to your room.' His voice sounded muffled through the barrier.

Private? Not any more when every porter on the street could likely hear him.

'Maybe I can be of help,' she began.

The door swung open slowly and Fei Long appeared. There was a slight flush to his cheeks and his eyes glinted with a dangerous light. 'There is nothing for you to concern yourself with here.'

She could hear the strain at the edge of his voice as he resorted to extreme politeness.

'Pardon us, miss, for disrupting your morning,' he continued. His chest rose and fell rapidly and the muscles of his face pulled tight as he fought for control. Maybe she could help. She was an outsider and he wouldn't dare yell at her…as loudly, at least.

'Everyone in the house is frightened. Lady Min is crying.'

The mention of the lady's name had Fei Long gritting his teeth. 'She's lost her mind.'

What would calm him? She tried to think of what little she knew of him and she could only think of one thing.

'Let me have some tea brought to you.'

Yes, tea. He did all his planning with her over tea. And he had come to the teahouse to ponder over his troubles when she'd first met him. He regarded her woodenly, perhaps thinking that she, too, had lost her mind. But slowly, as if with great difficulty, he nodded once.

A small victory.

They were seated with the tea tray arranged before them in his father's study. It was his study now, as was everything that had once belonged to his father: this mansion, the servants, all the troubles he'd stirred up like rats let loose in a storehouse.

Like rats, the problems gnawed away at what remained bit by bit. Like rats, they multiplied.

Yan Ling scooped the tea leaves into the special enamel cups. Her hand trembled slightly as she lifted the pot of steaming water. That small break brought him back to himself. These problems weren't meant for her or the other servants. He was wrong to involve all of them.

'I apologise for my anger,' he said.

He had been completely stricken senseless by the sight of his father's young concubine shaved bald. Even the thought of such foolishness made his pulse rise once more.

Steam rose from the cups and Yan Ling gently placed the lids over them to let the leaves steep. She sat back with her hands in her lap.

Her fingers twined together. 'Lady Min came to me last night—'

'We should speak of other things,' he interrupted.

'I think her intentions were well meaning.'

He let out a slow breath. She wasn't going to spare him this shame. 'How is bringing scandal upon this house well meaning?' he asked. 'Lady Min has no reason to complain. She was once a servant in our household before my father made her his concubine.'

Fei Long's own father had always let his passionate nature get the best of him. Shame soured his stomach once again. It was impossible to hide such personal family matters from Yan Ling while she lived here among them.

'She isn't complaining. Lady Min praised your father as a generous and joyful man.'

'Do you know how this looks? First my sister, Pearl, runs away, then Lady Min shaves her head to become a nun to escape. There is no discipline in this house. No harmony.'

'It is this woman's humble opinion—'

He raised an eyebrow at that. It was one of the phrases he'd introduced during their daily lessons and now she was wielding it. He didn't know whether to be pleased or irritated that she was putting it to practice to placate him.

'—that the women of this household may have enjoyed a certain freedom under your father's most generous care.'

He could see how she struggled with the words. How they lingered on her tongue, a bite too large to swallow easily.

'The lady came to me yesterday and asked for my help,' Yan Ling blurted out. She looked exhausted from speaking so delicately. 'I think she didn't want to be a burden, that was all.'

She was trying valiantly and his heart softened. 'What do you suggest?' he asked.

'Being a nun can't be the easiest life. Let the lady do as she's chosen and the good energy from it may come back to you.'

'Karma?' he offered.

She looked relieved. 'Yes. Karma.'

He leaned back, considering her argument. The difficult matter wasn't that his father's concubine now wished to become a Buddhist nun or that Pearl had been so devastated by being sent to a foreign lord that she went against duty and honour to run away. What Yan Ling could never understand was that he was responsible for all of them. Min had been utterly devoted to his father, yet she had gone to a stranger first to try to solve her problems. And his sister had become desperate enough to run away after he'd disregarded her plea for help. He was a failure at holding this household together.

'Will you abandon me as well?' he asked tonelessly.

She frowned. 'I don't understand, my lord.'

His throat closed tight and he had to force out the words. 'Our arrangement is an unusual one. I have no assurance you won't decide one day that it's no longer worth the sacrifice.'

If Yan Ling suddenly ran away like Pearl and Min, he'd be left with nothing. The family name would fall completely to ruin. Fei Long had also put his hopes on an outsider. The uncertainty left him vulnerable and darkened his spirit. The shadow of it had hovered over him during their journey and it clung to him now. This was the closest he'd ever come to admitting this fear to her.

'Is our arrangement what you truly want, Yan Ling? We have at least been honest with one another. If you have any doubt, tell me now.'

'I have no doubt, my lord.'

He didn't believe her. Her voice hitched and she ran the tip of her tongue over her lip before biting into it.

'Don't do that,' he reminded gently. She stopped this time.

'I have no doubt about this,' she repeated with more iron behind the words. 'I'll see this through to the end. I swear it.'

The tension in his shoulders eased. He'd been right about Yan Ling. She was a practical, logical woman. They were partners in this. Only she was audacious enough to carry out the ruse and she wouldn't abandon him.

She fidgeted as his gaze lingered. 'The tea is ready,' she deflected. 'Let us drink.'

They enjoyed their tea for a few peaceful moments. The stillness was welcome after all the drama that morning. A careful tap on the door interrupted the silence, but by then the throbbing in his skull had settled.

'Old Man Liang. Come in.'

His father's steward entered in a black robe and cap. He carried a thick ledger book, almost larger than he was, with a wooden abacus balanced on top. Liang had always been there at his father's side, older than time. And he'd always looked the same: same thin nose, same tapered beard hanging down to his breastbone. The widening bands of grey in it seemed to be his only signs of ageing.

Liang paused at the sight of Yan Ling. Fei Long had already explained her role to all of the servants as well as the old steward. That had been accomplished in the morning before his confrontation with Lady Min. They also knew that discretion was most important.

'Enquire today at the Temple of the Peaceful Lotus,' he told Liang. 'Tell the abbess that Lady Min wishes to join them and prepare a donation of alms to the temple.'

Across from him, Yan Ling straightened. Her eyes lit with surprise.

'I'll go tell Lady Min.' She set her tea down and rose to her feet.

Excitement brought a vibrant glow to her cheeks and he refrained from admonishing her for ending the meeting without taking proper leave. At least she remembered to bow to Liang, before rushing out the door.

He still had much work to do with her.

Fei Long got up to move to the desk. He and the steward had planned to go over all of the accounts that morning, without

the protective smoothing over of details that Liang had practised with his father. It was poor etiquette to give bad news
plainly, but Fei Long needed to know the truth about the family finances.

Old Man Liang seated himself and took his time opening
the record book and sliding the counters on his abacus back
to starting position. The steward coughed once and cleared
his throat.

'My lord is most generous.' He stroked his grey beard, a
habit that Fei Long had come to recognise as a stalling gesture. 'However, there may be a problem making a donation to
the temple as well as a few of the other payments.'

It wasn't until that afternoon that Fei Long was able to summon Yan Ling before him again. She was dressed in one of
Pearl's hanfu robes. The cloth hung loose as Yan Ling was
thinner than his sister. The embroidered sash accented her
slender waist and hips.

He stood in the parlour at the front of the house as she tried
to negotiate the layers of yellow silk past the entranceway. This
was supposed to be a reprieve from the dire financial figures
Old Man Liang had thrown at him, but Fei Long almost wished
himself back in front of the cursed ledger book as Yan Ling
stepped on the edge of her own skirt. The cloth pooled around
her feet as she tried to move forwards, wrapping about her
ankles until he was certain she would topple. Fortunately she
didn't. She kicked at the train, much like—heaven help him—
one would kick a stray dog. He raised a hand over his mouth.

'Are you laughing at me?' she demanded, looping the long
sleeves once and then twice about her arms so they would no
longer whip about while she moved.

'No.'

He was most certainly grimacing behind the shield of his
hand. He lowered it and held out his arm to catch her as she
stumbled into the room.

'This must be the sort of fancy garment only worn for big festivals,' she surmised.

He ground his teeth together. 'This is what Pearl wore nearly every day.'

She shot him a look of disbelief. 'This is not a robe. This is *three* robes.'

He was not going to lower himself to untangle her from the net of silk she'd woven about herself.

'Dao.'

The girl came running from her unseen location in the hallway. 'My lord.'

He tossed a curt nod in Yan Ling's direction. Dao rushed to her and worked to straighten out the hanfu, smoothing out the sleeves and rearranging the train. Yan Ling's face grew red as she stood still for the ministrations.

'Try walking forwards,' he said.

She took a few tentative steps toward the opposite end of the room. At the wall, she bent to tug the skirt straight with what she thought was a surreptitious movement. It wasn't.

'Again,' he commanded.

She turned and came back toward him. It was a little better this time in that she didn't pause to fidget with the clothing, but in truth it wasn't that much better.

'I'll practise,' she said sharply, cutting off the comment that hovered on his tongue.

Dao looked on in sympathy, eyes lowered.

He ran a hand roughly over his chin. Something was wrong, but on his father's grave, he couldn't say what. Her arms were wooden by her sides. Her step was heavy. She didn't seem to know what to do with her hands. Why hadn't he noticed anything when they'd travelled together? This was worse than he'd thought.

'This will take more than practice,' he replied.

She flinched as if he'd inflicted a physical wound, but he didn't have time to be gentle with words. He didn't know how to instruct her in how a lady should act and move. He looked to the servant girl Dao, but it was clear she wouldn't be able to help either, and Lady Min had the mental focus of a moth.

Yan Ling had to combat a lifetime of subservience. It wasn't her fault, he tried to tell himself as his head throbbed once again.

He was frustrated at her, but he was angrier with himself. It didn't matter whose fault it was; he needed to fix this. Yan Ling pressed her lips tight and he could see her reading the displeasure in his face.

'Let me keep trying,' she insisted with a stubborn lift of her chin.

A small part of him warmed with admiration, but feminine grace was a virtue while perseverance was not.

'Yes,' he said. 'Keep working.'

He dismissed Dao and accompanied Yan Ling as she walked the gardens from the first courtyard through to the second one. Occasionally she looked to him for approval and he'd oblige her with a nod, but he was no longer paying attention to her form. Instead, Fei Long was lost in thought. If Yan Ling was to become a princess, or at least pretend to be one, they would need to transform her. He needed someone who was a master at deception.

Chapter Five

'Nothing I do is right.'

Yan Ling winced as Dao wound a thread to the hairs at the edge her eyebrow and yanked. She reclined on the day bed in her sitting room with Dao leaning over her. Lady Min had entered the temple earlier that week after a tearful farewell to the household, despite her eagerness to begin her new life. This freed Dao to focus on making a lady of Yan Ling, which she was doing one hair at a time.

'Lord Chang is only trying to make sure you succeed,' Dao replied.

'I don't stand properly, walk properly. Pearl must have been a model of femininity and— Ow!'

Dao pulled the thread away on the other side. The skin around her brows stung like the bite of a hundred ants.

The mansion was arranged around the two courtyards with the private chambers in the back part of the house and the parlours, kitchen and storeroom arranged at the front. Even with Lady Min and Pearl gone, there were still fifteen people living within the residence. There was the kitchen staff, the hands who tended the stable at the side of the residence, and the various attendants and porters who handled everyday tasks such as cleaning and running errands. Old Man Liang was the eldest and most revered.

Yan Ling wondered why Fei Long wasn't married already. She would have thought a family such as this one would be eager to produce sons. It couldn't be possible that anyone would find him unsuitable. Women likely found him handsome enough…not that one needed to be with wealth and education. And not that she necessarily found him so.

She swallowed past a sudden tightness in her throat, embarrassed to be thinking about someone so far above her class. Maybe she had spent too much time listening to Fei Long's lectures. Even hidden thoughts had a proper place and standing now.

'You're very brave,' Dao was saying. 'Pearl was so frightened about going to Khitan. And all those people you'll need to convince. I couldn't do it.'

Her chest grew tighter as she thought of it. The Khitan court would be expecting a well-born lady. 'I'm a carp trying to leap over the dragon's gate,' she muttered.

'I'm surprised Lord Chang would think of such a thing.' Dao ducked in close to inspect the arch of one brow. 'He's always been so proper and upstanding.'

'This would be quite the scandal, wouldn't it?'

'Quite!' The servant lifted the thread again. 'But I think it sounds wonderful. To become a princess. The poets write lovely verses about the *heqin* brides, about how beautiful and treasured they are.'

Yan Ling pouted. She was neither beautiful nor graceful. In the afternoons, she sat through lessons on etiquette and diplomacy with Fei Long, but she questioned whether any of it was any good. She still felt like the same awkward teahouse girl while she strolled from the front courtyard to the back, trying to flow and glide like a cloud. Or a crane. Or anything much more elegant than herself.

'There.' Dao made one more painful yank and then handed her the mirror. 'See how it brightens up your face?'

Yan Ling stared at her newly shaped eyebrows sceptically. The ends narrowed in what was supposed to be the fashion of the day, according to Dao. 'So that was all I needed. Now I'm a lady. I thank you greatly.'

'Monkey.' Dao snorted and gave her a shove.

One of the attendants from the front of the house came into the sitting room then to announce a visitor.

'For me?'

The young man nodded. 'Li Bai Shen, by the lord's invitation.'

Fei Long had left that morning without telling her anything about a 'Li Bai Shen'. Old Man Liang wasn't present either. She didn't know if she was ready to carry on the deception for an outsider. She glanced once more in the mirror. Her eyes did look different—somehow more intense and focused—but she didn't feel it inside. She patted a hand over her hair. It had been pinned up on top and then allowed to fall loose in a cascade behind her.

The young attendant led her to the parlour at the front of the mansion. The gentleman was already seated on the couch. His robe was adorned with a brilliant border of maroon brocade and his topknot was affixed with a straight silver pin. He had narrow, handsome features, with dark eyebrows that accented his face in two bold lines.

He poured himself a cup of wine from a ewer that had been set before him and leaned back with his legs crossed at the ankles, taking in the sitting room décor with a bemused expression as if he were master of the house.

She stopped at the edge of the sitting area. 'Lord Li.'

Self-consciously, she executed a bow, keeping her hands folded demurely within the drape of her sleeves.

He smiled when he saw her. Setting his wine down, he lifted himself to his feet and came towards her with a powerful, yet graceful stride. He was deceptively tall in stature, his build lean and wiry. He circled her, head tilted as if to get a better look. His grin widened to reveal the indent of a dimple against his cheek.

'Not bad, Fei Long.' His voice held a hum of approval.

'My lord?'

He reached to tuck two fingers beneath her chin and she swatted at his hand. He chuckled.

'Who are you anyway?' she demanded.

He straightened and pulled back his shoulders dramatically. 'My good friend has asked for help. Li Bai Shen is here to honour that bond of friendship.'

He spoke his name with authority as if anyone would know it. She wrinkled her nose at him.

He tapped his chest twice. 'Bai Shen is one of the premier actors of the Nine Dragon theatre troupe and that, dear miss, is not a pretty face you're making. I can see why Fei Long needs my help.'

'I don't understand.'

'You have two months to become a well-born, well-mannered lady, correct?'

'Yes.'

Bai Shen made a sweeping gesture with his hand. 'I am here to ensure your success.'

'You?'

'No other. I played the Princess Pingyang at the Spring Festival before the Emperor himself.'

This was who Fei Long had enlisted to teach her how to be a woman? She knew that men played all of the female roles at the opera, but Bai Shen didn't seem at all womanly.

'This is a joke,' she scoffed.

'Have you ever known Chang Fei Long to joke?'

She couldn't argue with that.

Bai Shen leaned in close, a fellow conspirator. 'To be truthful, it is quite complicated being a woman.'

'It is!' she agreed wholeheartedly.

'There are a thousand looks. A hundred gestures. I've studied them all.' He circled his hand with a flourish. 'The secret is to create the illusion. You don't need it all. Emphasise certain characteristics and the audience will believe.'

He touched his fingers to his cheek in an affected feminine gesture, and she laughed aloud, irresistibly charmed. Bai Shen regarded her with warm approval. He certainly enjoyed having a receptive audience.

'And don't forget you have one grand advantage,' he said.

'What is that?'

He shrugged. 'You actually *are* a woman.'

Minister Cao Wei's offices were among the most ostentatious in the Administrative City. The government bureaucracy was a city unto itself that had grown around the bones of the former imperial palace. Each ministry was housed in a great assembly hall and surrounded by a constellation of bureaus, offices and courts. Located in the northernmost sector nearest to the palace, the Ministry of Personnel was one of the most influential branches within the imperial government. Fei Long and Old Man Liang were met at the door by a retainer who ushered them into the minister's meeting room.

The chamber was lavishly furnished. A round table stood at the centre of the room upon a woven rug. An ivory carving depicting the dragon-boat races spanned an entire wall. The minister entered through a beaded curtain. He wore the ceremonial headdress of state and his robe was forest green in colour and embroidered with a phoenix pattern at the front. It billowed around an expanding middle. Minister Cao had grown wider since Fei Long had seen him last.

'Fei Long, welcome!'

Another man also wearing the robe and cap of state entered behind the minister. Fei Long didn't recognise him, but

Old Liang murmured a warning to him as they bowed to the two officials.

Careful.

'Inspector Tong and I must both offer our deepest condolences for your father.'

'Thank you, Minister Cao. Inspector Tong.' Fei Long bowed again, acknowledging both of them in turn. He took a quick assessment of the second official as he lowered his head.

Tong was younger than Cao. His beard was trimmed to a sharp point and his eyes remained fixed on Fei Long as if targeting a pigeon during a hunt. Fei Long didn't recognise the insignia on his robe, but it was clear he held some authority even in the presence of a senior minister.

Cao gestured toward the round table in welcome. 'The last time I drank with your father, we enjoyed a flask of Guilin spirits together. Shall we have some in his honour?'

'Just tea is fine, my lord.'

Cao looked somewhat glum at his response, but Tong snorted. 'Not quite his father's son, then.'

The senior minister called for tea and the three of them sat, while Liang remained standing off to the side.

'I was just telling Minister Tong what a tragedy it is to lose Chang like that.'

'Who else would tell outrageous stories during all those serious meetings? One might mistakenly think there was work to be done if it weren't for Minister Chang,' Tong replied with an acid tongue.

Cao laughed heartily, either ignoring the slight or missing it completely. 'Yes! There really was no one else like Old Chang.'

The tea was poured while Cao continued to recount favourable stories of his father. For each one, Tong managed to add the slightest of cuts. Fei Long's grip tightened on his cup. It was ill-mannered to malign the deceased, but it was also ill-mannered to show his anger before his host.

Cao Wei served in the highest government circles where his

father had held a much more humble assignment within the Ministry of Works in the department of agriculture. Still, it was a position to be proud of and highly coveted. Cao seemed to have taken a liking to his father when he was still a student and had helped him secure the head position after the civil exams. The minister had become a benefactor to their family through the years.

Though Fei Long trusted Minister Cao, he was certain it was no accident that Tong happened to also be at this meeting. They were nearly through the first pour when Cao focused in on more serious matters.

'I was thinking about how your father's position within the Ministry of Works is still open. You were a candidate for the civil exams at one time, if I recall. I can put in a good word for you, my son.'

Tong's face twitched at the suggestion, but he covered it by taking a sip of his tea.

'The minister is too generous,' Fei Long replied. 'I'm afraid this unworthy servant is not qualified.'

'Nonsense.' Tong set down his cup and the lid rattled from the impact. 'Your father's name is enough. What need is there for qualification?'

Cao erupted again in laughter. 'Inspector Tong, you are always playing like that. Young Fei Long is more than qualified. Why, he passed the military exams with excellent marks. You should see him with a bow and arrow. I'm sure we can get a dispensation on the civil exams.'

The thought of serving in the administrative court made Fei Long's chest constrict. He didn't have the wile or charm for it. If he dared to accept, he'd be exposed as a fraud.

'Minister Cao, I must confess I have no talent for politics. It pains me to refuse such generosity, but my duty is with the imperial army.'

'Worthy! Very worthy. See?' Cao rapped his knuckles

against the table. 'I told you the son was a man of honour, serving the empire so dutifully.'

'So he is,' Tong said, his tone flat.

Cao poured the next round of tea himself, a great courtesy coming from the senior official. From that gesture alone, Fei Long knew there was another reason he'd been invited.

'How is your sister, Pearl?' Cao asked.

Fei Long kept his expression neutral. 'She is saddened by our father's passing, but otherwise she is well.'

Tong stared back at him, his face a stone wall as he scoured Fei Long for any sign of weakness.

Cao nodded gravely. 'Only two months until the journey to Khitan. A tragedy that Old Chang couldn't see his daughter wed.'

The senior minister bowed his head and Tong followed his example, but it was only a cursory gesture. Inspector Tong was working deliberately to get Fei Long's guard up. It was the sort of subtle power struggle that Fei Long had learned early on he had no knack for and one of the reasons he'd opted for the provincial garrison rather than the politics of Changan. His work in the imperial army was honest and straightforward, even if it was without glory.

'I apologise, Inspector Tong. I have been long away from the capital. I'm ignorant of how you knew my father?'

'The apology is mine. I should have introduced myself properly.' All the words that came from him were cold and correct. 'I serve in the Censorate.'

Tong let the silence take over so there could be no mistaking the seriousness of his purpose there. Fei Long should have guessed from the title that the dour-faced Tong was an imperial censor. These officials were responsible for investigating the inner workings of each of the government ministries.

'Inspector Tong has been assigned to oversee foreign affairs. He's been telling me about all the preparations for the caravan. The Emperor has bestowed a bounty of treasures for young Pearl's dowry. Silks, gold, jade treasures—'

'We have heard some disturbing news recently,' Tong interrupted. 'Rumours that Lady Chang has objections to the wedding. So much so that she may have left the city.'

'Rumours. Rumours.' Cao made a shushing noise at Tong's indelicate approach. He was the quintessential statesman, toiling away at keeping the peace. Even so, the senior minister looked at Fei Long expectantly.

'Who has started such vicious lies while our family still mourns for our father?' Fei Long demanded, while his palms began to sweat.

'Inspector Tong means no offence,' Cao soothed and Tong mumbled his apology.

Fei Long felt sick to his stomach; first for the lie he needed to perpetuate and second for using his father's death in such a way. He'd discussed the strategy with Old Man Liang and it was the only way they would be able to avoid scrutiny.

'My sister is in mourning at home. Pearl is very deeply stricken.'

Cao turned to the younger official, showing that he still held rank here. 'I told you there was nothing to worry about. I've known the family for over these twenty years.'

Fei Long had no doubt that it was Cao who had suggested Pearl to the imperial court as a candidate for *heqin*. There was more than his family honour at stake. Minister Cao's reputation also rested precariously upon it.

'I never expected such scandalous rumours to be true,' Tong deflected. 'It's good to hear that my expectations were correct.'

Twisting like a snake.

'Let us move on to more practical matters,' Tong continued. 'The date is approaching quickly. Normally, the *heqin* bride is a member of the imperial court. Under these unusual circumstances, the Censorate has suggested it would be wise to bring Lady Chang into the palace to complete her preparations.'

Old Man Liang jerked his head up in the corner. Fei Long prayed the censor missed the sudden movement.

'Pearl is still very distraught over our father,' Fei Long replied calmly. 'The pain of leaving our family is difficult enough. If I may humbly request that she be allowed to remain at home until the time of the journey to ease the transition?'

'The emotional nature of women,' Tong snorted.

Cao raised a hand to silence him. 'Listen here, Fei Long does have a point. Young Pearl has been tasked with a great duty when her family has suffered such tragedy. He's only acting as the new head of the Chang clan. At the same time—' Cao turned to Fei Long '—Inspector Tong also has a good point. The court would want to insure that your sister is prepared for her duty as a foreign bride. Let me propose that Inspector Tong be allowed to pay your family a visit in a week or so to speak with the lady. That way, we can be assured that young Pearl is receiving the proper instruction.'

Fei Long let out his breath slowly. It was a temporary reprieve only. They had less time to prepare Yan Ling than he had thought.

'A just decision, Minister Cao,' he said, fighting not to show any hint of anxiety. 'And I assure you, my sister is receiving the very best instruction possible.'

Chapter Six

'Lengthen your step and walk slower.'

Bai Shen stood with arms folded beneath the shade of the circular pavilion in the rear courtyard. He had her strolling from one side of the garden to the other while he watched like a hawk.

'Never hurry. The audience waits for you,' he barked out.

He turned out to be as strident as Fei Long when giving orders.

Yan Ling stepped carefully, trying to concentrate on keeping her head up, her steps fluid. By the time she reached the rock sculpture at the end of the garden, she felt as if she'd been running tea from table to table during the afternoon rush rather than strolling like a lady in a tranquil garden.

'Again,' he commanded.

She tried to turn around as elegantly as she could.

'Not so straight,' he complained with an impatient up-down wave of his hand. 'Sway a little. Like a young bamboo in the breeze.'

What was he talking about? He kept on telling her to look natural, which became impossible when she was concentrating so hard. Her muscles were tense and aching. The more she tried to follow his instructions, the more awkward she felt.

Bai Shen rubbed a hand over his chin thoughtfully as she came towards him. He stepped down from the pavilion to intercept her.

'Where did Fei Long find you?' he asked.

Find her. As if she were someone's discarded shoe.

'In a teahouse.' She dabbed at her forehead with the edge of her sleeve and wondered if ladies were allowed to sweat. 'I was a servant there. I fetched and carried, brewed tea, swept the floors.'

His expression grew intense. She could see why audiences were drawn to him. Every movement of his body was graceful, controlled and compelling.

'I would make myself as small as possible if I were playing a tea girl,' he went on. 'She would always be placed at the back of the stage and only appear when needed. Most importantly, she would never, never draw attention away from the leads.' His eyes lit up. 'You don't like being watched.'

'Not at all.'

'Your fear shows in every movement. You have always been the mouse.'

'Well, I am afraid.' She threw her hands onto her hips in agitation. 'I can't walk, I can't talk. I don't even know how to drink tea, which is the one thing I should know. And in two months I have to convince everyone that I'm fit to be a princess.'

Despair gripped her and held on tight. She should tell Fei Long it wasn't possible and that he needed to find someone else, but the thought of disappointing him sickened her. She'd sworn to Fei Long that she wouldn't abandon him.

'You need to become something grand.' Bai Shen puffed out his chest.

She tried imitating him by pulling her shoulders back and lifting her chin up.

'Not just outside, but in here. In spirit.' He placed a hand over his heart and miraculously seemed to grow in presence before her. 'Become a phoenix.'

A phoenix? He was mad. 'You're mad,' she said.

'There is a light that comes from you when you're angry.' He tapped her nose impetuously. 'Why only then? Don't you know, my pretty lady? There is a pleasure in watching a woman move. There is a joy in being that beautiful woman, admired by all.'

'But I'm not beautiful—'

He hushed her with a raised hand. 'Do you think Fei Long would choose an ugly girl?'

She considered telling him that Fei Long had simply chosen her because he had been desperate and she had been scared of being in the streets.

'Convince me that you're beautiful,' he said in a tone that would not be refused. 'Not by trying to hide the servant girl, but by overshadowing her with the woman.'

She laughed, part in disbelief, but part in hope. The heaviness within her lifted just listening to him. 'How did you do that?'

'Li Bai Shen is the best,' he boasted.

Bai Shen was a quintessential performer. He knew how to act the part on stage and that was exactly what she had to do. She needed to make the world her stage.

He worked with her for the rest of the morning, walking beside her and demonstrating the 'water sleeve' techniques he used on stage. Her robe swirled about her feet while Bai Shen stepped around her, sometimes nodding, sometimes frowning.

'The silk is a banner,' he instructed. 'Drawing attention to you.'

Yan Ling followed his lead and shifted her arms from one side to the other, feeling the fool, but doing it anyway.

'The clothing says, "look at me, I am an object of grace and beauty." Say it.'

She giggled. 'I am an object of grace and beauty.'

Though she knew she wasn't. Fei Long hadn't chosen her

or her manners or her appearance. Their paths had simply crossed at the right time and place.

'Good,' he finally declared. He affected a yawn. 'For a novice. Tell your Fei Long to plan his lessons later in the day next time. Li Bai Shen does not wake up before noon.'

With that, he raised his arm, palm flat to chest, and executed a sweeping bow.

Yan Ling watched as the handsome actor withdrew from the courtyard. She wasn't sure if half of the movements she learned could actually be used, but she was no longer thinking of every misstep and mistake. Instead, she was dreaming of becoming a phoenix.

Several hours later, she was actually excited when Fei Long summoned her to his study. He stood from behind his desk as she entered and she imagined herself catching his eye.

'Miss Yan Ling.'

She inclined her head and gave a bow, already feeling more graceful and feminine. 'My lord.'

When she glanced up, Fei Long's familiar stare greeted her along with the same rigid set of his jaw and hard line of his mouth that always hinted there was something more pressing on his mind. Something more important than her. Her spirits sank mid-flight. She supposed she couldn't expect him to fall to his knees with admiration.

'How was the morning lesson?'

'The lesson went very well! Your friend—' She stopped short, biting down on her lip to pull back her exuberance. He didn't want to hear about how she'd paraded and laughed. He wanted to see that she could be elegant and controlled.

'I learned something of great value,' she amended.

Fei Long nodded, yet he didn't seem pleased. The muscles of his jaw remained tense. 'It's of the utmost importance that you pay careful attention.'

'Yes, my lord,' she replied, feeling as if she was being unjustly admonished.

He was always so stern, his expression like stone. For weeks, she had worked at trying to gauge his displeasure or approval, but from what she could see, it was between the hard line as opposed to a slight curve of his mouth. Sometimes his eyes would light curiously when he regarded her. It was more cryptic than reading tea leaves.

He came around the desk to direct her to a smaller table against the wall. It was positioned directly beneath the window that opened into the courtyard. The blinds were rolled up and tied to allow the late-afternoon sunlight to flow into the room.

The chair had been arranged to face the desk. He urged her to sit. Yan Ling smoothed out her robe as she did so. A scroll of paper stretched out in front of her, weighted down by a smooth, black stone. Beside it, a slender brush rested against an ivory holder along with a shallow ceramic dish.

'We need to begin your writing lessons.'

She stared at the implements before her. 'But we have only two more months.'

'My father was known for his talent for words. He taught both my sister and myself.' He came to stand beside the table. 'You would be expected to know how to read as well as write.'

'But will anyone be sending me letters once I reach Khitan?'

She watched him as he struggled for an answer. 'The imperial court might send messages on occasion,' he replied.

'Wouldn't that be handled by ambassadors or someone more important?'

She didn't mean to be so contrary, but it seemed that she had just managed to climb one hill to find an even higher mountain beyond it. Fei Long's presence made her more nervous. While travelling together, they had begun to form a fragile familiarity, but he'd become distant again since their arrival in the capital.

'I might be expected to send you occasional messages as your brother,' he argued.

Only to uphold the deception. Loneliness swept over Yan Ling. She had no one to exchange letters with. No one would care what happened to her once she left the borders of the empire.

'Let's begin then,' she deflected.

'We'll start today with basic brush strokes.'

Fei Long described the process for making ink from the charcoal stick while she listened intently. Instruction always seemed to ease the tension from him. It was a ritual with expected roles and outcomes: teacher and student. She poured a few drops of water from a vial into the well of the ink stone. Then she ground the stick in small circles until the water became onyx black.

'The way you hold the brush is very important for proper technique.'

He handed her the brush. Her fingers curled clumsily around the delicate bamboo shaft.

'Press your thumb here. Curve your first finger.'

His steady hands enclosed hers and a ripple of warmth besieged her. The next breath lodged in her throat and she grew still, at a loss at what to do.

They had touched before. They must have every time she handed him something or he'd helped her onto the horse during their journey. Yet when Fei Long's hands moved gently over her fingers to position them, her heartbeat skipped.

'Don't grip it too tight. Now hook your middle finger around here,' he continued, unaware of how her pulse quickened beneath his touch.

'Keep the brush straight as you execute the brush strokes.' His voice was low, confident. Sensual without meaning to be as it pierced deep to fill her. 'More control that way. Understand?'

She nodded mutely, afraid to speak. He'd been nothing but Lord Chang up until then, her disapproving task master. This rush of feeling was unacceptable. She swallowed as he moved away from her.

My Fair Concubine

'Is there something wrong?' he asked.

Wrong? The brush held fast in her hand and she didn't move a finger.

'No, my lord. I…I must be more tired than I thought I was.' She was ashamed for making such an excuse, but she was more ashamed of the heat swimming through her. It would pass.

His tone hardened behind her. 'As you mentioned, we have only two months. Not much time.'

She kept her head down. If she looked up, he would certainly be able to see everything revealed in her face. 'I can continue,' she said apologetically.

'Good.'

He took the brush from her and stood to her right. She shifted aside in the chair to give him space. Suddenly, she'd become aware of everything about him: his wide shoulders and how close his arm came to hers. The rustle of his robe as he moved. She watched, transfixed, as Fei Long dipped the tip of the brush into the oily blackness of the ink, swirling to remove the excess. He then braced a hand against the lower corner of the paper and brushed a single dot over the pristine white paper.

'*Diǎn,*' he declared. The next stroke was a short horizontal one below it. '*Héng.*'

He continued, calling out the name after each stroke. A bold downward stroke, followed by a hook. Then a series of slanting marks to the side. There was confidence and strength in each movement. Eventually a single character emerged. She stared at it, uncomprehending.

'Forever,' Fei Long said.

'Forever,' she repeated softly, trying to imprint the character in her mind. The shape of it held mysterious power.

'There are eight basic strokes that make up "forever".' He broke down each stroke separately on the paper, moving from right to left in perfect even spaces. 'It is important to master each one from the beginning.'

He placed the brush back into her hand. She knew she was gripping it too hard again as she dipped it into the ink stone, but it was the only way to keep her hand from shaking. Before she could place the tip to the paper, Fei Long moved behind her. She closed her eyes as his hand rested against her shoulder to straighten her back. His other arm circled temporarily around her to position the brush and she flooded with fever. Her toes curled with the ache of it when he moved away.

'Repeat each stroke, moving downwards. Fifty of each, first one and then the other.' His tone remained steady.

He felt nothing. None of the unwanted fire within her. Silly girl, why would he?

Fei Long continued with his instruction, unmoved. All she was to him was a student. Under less favourable terms, she was a peasant, a servant beneath him that he'd chosen to bestow such learning upon. She had to remember that.

She attempted the first stroke. The single *diǎn* looked so simple, but the ink pooled on the paper and the dot lost its shape.

'Too much pressure,' he commented. 'And the stroke must be done quickly. The ink and paper will take in any hesitation and uncertainty.'

Would the brushstrokes show the turmoil of her emotions?

She tried again and the mark looked a little more like the one Fei Long had made. He watched over the next several attempts.

'Better. Continue.'

He moved over to his desk. Though they faced one another, she kept her focus on the brush, trying to keep her marks even. She could hear the rasp of paper each time Fei Long turned a page.

She finished practising the basic strokes and then fidgeted nervously while he stood and inspected her work over her shoulder. Her fingers were stiff from holding the brush. She'd been afraid of releasing her hold on it in case she couldn't find the right position again on her own.

Fei Long hardly spoke as he replaced the sheet of paper before her. He wrote out several simple characters. The first set she recognised as numbers. Then there were a few examples that only used a few strokes. Once again, he instructed her to copy the examples.

'The order of each stroke is important,' he told her. 'The direction of each stroke is also important.'

Everything in its place with him. Fei Long believed in order and boundaries that should never be crossed. Hadn't he assured her of that the first night of their journey?

For the next hour, she meticulously worked on the new characters. When she set down her brush to grind more ink, her throat seized when she saw Fei Long watching her. His dark eyebrows pulled close into a frown and his mouth tightened in displeasure.

She didn't know what he could possibly be unhappy about. She'd been even more meticulous today than ever before. Her brushstrokes were as neat as she could possibly make them. She had taken special care not to spill any ink.

'My lord?'

'There is something I need to tell you.'

It wasn't fair that one look could pour so much fear into her. All she could do was wait in silence.

'I made a visit to the Administrative City today. The Minister of Foreign Relations wishes to send a representative to meet with you.'

'When?'

'Two weeks.'

At first she was relieved that his foul mood wasn't because of her, but too quickly her relief was replaced by panic.

'Two weeks? But that isn't enough time.'

Fei Long remained impassive, though his frown deepened. Her hands clenched just seeing how the muscles along his jaw tensed.

'They wanted you to relocate to the imperial palace, but I managed to negotiate for you to stay here,' he said.

The imperial palace. She hadn't realised the enormity of what they were trying to do until now. What had foreign lords and princesses been to her before but faraway stories and dreams? This was a matter that involved the imperial court and perhaps even the Emperor himself.

He must have seen the sudden sick look on her face. 'You won't be alone. I'll be with you. It will be a courtesy visit, I'm certain. Unfortunately, Inspector Tong will most likely come himself rather than send a retainer. He's taken an unusual interest in this alliance.'

She didn't know one minister from another, but it was clear that this visit could be the end of everything if she failed.

'Do you think I'll be ready?'

'You will do well.' His tone was more of a command than a comfort. 'We just have to work harder. I have faith in you, Yan Ling.'

She nodded. Her palms grew damp and she wiped them against her robe when he wasn't looking. The only thing that could make her more anxious than Fei Long's disapproval was his trust.

After the evening meal, Yan Ling retired to her chamber early, but she didn't sleep. She lit the oil lamp and unfolded the list of characters that Fei Long had given her to memorise. He hadn't dined with them that night or any night for that matter. She always took her meals with Dao in the servants' dining hall. She kept on reciting the characters to herself over dinner, afraid she'd forget.

Now that she was alone, she went through each character, matching them up with the words they represented. There were fifty or so on the paper. Strung together, they meant nothing. They were only practice words.

In her first days there, Yan Ling had looked through Pearl's belongings. It wasn't right to think of this chamber or the personal items within it as hers. She was there for only a few more months before she would be making an even longer journey. In one drawer, she'd found several books. When she'd looked through them, the characters had blurred together, black lines and dashes on the page with no meaning. It was hard to believe she'd ever be able to understand the knowledge held there, but now a faint promise dangled before her.

She looked through the first characters again. Each one reminded her of Fei Long. He was adamant about teaching her as much as she could learn in the next months. She wouldn't fail him.

Soon she wasn't thinking of the words. Instead, her mind drifted to the careful pressure of his hand around hers. The roughened texture of his fingers.

It was only because they were forced to spend so much time alone, she insisted. Her former master had been old and married. And fat. Fei Long was young and not unhandsome. And strong. That was the closest she would come to admitting she liked the way he looked. She squeezed her eyes shut as if that would stop the images of Fei Long from haunting her.

She'd made a habit of trying to read his expressions, which only seemed to shift from stern approval to controlled disapproval. Whenever the hard line of his mouth softened so much as to allow a smile through, her stomach swirled like a flight of sparrows.

This was stupid of her. She bent to look at the next line of characters and reminded herself that these things just happened: yin and yang and clouds and rain. Fei Long must never know. She'd die of shame if he ever found out.

'Yan Ling?'

She jumped at the sound of her name. Dao stood at the edge of the sitting area, looking at her curiously.

Without thinking, Yan Ling sat up and slipped her arm behind her back. The pulse in her neck jumped as the paper in her hands crinkled mercilessly.

'I saw the light from the hallway and thought you must have fallen asleep without blowing it out,' Dao said, but her almond eyes narrowed with awareness.

'I wasn't as sleepy as I thought.' Yan Ling's heart pounded guiltily as she tried to fumble the paper into her sleeve. It burned against her palm like an illicit love letter. 'I think I will go to bed now, though.'

Dao came forwards with the feigned uninterest of a cat on the prowl. 'Let me help you with your robe then.'

'No, you don't need to—'

The clever servant manoeuvred around her and grabbed the paper with a triumphant laugh.

'Fox demon!' Yan Ling sprang at Dao, but the girl had already run to the far side of the room beside the dressing screen.

Her ears burned while Dao unfolded the paper and held it up to the light. 'Oh.' The delight faded from her rounded face and her lower lip stuck out in a pout. 'Well, this isn't nearly as interesting as I'd hoped.'

Yan Ling stalked over to retrieve the paper with a vicious swipe. 'Those are the words I need to memorise.'

The act of studying the characters Fei Long had given her kept him close like a secret, gossamer thread tying them together. She knew it was girlish nonsense, yet her blood still heated at being caught. Excessive irritation was the only way to account for her guilty behaviour.

'You're like an alley cat, prowling for gossip,' Yan Ling accused.

Dao folded her hands before her with embarrassment. 'I'm sorry. I didn't mean to intrude.'

Of all the servants in the mansion, she was closest to Dao. Yan Ling didn't want to do anything to ruin their relationship.

'I'm sorry for raising my voice.' The unexpected feelings she'd discovered about Fei Long made her anxious. 'There's so much to learn and it feels as though there aren't enough hours in a day.' What she meant was that everything was forgiven. Could they please continue as if nothing happened?

'What are the ones with the dots?' *That moment is passed,* Dao responded silently. *We can be as we were before.*

'Those are the words I've forgotten the meaning for. I'll have to ask Lord Chang tomorrow, I suppose.'

'There are only a few of them. You must be doing very well.'

'I don't know. There must be hundreds of characters to learn.'

'Well, thousands really,' Dao replied. 'If you want, I can tell you what they are.'

'You can read?'

'Only a little.' Dao fluttered her eyelashes demurely. 'If I may?'

Yan Ling handed the paper to her and Dao read the dotted characters out loud before handing it back.

'I was allowed to sit in on the same lessons as Miss Pearl when we were younger. The elder Lord Chang believed in educating his servants.'

A ray of light peeked through the clouds. 'Can you help me?'

Dao seemed hesitant. 'I never learned as much as Miss Pearl and the lessons stopped when I had too many chores to do—'

'But you read so wonderfully just then.'

Dao's smile widened, rounding out her cheeks. 'If you would like me to, I'll try. Your success is important to all of us.'

Fei Long had only a few hours each day for lessons, but if she studied at night with Dao as well, she wouldn't seem so hopelessly lost. She would devote every moment of her day to transforming herself into a suitable bride. Much like Lady Min had done, she flew at Dao and hugged her.

Chapter Seven

Bai Shen stepped into the parlour from the entrance hall and Fei Long stood as he would have for an imperial official. Beside him, Yan Ling did the same. She waited in the sitting area as he went to greet Bai Shen, who was playing the role of Inspector Tong that morning.

Over the last week, Yan Ling's training had become his singular focus. The keen-eyed inspector would be looking for reasons to discredit them.

She bowed with a graceful tilt of her head as Bai Shen approached. Her jewelled hairpin caught the light.

'I am humbled to meet you, illustrious sir.'

Bai Shen bowed in turn. 'Miss Pearl.'

Fei Long tried to distance himself and assess her appearance objectively. She was benefiting from the generosity of the kitchen. The hollows of her cheeks had rounded out slightly, losing their sharpness. The paleness of her skin had taken on a new brightness and warmth.

Yan Ling presented herself well, he decided. Her shoulders had lost their slouch and her expression was soft. She managed to project a tranquillity about her that must have required hours of practice. Usually she never stood still.

'Miss Pearl, you're as beautiful as they say,' Bai Shen drawled garrulously.

'You flatter me, Inspector Tong.'

Fei Long stopped them. 'No government censor would open with that.'

'Why not? It's perfectly acceptable.'

'This is an official visit. Be serious.'

Bai Shen wrinkled up his face in disdain. His friend was in less-than-perfect form. He'd asked the actor to come early, which meant that Bai Shen was hung over, if he wasn't still drunk.

Yan Ling valiantly tried to continue in her role. She averted her eyes shyly. 'The inspector is too generous. Will you have some tea?'

'Tea would be wonderful.' Bai Shen strode into the sitting area and slumped down into a chair. His head fell back, eyes closed. 'And food if you have it.'

Yan Ling stifled a laugh, lifting her sleeve over her mouth in true lady-like fashion. The scoundrel Bai Shen opened one eye at the sound, a crooked grin cutting through his sickly pallor. The only thing Bai Shen craved more than a good party was attention.

'Get up.' Fei Long went over and gave Bai Shen a swift kick. 'Let's do this again.'

Dao, who had just stepped into the room with a tea tray in hand, promptly turned to head back into the corridor. They took their positions again.

'Inspector Tong, an honour to meet you.'

'Lady Chang, the honour is mine. And what an exquisite vase this is,' Bai Shen gushed. Fei Long shot him a look, which he ignored. 'Your father must have had impeccable taste.'

'He would be pleased to hear it, sir.' She bowed and her eyes turned downwards with a hint of sadness.

'My condolences for your family's recent loss,' Bai Shen continued. 'But there are important matters we must discuss today.'

'I understand. Will you sit and have some tea?'

They arranged themselves in the sitting area with Yan Ling upon the couch and the two of them seated across from her in wooden chairs. Dao entered again with the tea tray. They waited until she finished pouring.

'This is a very important duty you're to fulfil,' Bai Shen declared with a suitable amount of pompousness. 'We must be assured that you are completely prepared.'

'I've been working very hard to get ready—'

'No, no,' Bai Shen cut in. 'This is all supposed to be effortless. You must say, "I am humbled by the task and hope to bring honour to the empire".'

Yan Ling repeated the actor's words to herself, her expression thoughtful. Her mouth moved silently while Fei Long watched the curve of her lips: soft, rounded, pleasing to the eye. His breathing deepened unexpectedly.

'Mention humility and honour and the greater good of the empire whenever you can. I learned that from listening to this fool.' Bai Shen jabbed an elbow in his direction before taking a sip of his tea. Then he sat back, groaning. 'I'm dying. Will someone be merciful and kill me?'

Yan Ling leaned towards him in concern. 'I know of a brew that might help. Many of our customers ask for it after a night of heavy drinking.'

'You're a goddess, my lady. We had a show last night, so of course we had to celebrate afterwards.'

'Oh, what story?'

'"The Maiden of Yue."'

Fei Long glared at the too-familiar exchange between them. 'Can we concentrate on the problem at hand instead of this dog's theatrics?'

'Who's the dog so worried about his masters?' Bai Shen retorted.

'Let's not fight,' Yan Ling soothed.

'We have another show in three nights.' Though Bai Shen dropped his voice to a whisper, there was no subtlety there. 'You should come see it.'

Fei Long turned on her. 'You need to convince Inspector Tong that you're a well-bred lady prepared to go to Khitan. Humouring this drunkard won't help your cause.'

'Promoting harmony is one of the four virtues,' she replied stiffly.

'The infamous *Four Virtues*.' Bai Shen chortled. 'Stricken by your own poison!'

Fei Long wanted to strangle him.

'All this proper sitting and standing is good practice, but shouldn't I learn more about your family?' Yan Ling interjected. 'What if they ask me about your father? Such as, how did he get his government position?'

Her questions took him aback. 'Minister Cao Wei took a liking to him and gave my father an appointment after he passed the imperial exams.'

'I don't even know the most basic things,' she insisted. 'How much older are you than Pearl? Were the two of you very close? And when did you leave home for your military appointment?'

'There's no need to know such details. It would be rude to ask anything so personal.' These weren't the most intimate of questions, but even so they raised his defences.

'She's right, you know,' Bai Shen said. 'The two of you don't seem like brother and sister at all.'

Fei Long sensed a rebellion brewing in the ranks. 'I'll be there beside you in case Tong decides to ask anything of that nature. It's best that you say as little as possible. Let's practise that.'

Yan Ling blatantly ignored his suggestion. 'According to Bai

Shen, I should be over-prepared for the performance. I should know everything about Miss Pearl.'

Fei Long rubbed a hand over his temples. 'You don't have to become my sister. Inspector Tong has never met Pearl.'

'But what about Minister Cao Wei?' she asked. 'If he's your father's benefactor, won't he be there as well?'

Yan Ling and Dao stared at him expectantly. Even Bai Shen had straightened to raise a questioning eyebrow.

'I've already been thinking about that,' Fei Long said. 'This will only work if Cao Wei doesn't attend.'

More subterfuge. More deception.

'Can't we let the minister in on the secret?' she asked nervously.

'That is impossible,' Fei Long explained. 'Cao Wei is a senior official within the imperial court. He would never let such a transgression pass.'

Yan Ling wrung her sleeve, crinkling the silk beneath her fingers. Her poise was faltering under pressure. Ill-fated indeed.

'All you need to do is concentrate on your part and I'll take care of the rest,' he assured.

She nodded blankly.

'Yan Ling.' He waited for her to meet his eyes. If they stayed focused, they could do this. Together. 'Pearl and I are seven years apart. I left the city nearly five years ago after the military exams.'

The information seemed to calm her. 'Were you and Pearl close?'

'Our relationship was a harmonious one.'

Her nose wrinkled. 'Harmonious?'

What else could be said? He and Pearl had got along well enough.

'I've never had a brother or a sister,' Yan Ling insisted. 'It would help to know what it's like.'

'Miss Pearl worshipped her older brother,' Dao supplied helpfully.

'Fei Long was very strict about her upbringing.' Bai Shen chimed in, his voice muffled. He was resting his head against his hand as if it had become too heavy to lift.

Fei Long shifted uncomfortably in his seat. How had this conversation become about him? He thought of how his sister had depended on him. Their mother was gone and there was no one else in the household to ensure her education and well being. When Pearl had been betrothed to Khitan, she'd written him impassioned letters. He'd assured her it was a great honour and the marriage promised a bright future for her. Even when she'd begged for his help, he'd remained steadfast.

'Pearl was always diligent in her studies,' he told Yan Ling. 'Sometimes she was impetuous, but only because she was young. She was well-mannered, thoughtful and obedient. Remember that and you'll do well presenting yourself to Inspector Tong, I'm sure of it.'

Yan Ling absorbed each description with quiet concentration. He always admired how seriously she took her role. So much depended on it.

He moved closer and considered taking her hand, but decided against it. 'If I had seen you for the first time today, I would have never known that you were that impulsive teahouse girl from the provinces.'

Her hopeful gaze held on to him. 'Really?'

'Yes. That's the truth.'

The scouting mission was underway the next morning. To Fei Long's surprise, Bai Shen appeared at the gates with a determined expression and they ventured together to the Administrative City. On foot, the journey took them the first half of the hour and they arrived at the section gates once the many offices and functionaries had had a chance to settle into their daily routine.

They watched from the street as the army of clerks and messengers travelled between the various offices. A good portion of the northern part of Changan worked for the imperial government in one form or another.

'I can't imagine you working here,' Bai Shen remarked.

'It's reputable work,' Fei Long argued. His father, his grandfather, and on and on back, his line of ancestors had held government positions in one form or another.

'Unlike the theatre.' Bai Shen tossed him a sideways glance before continuing along the colonnade toward the central ministry buildings.

The imperial palace had moved just beyond the city walls at the start of the dynasty, to a secluded area cordoned off by more walls and gates. These government offices were the closest most citizens would ever come to being in the presence of their imperial ruler. Of the illustrious officials of the Six Ministries, only the most senior and highest-ranking were ever given an audience within the palace itself. Unlike the bureaucracy of the ministries, the Censorate reported directly to the Emperor, which was why men like Tong were treated with such care.

They passed by a patrol of city guards without a blink in their direction.

'It should be easy to blend in,' Bai Shen assessed.

Fei Long smirked. 'Not in those robes.'

As usual, Bai Shen was the most colourfully dressed in the crowd. He dismissed the comment with a wave.

'The Ministry of Personnel resides in that building with the green rooftop.' Fei Long gestured toward the towering assembly hall at the end of the avenue. 'Minister Cao is there every morning overseeing special petitions.' He turned to Bai Shen. 'Are you still in good with that crew of rascals?'

'Everyone loves Li Bai Shen.'

'Can you position yourselves near Minister Cao's offices that morning?'

'A diversion.' Bai Shen looked thoughtful. 'Yes, a grand one.'

'No. *Not* a grand one.' Fei Long stared him down. 'Just delay him.'

He imagined having to stand before the magistrate on behalf of Bai Shen and his entire acting troupe. It was something Fei Long had done years ago when the crew had been thrown into prison after being disrespectful to the city guards. Loudly and drunkenly disrespectful.

'And nothing illegal,' he added on the heels of the unpleasant memory.

'Of course. But you're going to owe us a round of drinks after this.'

They walked the perimeter, with Bai Shen surveying the gates and exits as if planning a siege.

'We'll need to be sure he doesn't slip past us,' the actor said. He peered intently down the deserted alley along the western side. 'Six of us could cover it. Maybe seven.'

'What are you planning?'

'Better you don't know.' Bai Shen started down the empty lane, head bowed in concentration. Fei Long imagined he was scripting out his performance line by line.

He followed Bai Shen into the shade cast by the high wall. The hum of the street faded behind him in a rare silence seldom found in the crowded city. It seemed as if had been ages ago when he and Bai Shen had walked the streets of Changan together. Not since his days as a student.

It was tempting to think of those days as carefree. He'd had his wild times carousing in the entertainment district, but Fei Long had always felt the weight of responsibility. He'd never forgotten it, even when he'd left the city to try to make a name for himself. The sense of duty just hadn't been as palpable until his father had left them.

'Thank you,' he said, putting as much feeling as was proper into his words.

Bai Shen's back was to him, but the actor stopped in the middle of the alley and turned. 'What, we're friends here, right? No need for thanks.'

Fei Long never imagined he'd have to lean on the hapless companions of his youth or a stranger he'd just met in a remote teahouse. He never thought he'd have to deal in deception either or hide so completely from their family's respectable associates.

'Not just for this,' Fei Long said. 'For the work you've done with Yan Ling as well.'

Bai Shen raised an eyebrow. 'Done with?'

'Whatever you're teaching her, it must be working. The other day we were discussing a poem—or I was explaining a poem to her—and it was almost as though she understood its deeper meaning. At first she asked so many questions. Incessant really. Enough to make one's head hurt.'

'So she *seemed* intelligent enough,' Bai Shen mused.

Fei Long couldn't quite decipher that tone. 'Well, poems are simple—'

'Deceptively simple.'

'What I'm trying to say is, if I hadn't known where she had come from, I might have believed that she was an educated lady. She sounded like she had a true interest in the discussion. Of course I know she's only pretending.'

'Pretending to have some wit and intuition.'

'That's what you've been teaching her to do, isn't it? Acting lessons.'

Bai Shen made a snorting sound that raised Fei Long's ire considerably. The actor's eyes were gleaming as if there was some joke here that only he understood.

'So during all these pleasant conversations you've been enjoying with the young lady, she's been only acting.'

'I didn't say I was enjoying—' He hadn't said anything like that, had he?

'Playing a role,' Bai Shen continued relentless. 'And you

were playing a role, too, of course. That's the only way to explain how you could *pretend* to have a conversation of equals with your little tea girl.'

'That's insulting.'

'To you or to Yan Ling?'

His pulse was rising. The conversation had got out of hand. 'She's not a "little tea girl" and it's insulting to refer to her as mine—'

Fei Long stopped himself. Bai Shen was baiting him for his own amusement and he should have known better than to react. The situation was black and white in his head and no amount of taunting could change that.

He took a deep, steadying breath. Yan Ling didn't belong to him. She was here to fulfil a role, as they had agreed upon. And of course any intimacy between them was only for the purposes of her training. They were co-conspirators in a grand scheme.

Bai Shen laughed and the sound clanged in Fei Long's skull like a dissonant chime. 'Look at you! Ready to give me a thrashing over the slightest insult. It's not as if she's really your sister.'

'No,' Fei Long said after a pause. 'No, she's not.' He was confused and he did want to hit Bai Shen, now that the rascal mentioned it.

His friend grew serious. 'You're really going to do this, aren't you?'

'We have to. If we don't, my family name will be dishonoured. We'll be left with nothing.' It wasn't only him. Yan Ling, his steward, Dao—the entire household was involved. They had served his father and now him in good faith. 'They're all looking to me to do something, Bai Shen. I need to make this right.'

'Then maybe you should take credit for Yan Ling's transformation. You're the puppet master, after all.' There was no hint of amusement or teasing in his friend's remark. 'Though you're right. I have noticed a significant change in her.'

'I don't know what we would do if I hadn't found her.'

Bai Shen regarded him with an oddly contemplative look. It was the sort of look he might take on at the end of a late night, after several rounds of wine had made him melancholy and reflective.

'Be careful, Fei Long,' he said sombrely.

'I'm being very careful. Tong is as sharp as an eagle and he seems out to destroy our reputation. I'm taking every precaution when dealing with him.'

With a sigh, Bai Shen turned around to continue surveying the perimeter. 'You fool,' he muttered. 'That's not what I was talking about at all.'

Fei Long bit back his reply and watched Bai Shen retreat down the alley. He *was* being careful about Yan Ling. Diligently so. All of his senses sharpened when she was around. He was always on guard now, even in his own home. That was how careful he was.

Chapter Eight

Yan Ling lay on her back in bed and blinked at the alcove overhead. She had been up for an hour, staring sightlessly into blackness and waiting for the first sound of the morning birds. She had only slept fitfully through the night. An official notice had come from the ministry offices earlier in the week that the ministry would visit that morning.

Her worries about the dreaded Inspector Tong had chased her deep into her nightmares. She would open her mouth to speak only to find her tongue wouldn't move. All she could do was sit like a stone statue in her chair, blinking helplessly, while Fei Long glared at her in horror, dishonoured and disappointed.

She woke up and couldn't fall asleep again. Instead, she waited for the household to awaken. At the sound of footsteps outside, she rose to call Dao into her room.

'Look at you,' Dao bemoaned. 'I told you to get your rest.'

'Is it that bad?'

The sun hadn't risen yet and they had to light a lantern in order to comb and pin her hair. Dao frowned as she dusted fine powder beneath her eyes to try to mask the dark circles.

'I'll just say I'm losing sleep over the elder Lord Chang— I mean, my father's death,' Yan Ling said.

Dao's frown deepened, making Yan Ling even more agitated. She had been filled with advice over the last few days. Bai Shen told her to speak with her eyes while Fei Long insisted she say as little as possible. She needed to succeed for everyone's sake.

Once dressed, she went to walk the garden to gather her thoughts, but after a half an hour of that, her feet were sore and her nerves just as taut. She settled onto the stone bench at the edge of the garden as sunlight peeked over the rooftop.

The morning chill settled in around her, but she didn't want to go back to her chamber. Instead she huddled inside herself, tucking her hands together within the folds of her sleeves.

The kitchen stirred with activity over at the far corner and the scraping of pots and the clatter of dishes reminded her of mornings at the teahouse. If given the choice, would she want to go back? Certainly not. The last weeks in the Chang household had been the happiest time she'd ever known. She wore the fanciest silks and ate delicious meals from painted plates and bowls.

More precious than that, she had companionship. True companionship that came from the time that was her own. Her mornings were spent with Dao or Bai Shen. The afternoons with Fei Long were made of gold and jade. From the moment she woke each morning, she'd wait for their lesson.

All her life, she'd heard only commands. Her master and mistress would tell her what to do and to do it faster. The snatches of gossip and laughter with the cook and the kitchen boy could hardly be called conversation, not after the discussions she had now with Fei Long. Whenever she asked something or said something that made him pause and think, the thrill of victory would rush through her.

Yan Ling was no longer merely mimicking the actions of

an educated lady. She was learning. Something was changing inside of her, but was it enough?

'You're up very early.'

She knew it was Fei Long before he spoke. She'd sensed him from the moment he came out into the courtyard, yet her pulse still jumped with pleasure as he neared. Every day, she strained to recognise the weight of his footsteps and the echo of his voice from the far reaches of the house. She always knew when he left in the morning and always noted his return. It was a game she played only with herself and there was no way of winning.

Whenever he was home, there would be a chance of meeting in a hallway. She might catch a glimpse as he left a room. How she hungered for those accidental meetings. This time there was nothing accidental about their meeting. Fei Long quite deliberately lowered himself beside her. She shivered as his sleeve brushed against her arm.

'Are you cold?'

She shook her head, though she pulled her arms tighter around herself, her pulse racing. Fei Long breathed deep to take in the clean essence of the morning, then exhaled slowly. She was already reaching out to take in as much of him as she could: the broad shape of his hands, the quiet strength of his presence. Warmth and security radiated from him.

'Please don't give me any more advice,' she said as he started to speak. A hundred crickets were already chirping away in her head.

'I was only going to say that you don't have to worry.'

She nodded, even though she could already feel her tongue growing thick at all the proper speech she would need to coax from it that day.

'As long as you don't throw any tea on Inspector Tong, you'll be all right,' he continued, amused.

The reminder of their first meeting unsettled her even more.

It hinted of a false intimacy between them. They had no right to share such memories.

I'm only doing this for you, she wanted to cry out. Instead it wasn't even a whisper. He would never truly understand and the knowledge wounded her.

She smoothed her skirt over her knees nervously. 'I wish Inspector Tong was here right now so it could be done with.'

'I know.'

'Maybe you should have asked Bai Shen to stand in and play Pearl instead,' she suggested.

Fei Long laughed and the warmth from it penetrated the coolness of the morning. 'You're much better for the role.'

He sat with her in silence on the stone bench while the sky lightened to purple, then pink. Gradually the morning chased back the shadows.

'Are you sure you can count on Bai Shen, as unpredictable as he is in the morning?' she asked.

'He can always be trusted when there's a performance. That's exactly what this morning will be for him.'

Fei Long had moved closer to her, or somehow she had inched closer to him. In another time, in another life, he might put his arm around her. There would be no arranged marriage and no alliance. She'd have more than a few glances and incidental moments between them.

But then, what next? She didn't even know enough about proper courtship to fill out her misbegotten fantasies.

'A performance for us as well.' She looked to him, admiring the strong lines of his profile in the morning light. When he turned to her, she refused to look away. 'Promise me you'll stay beside me the entire time.'

'I promise.'

His gaze held on to her and she knew then that Fei Long wouldn't let anything happen. She would do this for him. So he could be proud and think well of her.

* * *

Old Liang sent the stable boy to keep watch at the ward gate and he returned with news shortly before the Horse hour. Inspector Tong was heading towards them accompanied only by a single attendant.

'Minister Cao isn't with him,' Dao confirmed as she rushed inside to take her place.

Yan Ling sat upon the couch in the front parlour as they had practised. Fei Long was seated across from her. Her heart pounded so hard she feared it would seize up. Her palms sweated. She rubbed them against her sleeves, but within moments they were damp again.

'Don't worry.' To her surprise, Fei Long reached out to squeeze her hand before rising. 'You'll do fine, *Pearl*.'

He gave her a reassuring nod. The look she returned him was wide-eyed with fear. She felt like a hunted animal caught in a snare while she waited. Voices came from the front of the house and Fei Long disappeared around the corner. This was it. The deception began here and they couldn't turn back.

'Dao!' she whispered fiercely.

'What?' The hissed reply came back from behind the screen.

A wave of light-headedness took hold of Yan Ling and her stomach churned. 'I'm going to faint.'

'Don't you dare!' Dao warned.

And that was the final word. Fei Long had returned with a middle-aged man wearing an indigo robe. His headdress marked him as a government official of high rank. His severe expression marked him as one who hadn't set out to be cordial.

Yan Ling stood. She didn't know if the motion was suitably graceful or not. Her knees were shaking.

'Inspector Tong.' She bowed and sent a prayer of thanks to the Goddess of Mercy that her voice didn't shake as well.

'Lady Chang.' The minister fixed his slanted gaze on her. His thick beard and stark eyes reminded her of pictures of the judge of the underworld. 'This servant is humbled to make your acquaintance.'

Already the exchange had become confusing. Tong was her elder and of unquestionably high rank. Yet he referred to himself as if he were of lower rank. Was it because she was a lady? Being a woman never afforded her any respect in the teahouse. Or was it because she was supposed to take on the rank of princess?

Caught speechless with doubt, Yan Ling bowed again. She was doing that too much, but she couldn't help herself. 'Welcome, please. Won't you have some tea?'

Thank the heavens for tea. How did people ever come together without it?

They took their places in the chairs around the low table. Fei Long sat beside her on the couch, much as he had that morning on the stone bench. He gave her a reassuring look.

'Are you well, Lady Chang?' Tong's voice boomed in the parlour, entirely too loud and strident for such a casual setting. 'You seem pale.'

'Umm…perhaps I've been avoiding the sun lately. It…umm…makes me dizzy.'

Tong frowned. 'I hope you're well enough for the long journey.'

'My sister is quite well,' Fei Long cut in. 'Though perhaps nervous. She has lived here all her life.'

'Yes, but I'm also quite excited,' Yan Ling chimed in, a bit too emphatically. 'And I hear the Khitans like fair-skinned women.'

What were these words coming from her lips? Fei Long stiffened beside her, but said nothing. Dao came out with the tea tray as rehearsed. The porcelain cups rattled together as she set the tray down on the table in an echo of Yan Ling's jostled nerves.

In her flustered state, she made another mistake, reaching

out to grab the teapot. Dao's hand collided against hers. Inspector Tong's gaze bore down on her.

How long was this visit going to last? She was already sweating beneath the layers of gauze and silk. Yan Ling poured the tea for all of them and then sat back, her hands folded so tightly in her lap that her knuckles ached. That would keep her from doing anything else inappropriate with them.

'First we must thank Lady Chang for her sacrifice to the empire.'

Sacrifice? She looked questioningly to Fei Long, who responded calmly. 'Our family is happy to be able to perform such a duty.'

The minister went on. 'The lady must know that this is a most important task we have entrusted to her.'

'Yes. Very important, indeed.'

'The Khitan lords have been growing more aggressive. There are rumours of a power struggle in the region. We must secure an alliance with their leader as soon as possible. Easier to send one princess than an armed legion.'

His words echoed in her ears. *Aggressive. Power struggle.* She swallowed past the lump in her throat. 'A wedding is always preferable to a war,' she said, her voice thin.

'Inspector Tong.' Fei Long addressed the official with a sternness that surprised and impressed her. 'Khitan has been our ally for decades now. I don't see why you've chosen to present them in this way to my sister.'

'Lady Chang should know the reality of this alliance. A woman might become frightened if thrown into an unexpected situation.'

'Pearl doesn't frighten easily.' Fei Long covered her hand with his. Whether it was an act or not, she was grateful. 'And keeping the peace is the duty of the foreign ministry and the ambassadors.'

'So it is,' Tong replied coldly.

What was all this talk of strife and power struggles? Wasn't she going to become a princess and a bride?

The minister continued with more neutral topics. The Khitan delegation was set to arrive in two months, in the middle of the summer. She would be escorted to the palace first and then she would be presented to the delegation by the Emperor himself.

'What happens if they find out I'm not truly a princess?'

She'd said the wrong thing again. She knew it from the way Fei Long tensed beside her. Duty and humility, Bai Shen had instructed. None of these meddlesome questions.

'But you are a princess,' Tong replied. 'Our divine Emperor has declared it so.'

She was beginning to understand. *Heqin* wasn't about marriage at all. It was an arrangement between kingdoms and ambassadors. She would serve as a puppet. Well, that was fine. An imperial puppet was regarded more highly than a teahouse girl.

'I will do my best to be worthy of such an honour,' she said gravely.

At the end of the visit, Tong rose to go, but he threw one last question at her like an unexpected dagger.

'It must be hard for a young woman to be going so far away from home,' he said.

The words sounded like kindness, but she knew better. She chose her words carefully, trying to make them as obsequious and flattering as possible. 'I will miss my home and our beautiful empire without question. Every woman must leave home at some point in her life.'

'What of imperial candidate Zheng Xie Han? I hear he was a childhood friend of yours.'

The name meant nothing. She glanced at Fei Long and was met by the stone wall of his expression. A prickle of sweat began to gather at her brow, but she didn't dare wipe it away.

'Of course, I will miss all our neighbours and friends, Inspector Tong,' she ventured. 'They have been unbelievably kind upon my father's death.'

And at that mention, Tong was forced to bow his head reverently and say a few kind words about the elder Lord Chang.

As he gave his final farewell, Tong lowered his voice and spoke directly to Fei Long. 'Did you know that candidate Zheng is missing?'

'I wasn't aware. Our families are not very close.'

She stood respectfully and watched as the two men exchanged bows. Her stomach knotted as she went over each one of her stumbles. As soon as the censor was gone, Yan Ling let out a long sigh of relief. It was the deepest breath she'd taken in over an hour. 'I'm so sorry. I had no idea who Zhang Xie Han was.'

'No need to apologise.' A light smile touched Fei Long's lips. 'Tong was trying to break your focus, but you were perfect. Absolutely brilliant.'

Brilliant, despite the way her throat was dry and her nails dug into her palms. Her face ached from forcing a blank and pleasant expression for so long. Yan Ling didn't know what she had done to earn his praise, but to hear such words coming from Fei Long—she glowed like a lantern inside.

Chapter Nine

The soft, warming glow continued the next day as Yan Ling floated from the gardens to the study to the parlour. An official-looking letter came for them. Minister Cao was sending his apologies for his detainment and complimenting Pearl on the report he'd received about her gracious and honourable conduct. Fei Long cast a meaningful glance at her while he read the praise, making her shiver with happiness.

Over the next days, Fei Long fell back into pattern and ritual. Their afternoon lessons continued in earnest. He would spare a few precious moments of instruction before becoming absorbed in the ledgers on his desk. Yan Ling would steal glances at him from across the study. That deep crease between his eyes could have been painted on; she rarely saw him without it.

They were working on more complex characters that afternoon. Yan Ling stared at her brush in a trance, still seeing that one conspiratorial look Fei Long had given her. She drew the ink across the paper in lazy strokes, imagining that the secret glance held much, much more that was unspoken.

'You're distracted,' Fei Long declared from his desk.

She looked up, startled. 'No, I'm not,' she argued more from impulse than thought.

'Your calligraphy is uneven. I can see it from here. It's important that you concentrate.'

'Oh, yes,' She drawled lightly. 'I heard once of a princess who was to be married to Khitan, but they saw how her calligraphy was all wrong and they *sent her back*.'

'Keep writing,' he commanded, turning his attention back to his affairs.

Yan Ling thought she caught a smile hidden behind the letter he was reading.

She dipped the brush again, but only started writing after casting a glare at Fei Long to make it clear that she was not continuing without protest.

By the end of the hour, she'd filled several sheets of paper. She was cleaning her brushes when Fei Long set a package on the edge of his desk. The crinkle of the brown paper wrapping caught her attention.

'What is that?'

The package was tied with string. Fei Long sat back, his expression revealing nothing, which only lured her even more.

'For you,' he said finally. She was already pulling the string free when he spoke again. 'For tonight.'

'Tonight?'

'"The Maiden of Yue."'

Her heart leapt and immediately she forgave him for his difficult disposition. She didn't think he'd paid any attention when she and Bai Shen had spoken of it.

'You'll need to go in disguised as my servant,' he said.

She pulled away the paper excitedly, revealing a bundle of cloth. She lifted the garments up one after another: cloth cap, black trousers and a dark cotton robe.

'When will we go?' She scooped up the outfit, eager to change as soon as possible.

'Much later. Not until after dark.'

He didn't appear pleased at all. Looking at the masculine garb in her hands seemed to make him uncomfortable. She didn't care. She was swept up in the prospect of going out into the city.

'I'll come get you,' he instructed.

'Thank you, my lord.'

She couldn't wait to try on the disguise. Pressing the clothes close to her breast, she rushed to the door.

'Only this once,' he called after her. 'We need to keep you hidden.'

Back in her room, she tugged free of the layers of gauze and silk and then pulled the robe over her shoulders, fixing the sash around her waist. The sleeves only extended two hand spans. These were servants' clothes after all. The material was heavier and didn't mould to her the way silk did. The cut of the robe broadened her shoulders and straightened out the curve of her hips.

This was going to be such an adventure. Her first time out of the mansion since she'd first come there. She took a few practice steps, lengthening her stride and swinging her arms as she threw in a swagger. Li Bai Shen might even be proud of her.

Several hours later, she was wearing the entire outfit, including the trousers and cap, when she greeted Fei Long at her chamber door.

'My lord.' She raised her arms, palm to fist, and bowed ceremoniously.

A short laugh broke out of him. She didn't know if it was out of genuine amusement or whether he was mocking her, but it didn't matter. Nothing could darken her mood tonight.

'What are you doing?' he asked as she strode past him out into the hallway.

She stuck her chest out and chin up. 'I learned this from watching you.'

'I do nothing of the sort.'

'No?' She turned crisply, enforcing a stern expression while she ran a hand over the front of the robe. A cloth wrapped tight around her breasts further straightened her figure. 'You hardly move any other part of your body when you walk. Rather like a tree. This is much easier than being a lady.'

He smirked. 'Indeed.'

They'd reached the portico to the courtyard. As Fei Long promised, it was dark outside.

She pitched her voice a notch lower. 'What shall my name be?'

'You won't need a name. I'll call you "you" or maybe "boy".'

She made a face. 'That's it?'

'Yes. Remember, you're a servant. Be humble, unassuming. If no one notices you, then you've succeeded.'

No matter. He could call her whatever he wanted if she got the chance to leave the confines of the mansion. They were going to explore the city at night! See the theatres and drinking houses and what other delights the capital had in its walls. She'd only seen Changan through one brief peek from behind the curtain of the palanquin. It was enough to make her hunger for more like a child teased with a sweet.

'If you need to speak to me, lean close and speak quietly as if it's a delicate matter,' Fei Long said.

Always instructing. She nodded dutifully.

'There is one more thing.'

Fei Long directed his gaze downwards to where her slippers peeked out from beneath the trousers. The embroidered flower pattern swirled delicately over her toes.

'Oh!'

She ran back inside. After a short delay, she was able to borrow a pair of felt boots from one of the stable attendants. They were still too large for her feet, but she stuffed a handkerchief into each toe and was able to walk without them slipping off.

Out in the courtyard, Fei Long gave her another head-to-toe inspection, finally meeting her eyes. He held his gaze there for a moment longer than proper. Yan Ling squirmed in the disguise, growing uncomfortably warm in the cool evening.

'Do I look like a man now?' she asked.

'No,' came his curt reply.

Regardless, he turned and headed to the side gate, which meant she was to follow. Yan Ling took hold of the bamboo stick with the hanging lantern attached and fell into step behind him. From there, she had a chance to observe him without risking his attention. Fei Long wore a tan-coloured robe with black-embroidered trim along the edges and sleeves. He presented a stately sight as he walked through the gate; understated, yet refined.

As they followed the alleyway into the main street out front, Yan Ling was surprised to see how many others were out that evening. A sparse, but steady, stream of people passed by on either side. In her home town, the customers in the teahouse would have thinned by this hour. Here in the imperial capital, it seemed the citizens were just emerging for the night.

Yan Ling ducked away nervously from the first passers-by, but soon realised no one gave her more than a passing glance, if even that. She was a servant, unseen and insignificant. The tension eased from her shoulders and she let out a breath.

She was no one again. She didn't have to worry about impressing or pleasing anyone. Her attention swung down the opposite side of the street. The courtyard mansions of the neighbourhood stood side by side, with narrow alleyways in between. Some of the gates had wooden plaques fixed over them, but she was unable to make out the characters as they strolled by. Dao had told her that many civil servants and city officials lived within this ward. Not excessively wealthy, but certainly prosperous families.

Fei Long glanced over his shoulder as her forgotten lantern bumped against him. She smiled in apology and righted the bamboo pole. He didn't seem too disapproving as he resumed his step.

The entire ward was encircled by a low wall that rose just overhead. It wasn't impossible to scale, except it appeared to be patrolled by armed guardsmen. At the ward entrance, Fei Long paused to show the gatekeeper a marker before they were nodded through.

They didn't spend much time along the main city street before passing through the adjacent ward. They were going to the entertainment district in an area called the North Hamlet. Inside those gates, the crowd thickened, everyone moving a step or two faster. She crowded close to Fei Long so as not to lose him while she stared at the surroundings.

A collection of tea rooms and pavilions gathered along the main avenue. Red-and-yellow lanterns hung at the front of every building and the sky brightened above with the soft glow of the floating orbs. She doubted her lantern was needed at all any more, but she held on to it dutifully. There were shops still open as well and an endless maze of food carts with steaming baskets and delicious smells.

She wanted to see it all, peek inside each open door and stop at each stall. But Fei Long wove a confident path through the crowd and she had no choice but to follow, absorbing the quarter in tantalising sips. A stringed instrument played inside one doorway. The slow melody spoke of romance and longing, only to fade once they reached the corner. Yan Ling stared up to the second balcony of a teahouse, which put the humble one she'd grown up in to shame. Gold curtains and floral lanterns with well-dressed patrons engaged in lively conversation. Could one taste the luxuriousness in the brew they poured? It must have been as refined as a hundred-year wine.

Beyond the street, another entranceway greeted them. She could see the grass-covered area graced by willow trees just inside the arch. This time she did pause to try to read the plaque overhead. It would give her something to hold on to. She'd write the name onto a slip of paper once she got home.

'Gardens,' she recited softly, making out one character amongst the three. She struggled with the others, trying to capture the shapes in her mind.

Fei Long came to her side. He read out each character to her, pointing to it in turn. 'Pear Blossom Gardens.'

She repeated it, much like she did in their lessons. Then she smiled, swept up in a rush of happiness and gratitude. People brushed past them to enter the park, but Fei Long remained beside her for a moment longer while she floated like the moon, filled with warmth and light.

Finally, he directed them inside with a short nod. Dots of lights and coloured flags marked out different areas within the park. Clever vendors had set their food stalls within the gardens and their carts were arranged beside small clusters of benches and tables. Fei Long chose one beside a carp pond and Yan Ling waited for him to be seated first before settling in across from him. Grass sprouted up in tufts around the bare spots at their feet and the square table teetered when she rested her arm on it.

A pot of hot tea was set down between them. Fei Long faced her as they dined on parcels of sticky rice and pork steamed in banana leaves along with red-bean pastries and a bowl of boiled peanuts. Yan Ling unwrapped the leaves, careful to keep her fingers from sticking to the rice, and took a bite.

It was a perfect mouthful. The rice was fragrant and slightly sweet against the saltiness of the pork. She chewed happily and washed it down with a sip of tea, already glancing wistfully towards the cart to see if there was the possibility of more. The benches beside them filled with customers. Strangers jostled in beside her, but everyone was focused on their own meal.

'Is it like this every night?' she asked.

Immediately after, she remembered she was supposed to speak quietly and confidentially to him, but Fei Long didn't seem upset by the familiarity. She breathed a little easier.

'In the spring and summertime,' he answered. 'This has always been the best time in the city.'

It was the only time Fei Long had sounded remotely wistful. She imagined he and his sister had grown up in the magnificent capital, discovering it bit by bit as children.

'Only during festivals would you see it like this out in the provinces.' She swept her gaze across the park once more before taking a pastry. It was almost as good as the sticky rice.

'You should eat more,' Fei Long remarked.

He sat back to watch her with one arm draped over the edge of the table. There was a rare carelessness to his posture.

'Are you developing a brotherly affection toward me?' she teased.

Her heart raced at her boldness. To be with Fei Long like this, exchanging idle conversation. The two of them weren't like master and servant at all. Nor brother and sister.

'The Khitans would expect a princess to be well fed. Not a waif like you.'

He meant it as a jest. The casual warmth of his tone said so. Yet her bright mood flickered and died. She reached for another sticky rice ball, peeling the banana leaf away slowly.

'Ah, of course.' Her throat tightened around the words. 'The grand scheme, above all else.'

She chewed without any enjoyment. The delicacy had lost its flavour. Chang Fei Long wasn't prone to dreams. That was her failing, and hers alone.

'You're looking thinner yourself.' She fought to recapture

their light banter. 'Dao says you haven't been eating well and that you rarely sleep.'

'Dao seems to talk a lot. Not a favourable disposition for a servant.'

'She says it's because there's so much on your mind. I know I've been a burden—'

'You're not a burden,' he cut in roughly.

She fell silent, not knowing what to make of the vehemence of his reply. Her heart was pounding. If she wasn't another servant under his charge, what was she? The ever-present question.

'The stage is at the centre of the gardens, beyond those trees there,' he offered as a kindness after a pause. 'You can see them lighting the lanterns now.'

'My lord has been here before, then?'

'In my younger days.'

'When you were a student?'

He looked surprised. 'Did Bai Shen tell you?'

'He must have mentioned it in passing,' she said, trying to sound casual.

She couldn't have him thinking that they discussed such personal details, though she vied for every morsel she could scavenge about Fei Long from Bai Shen and Dao. She'd never dare to ask Fei Long so directly. Detached courtesy was all that he wanted from her.

They finished the meal and she fell back into her role as attendant, remembering to leave the money for the seller and thank him with a courteous bow. She followed Fei Long down the slope of the hill toward the ring of trees at the centre of the park. They were out in the city and she would enjoy this night.

The stage emerged beyond the tree line. The open pavilion was set on a raised wooden platform and a painting of blue sky and mountains in the distance served as the backdrop. Lanterns had been strung up around the stage to surround it with a welcoming glow. A handful of spectators were seated on the benches around the stage and more continued to gather.

Fei Long chose a seat near the front and she seated herself in the row just behind him. As instructed, she was to keep a respectful distance. It wasn't long before they were surrounded by eager attendees on both sides. She stuck her arms tight against her sides to avoid bumping against anyone.

The audience hushed as the first strains of music rose to fill the empty space above the stage. The blend of stringed instruments, flutes and drum beats wove together to create a majestic mood. Yan Ling searched the stage for the hidden musicians, but saw no sign of them.

The play opened with the King of Yue and his adviser. She marvelled at the richness of the costumes. The king wore a spectacular robe of black and gold with a bold dragon emblem curving along both sides. His headdress was embellished with strings of pearls and his thick black beard spoke of age and authority. The advisor was dressed in vermilion with a black-tasseled minister's cap. They sang out their lines with voices that rang through the clearing, holding the audience in thrall.

It was a well-known folktale. The king was looking for a master with extraordinary skills to train his soldiers. His minister, Fan Li, had heard rumours of an unnamed maiden within the southern forest.

Yan Ling leaned forwards with excitement as the music changed to depict a journey. A maiden in a flowing green robe entered the stage. Her face was made up with white powder and rouge. An elegant sweep of black paint accented her eyes at the corners. Lifting her chin, she raised her arm in a regal pose and turned to the audience.

Yan Ling gave a little squeal, but pressed her hand over her mouth when Fei Long glanced back to her. It was Bai Shen! Bai Shen dressed as a woman, and a handsome one at that. He barely looked like himself beneath the stage make-up and the costume was cleverly draped so he took on a more feminine form.

Bai Shen flashed her a secret smile, his face partially hidden behind the drape of his sleeve. His mannerisms were exaggerated for the stage, but undoubtedly feminine and graceful. The drums began to beat in a driving rhythm as the forest maiden encountered her first challenge: an elderly swordsman who challenged her to show her skill.

The maiden accepted the challenge with a humble response and a demure tilt of her head. Then she took hold of a wooden staff painted to look like a bamboo stalk and transformed into a warrior.

Chapter Ten

Fei Long enjoyed the staging as Bai Shen duelled with the old swordsman, who was of course played by a young actor. The swordsman showed off by spinning his staff in a windmill motion; one hand over the other, the lines of the staff blurring while its shadow danced over the stage. He finished his routine by twirling and tossing the staff so high that it was lost in the night before it spun back down into his hands.

The audience murmured with appreciation and applauded. After a few drumbeats, the 'maiden' responded with an acrobatic routine that was fluid and graceful. She leapt and turned, her robes emphasising her movements so that she seemed to float through the air.

Bai Shen made up for his lack of discipline in the drinking house with rigorous dedication to his art. Fei Long knew that the actors of the troupe trained as hard as imperial soldiers every day to be able to work their physically demanding roles.

'He's good!' Yan Ling exclaimed with delight.

Fei Long glanced over at her and she seemed to remember herself. She leaned forwards and he bent his head to accommodate her.

'Bai Shen is really good,' she whispered, her breath soft against his ear.

'It takes many years,' he explained, ignoring the warming of his body. 'He trained in acrobatics and dance from an early age.'

She straightened to watch the performance. As she moved away, her cheek brushed against his in a butterfly movement and every muscle in his body absorbed the touch. He stared ahead, but was only nominally aware of what was happening on stage.

The maiden defeated the old man and journeyed to meet the king. There she was challenged by a hundred champions, ushering in a major acrobatic routine involving tumblers and dancers dressed in all different colours.

Fei Long couldn't resist looking to Yan Ling once again at the height of the scene. Her gaze was fixed on the stage, face upturned. The halo of the lanterns illuminated her so that he had no choice but to see.

They had spent every moment together for the past few weeks, on the road and then at his home and yet he hadn't seen. They had shared meals, slept in close quarters, and he had never noticed. She was just a teahouse girl. A grey shadow. A stray kitten.

Now Yan Ling seemed too far away. He wanted to be next to her so they could watch the adventure unfold. She would whisper questions to him. What does the story mean? Who does that figure represent? And he'd answer. He'd make up answers just to have something to say to her.

He'd fooled himself into thinking Yan Ling was reserved and unassuming. She was so conscientious about her lessons, anxious over even the smallest of mistakes. Seeing her like this reminded him of how she'd been during that first journey. She had been endlessly curious and eager until he'd stolen the light from her eyes.

Perhaps he needed to remind himself of his duty to the empire and to her. By summertime, she would be gone, sent to some faceless Khitan lord in the untamed grasslands of the north.

Fei Long turned back to face the stage before she could notice his unseemly attention.

Bai Shen finished his dance with a dramatic thump of his spear as he stood to attention, the courageous maiden ready for war. The audience applauded loudly, then the drums beat out a pounding staccato as the troupe scattered to set up for the next scene. Bai Shen, the incorrigible creature, turned to them and winked. Fei Long could hear Yan Ling's laughter just over his shoulder while he sat in isolation, unable to share in it.

He was the only one not in disguise that night, yet he was the one hiding.

After the show ended, he tried to impress upon Yan Ling that it was late and they needed to return, but she insisted they find Bai Shen.

'We have to tell him how wonderful he was,' she said.

'He may hear that too much already,' Fei Long replied drily.

She was already trying to weave her way through the crowd towards the stage and having little success. He caught up with her easily while she stood on her toes, trying to search around two tall men blocking her path. It was impossible to resist Yan Ling in her exuberance.

'Come along,' he conceded. 'I know where to find him.'

They circled the stage area to the far end of the gardens to exit through the rear gate. The streets on this side of the gardens were quieter. Sounds of celebration from the main thoroughfare remained an enticing murmur in the distance.

It had been a few years, but Fei Long was able to navigate his way through the *hutong* alleyways to the familiar entrance. Performers slipped in and out through the gate, but no one paid the two of them any attention as they entered.

The courtyard had the same hapless appearance he remembered, with shrubbery that was overgrown and clinging to life. The complex was divided into many small apartments where the actors and musicians of the theatre troupe stayed. Laughter and lively conversation echoed from within the depths of the building. Spirits were high in the wake of a successful performance.

'Bai Shen's chamber is at the west end,' he told Yan Ling. 'Far away from the rising sun, he always said. I've put him there enough times after a night of drinking.'

'What interesting times you two must have had in your youth.'

Fei Long had no desire to drag out those stories. He shot her a cryptic look and proceeded to the apartment situated in the western corner. The door was open and light streamed from it. For propriety's sake, what little propriety could be preserved, he held her back while he looked into the room first.

'The illustrious Fei Long!' Bai Shen crowed. He stood before a dressing table and mirror, still in full costume.

'Someone wanted to tell you what she thought of your performance.'

At his signal, Yan Ling came bounding in excitedly. 'Bai Shen, you look so *pretty*.'

Bai Shen did a half-turn to show off the jade-green robes. 'And you, young sir, look quite handsome.' He nodded at the servant's robe with approval.

'I didn't know you could tumble like that. Can you show me?'

'You'd hurt yourself.'

The three of them crowded into the room, which was cluttered with costumes and props. Bai Shen and Yan Ling chattered away like excited children. Yan Ling took the elaborate warrior headdress from him and tried it on. Fei Long laughed at the sight of her, his entire being lifting and lightening in the intimate refuge of the chamber. He crossed his arms over his chest and leaned back against the door frame, content to watch while she asked question after question about the performance as Bai Shen washed away his make-up.

'What about your little performance, pretty lady?' Bai Shen asked, once he had cleaned away the white paint and dark kohl around his eyes.

'I was so nervous. I think I said too much.' She looked to Fei Long for a final report.

'She was exceptional. Inspector Tong has no reason to doubt.'

Yan Ling smiled happily.

Maybe he'd been wrong to keep her so isolated within the house. There was always the risk of being discovered, but she seemed so vibrant tonight when no longer trapped within the confines of the inner chambers. Yan Ling hungered for new sights and sounds. Perhaps if they were careful, she could go out into the marketplace and explore the gardens and temples of the city. He could take her himself. The thought sent unexpected warmth to his chest.

'We should celebrate, then.' Bai Shen peeled away the outer layers of his robe and hung them on to a hook on the wall. Bit by bit, the man re-emerged. 'Besides, Fei Long here owes my friends for detaining the honorable Minister Cao.'

'Another time,' Fei Long said.

Yan Ling looked mournful. 'But it's still so early.'

'It's the nearly the end of the twelfth hour.'

'Quite early,' Bai Shen scoffed. 'Don't worry. None of your courtly folk will be at this drinking house.'

It wasn't so much he feared discovery. Maybe he just wanted to have Yan Ling alone for a moment away from the crowds. Away even from Bai Shen.

'An hour,' she negotiated, fixing a shrewd look on him as if she were haggling in the morning market.

He was being selfish. If she wanted adventure, he supposed this was an innocent way of giving it to her.

'An hour,' he conceded.

'There,' Bai Shen declared. 'I should have told you the men of the Chang family could never resist a charming lady.' He pinched her cheek. 'I have to teach you a prettier face than that one you used.'

'Hurry up and get dressed,' Fei Long said with a scowl. He ushered Yan Ling out into the courtyard. 'Bai Shen flirts with everyone.'

She blinked innocently. 'He was flirting with me?'

Lately, he found himself growing impatient with the actor's antics. Bai Shen seemed to think that he had complete freedom to exhibit whatever outrageous behaviour required to get attention. He scattered compliments to the breeze without thought or care.

'Bai Shen and his friends are shameless. Things can get rowdy,' he warned.

'You wound me, Fei Long.' Bai Shen emerged, looking more himself. He'd thrown on an embroidered robe with blue-and-crimson accents, just a touch less ostentatious than his stage costume. 'Have you forgotten your adventurous student days?'

'I was recalling them quite clearly.'

'Fei Long could outdrink the best of us.'

'Or the worst of you,' he countered.

She smiled at their exchange. 'All I've ever seen him drink is tea.'

'I could tell you some stories…'

Bai Shen took Yan Ling under his wing conspiratorially, but Fei Long stopped them before they got too far.

'Appearances,' he reminded, looking pointedly to the arm draped over Yan Ling's shoulder.

The actor removed his hold with a smirk. 'Of course. One must always keep up appearances, Lord Chang.'

The scoundrel was looking for mischief. Fei Long positioned himself securely beside Yan Ling as they continued towards Bai Shen's favourite establishment.

The place was close. Just a stagger away, if it came to that.

The drinking house was much as he remembered it. Unassuming, with none of the banners and embellishments of the businesses along the main avenue. A scroll of two golden carp circled on the wall just inside the door.

The first floor was divided into two parlours, left and right. The décor was also simple. Low wooden tables upon bamboo mats. Patrons would crowd into the room, find a comfortable spot on the floor among the pillows and rugs, and spirits would be passed around.

It was common, almost required, for scholars to engage in nights of drinking and poetry. When he'd been a candidate for the imperial exams, Fei Long had found himself drawn towards these lesser-known houses, mixing with people like Li Bai Shen and his nameless friends. His father's reputation glared too brightly in the renowned establishments along the main avenue.

The performers had already gathered in one of the parlours. One of their own sat at the centre, plucking the strings of a *pipa*. There was a cup of wine in every hand.

'Chang Fei Long!'

A chorus of greetings rose up. A few he recognised as old comrades. Others were simply joining in with the crowd. They cleared away a spot at the table and he directed Yan Ling to sit beside him. She stared from one end of the room to the other with curious excitement.

'Penalty drink,' someone declared. 'Penalty for arriving late.'

'Hot tea,' Fei Long said to the serving girl as she came to set more flasks on the table.

A round of jeers met his request, which he accepted good-naturedly.

'Now hear this.' Bai Shen quickly took position as the centre of attention. 'Fei Long is a reformed and respectable gentleman now who has very honourably offered to pay for our drinks tonight.'

More cheers at that. Fei Long thought of the   readed ledger book. More numbers to subtract, but he did owe this crowd a debt for whatever they had done to detain Minister Cao. He nodded graciously as a rain of toasts came at him.

Bai Shen was still going. 'Now, I'll take my punishment as deserved, but since his lordship is enjoying his tea, his servant there will have to drink for him.'

Someone pushed a cup into Yan Ling's hand while Bai Shen looked on with great amusement. She peered at the clear liquid.

'My lord,' she whispered. 'What is this?'

'Baijiu.' Fei Long was quite familiar with the distilled rice liquor that this crowd favoured.

'All at once is how it's done.' Bai Shen lifted his cup to her. 'I know how important it is for you to uphold the Chang family honour.'

Fei Long eyed the actor. 'What are you playing at?' he asked quietly.

His friend grinned before tossing back his drink. Yan Ling tried to do the same. She swallowed with difficulty. A moment later her eyes shot wide and her mouth contorted into a grimace.

'It doesn't taste so bad if you don't make that face,' Bai Shen said with a laugh.

The crowd roared with approval as she doubled over coughing. Fei Long closed a hand over her shoulder to steady her.

'Are you all right?'

Yan Ling finally righted herself and looked at him, eyes watering. 'Fine,' she choked out. Then, 'That was awful.'

She pressed her fingers to her throat in a gesture that was all too delicate. Already there was a slight flush to her cheeks that he couldn't describe as anything but alluring. The party had resumed around them in a swirling mass of conversation. This crowd of actors likely recognised she was female, but they'd go along with the ruse.

'I suggest you don't do that again.' He handed her some tea to help soothe her throat.

'There's no danger of that,' she promised, taking a grateful sip.

But within minutes, the burning in her throat had eased and she decided that perhaps *baijiu* wasn't so bad after all. A slow, not unpleasant warmth spread through her muscles. Someone else pushed a cup of warmed wine into her hands. She looked to Fei Long uncertainly, but he was in conversation with the fellow next to him.

Why did she have to ask for permission? She was always searching for approval and acceptance from him. It was exhausting.

This time she sipped slowly. Unlike the liquor, the wine was slightly sweet and the burn of it on her tongue was even enjoyable. Gradually the flush of it crept all the way to her fingertips and the crest of her cheeks.

At first she tried to follow the conversations as they were tossed across the room. There was poetry, interwoven with riddles, interwoven with bawdy insults. It was an intricate puzzle with no beginning, no end. She found herself smiling, nodding.

'So you have to hear how we distracted the minister,' Bai Shen was saying.

The room quieted somewhat to listen. Apparently several of the performers had been involved in the caper as well, but Bai Shen was designated as the storyteller.

'We had three plans.' He held up a finger dramatically. 'One: delay him in the ministry building with a civil dispute. Two: if the first one failed, we'd pose as porters and carry his sedan off on a wild chase through the city. Three: we'd simply have to accost the senior minister and steal all his clothes.'

'I told you nothing that would get you thrown in jail or I would disown you,' Fei Long protested.

'Disown me?'

'No, honourable judge. I've never seen this man before,' Fei Long intoned.

'That's because it was dark and I was dressed as a woman.'

The crowd hooted at Bai Shen's jest.

'He said I was as pretty as a spring flower,' Bai Shen finished, to the roar of the audience.

Fei Long's deep laughter resonated beside her. It filled the room wonderfully and warmed her even more thoroughly than the wine.

'You should laugh more often,' she told him before she could stop herself.

He regarded her closely. The laughter remained in his eyes as he gently pried the cup from her hands and set it aside. Bai Shen went on to describe the elaborate show they had performed before Minister Cao, but she was more curious about Fei Long.

'How long were you studying for the imperial exams?'

He had to lean in to hear her and she repeated the question.

'Only a year,' he replied.

'Is that long?'

The spirit of the room was boisterous and full of joy and celebration. Fei Long had also relaxed. He seemed to be genuinely enjoying himself, as if this night wasn't just a chore and a duty. The clamour of the others around the table pushed them closer together. Her knee brushed up against his, but he disregarded it. Her pulse skipped faster, swept up in the recklessness and the gaiety.

'It's common to study for the exams for two or more years,' he said. 'But I never took the civil exams.'

'Why not?'

'I decided to go into military service instead.'

'Are there exams for that as well?' she asked.

'There are indeed,' he said. 'There are military classics

to study and then the physical tests. Horse riding, archery, sword skill.'

Casually, he reached behind her to pull one of the pillows closer for her. She leaned back against it, before realising how odd the gesture must have looked to anyone who was watching. She was supposed to be his servant.

'Why did you decide to change? Your father was already a highly respected official.' She became a bit flustered when she realised how much it seemed like she was questioning his decision. 'I mean, your military appointment took you so far away from home.'

Fei Long frowned and for a moment she feared she had been too impertinent, but he was only considering her question.

'Perhaps I didn't mind seeing what was outside of Chang-an. Otherwise I might have drowned in the pleasure quarters with these fools here.' He nodded indulgently at the crew surrounding them.

'I don't believe that,' she said.

'No?' He leaned closer to her as they spoke, the crowd jostling them together. 'I was young, brash, with no knowledge of limits—'

She giggled at that. 'As if you're *so* old now.'

He shot her an admonishing look, but there was a warmth behind it that made her toes curl happily.

'I found I wasn't any good at being a scholar,' he confessed.

'Fei Long!' The man who played the King called out from the other end of the table. 'Are you still a master with the bow and arrow? I won a lot of money at that match.'

Their conversation had been overheard. For a moment, she was embarrassed that she had been quite so personal with her questions, but Fei Long never spoke so openly when they were alone.

'Our Lord Chang is like the legendary Houyi,' Bai Shen boasted.

Fei Long waved his hand in modest denial. She lit up when

he turned back to resume their conversation rather than banter with the others.

'They're talking about the Great Shoot,' he explained. 'I competed in one before passing the military exam.'

The hard lines of his face had softened. Usually she grew anxious whenever he focused his attention on her, but tonight he wasn't looking to instruct. Fei Long was more relaxed and they could speak as if they were…she didn't know what they were. Friends?

'Is it dangerous being in the imperial army?' The question brought on a bout of shyness. She tried to mask her concern behind simple curiosity.

He paused to consider it. 'I've sworn to protect our land, but we have been free from rebellion for many years now. And this Emperor prefers diplomacy to warfare with the neighbouring kingdoms.'

'Like with the peace marriages?'

His gaze fixed on her, the sudden depth of it making her stomach flutter. The knot in his throat lifted and lowered as he swallowed.

'Your face is red,' he said lightly, not answering her question.

'What?'

'The wine.' He smiled, amused, but there was a hint of strain beneath it.

'Oh! Does it look awful?'

She pressed her hands over her cheeks. Her skin flushed hot, but she couldn't tell if it was from the spirits or how Fei Long had looked at her. It was a drawn-out, thoughtful look. The way a man regarded a woman.

'I've never had much to drink before,' she confessed.

'I can see that.'

The moment between them broke and she turned away to seek some diversion. She could feel Fei Long's gaze, heavy and thoughtful, on her. She didn't dare ask what it was that he saw.

The musician had pulled out his *pipa* again. He'd started up a song and the troupe joined in, singing loudly as if each one were trying to outdo the other. She fell silent, letting the music and the laughter hide her while she cradled the gem of her conversation with Fei Long close to her breast. She'd often wondered what his life was like before he had returned to Changan. She wondered if he would go away again once she left.

Soon the banter droned hazily around her and she fought to keep her eyes open. She waved away an offer of more wine. Vaguely, she registered the start of some drinking game, but her head was starting to feel heavy.

The next thing she knew, she was leaning against something. She'd fallen asleep while the party continued without her. Blinking drowsily, she opened her eyes to see Bai Shen watching her with a wide grin.

'Wake up, young sir. You don't want Fei Long to have to cut off his sleeve for you.'

Fei Long. Her cheek was pressed against his shoulder and she could feel the steady rise of his chest beneath her fingertips where she rested them against him almost possessively. She'd fallen asleep on him, of all things!

Her cap fell off as she righted herself in horror. She fumbled with it hopelessly. 'I—I'm sorry.'

Fei Long didn't appear angry as he looked down at her. 'It's time to go.'

She stumbled as they untangled themselves from the troupe, but Fei Long steadied her and soon they were free, standing on the edge of the party.

Bai Shen bowed, palm to fist, in a formal farewell. His regret at their departure didn't last long as he was caught up in another conversation. The festivities would no doubt continue once they left.

'I should pay…' She realised it only once they were beyond the threshold of the entrance. Her mind was still clouded with sleep. She was posing as his servant and supposed to open doors and handle money.

'I've taken care of it.' Fei Long guided her onto the street with a hand against her back.

The city became a maze of alleyways and unfamiliar streets in the haze. Dutifully, she followed along beside Fei Long, her step not quite steady. The lanterns of the drinking houses were still burning along the main avenue. Their halos became fuzzy and distorted before her.

What time was it? She yawned again.

Dimly, she recalled passing through the ward gate. She waited while Fei Long showed his pass. One moment, she was awake. In the next, she'd drifted into sleep on her feet.

'Come,' he said.

She plodded along beside him again. The way back seemed so much further than the way there, if that was possible. The oversized boots were more a hindrance now as they wobbled about her ankles. At some point, she stopped to adjust them and found herself once again dozing, her back propped against the brick wall of an alleyway.

'It's not far now.'

She opened her eyes and Fei Long was right before her. He was holding the lantern now, as she could no longer be trusted with it. His face was partly in shadow and she could see the glow of moonlight beyond him.

'I didn't drink that much,' she said.

'I know. Come on, you.' He looked so pleasant and indulgent and wonderful.

She should tell him now. Tell him something about the feelings growing inside her.

Once they returned to the mansion, there would so many barriers between them. Heavy veils of propriety and class, like the silken layers of those cursedly beautiful robes. Those walls were down tonight and he was standing so close, looking at her in that way again. She didn't know what that way was, only that it was different. She wanted to confess right here in this darkened alley. It was irrational, but it made more sense now than it ever would.

'Fei Long.' She held her breath.

'Yes?'

Her voice sounded soft, plaintive. Vulnerable. She was being stupid.

'I enjoyed tonight very much.'

'Good.'

She couldn't tell if he was irritated with her. He just sounded like he always did: solid, steady, unreadable.

'I mean tonight was so very…good. Thank you.'

'It was nothing.'

Her face burned at the warmth in his voice.

In the end, she couldn't do it. Soon, they were walking again. Such a confession—unsightly with feeling, like some lovesick maiden's lament. She'd do nothing but shame herself and embarrass Fei Long. Even worse, she might bring his derision upon her.

At some point, her left boot slipped and she stumbled. Fei Long caught her, but before she could mumble an apology, he cast the lantern aside and lifted her in his arms. Her breath caught in her throat as he cradled her against his chest. His muscles tensed against her weight.

'But we'll be seen,' she protested.

'It's not far now.'

He adjusted his hold and started walking, making much better time without her stumbling beside him. Nervously, she curled her arms about his neck. There was no good place to hold on otherwise.

She was close enough to feel the beat of his heart against her, the soft labour of his breath. She stared at the strong cut of his jaw in profile and then she was drifting again, lulled by the confident rhythm of his stride and the enfolding heat of his body.

· * * *

The next time she opened her eyes, she was gazing at the familiar rooftops of their courtyard. The view faded and then they were in her room and Fei Long was easing her into bed. Her heart thudded while she lay as still as she possibly could.

The darkness of the chamber made it impossible to see, but she could sense Fei Long above her. She could hear the sound of his breathing and feel his weight as he moved. He bent to reach for her boot and tugged it free. His touch just above her ankle was wickedly out of place and too intimate. A nobleman performing this servant's gesture.

She should tell him she was awake, that he could go, but she couldn't find her voice. Her breath came only in shallow gasps. Fei Long placed his hand firmly on her calf. Sensation radiated from his simple touch. Beloved heat coursed through her veins, pooling as a low tremor in her belly.

The second boot was off. Fei Long pulled the blanket over her and when he moved to tuck it about her shoulders, she found herself eye to eye with him. She hadn't even enough sense to close them and pretend to sleep. Her skin flushed hot, though the wine had long burned away.

He didn't say anything. The back of his fingers brushed gently over her cheek. A touch so brief, she couldn't be sure it wasn't inadvertent. She did close her eyes then, inhaling once, then exhaling.

Yan Ling didn't know if she slept. When she opened her eyes again, it was still night time, but Fei Long was gone.

Chapter Eleven

It was a familiar scene now. Fei Long was at his desk in the study. She stood before him in a sun-yellow robe as if presenting herself before court.

She bowed slightly. 'My Lord.'

He acknowledged her with a nod, not standing to greet her.

Excruciatingly familiar. She had been hoping for something different this day after their evening at the theatre. Fei Long didn't even inspect her appearance to see if it was acceptable, as he usually did. Instead, he was intent on writing. His brush moved in fierce strokes over the paper. He even dispensed with the few lines of polite conversation they usually exchanged. His requirement, not hers. It was one of the methods he used to train her on etiquette.

Perhaps he expected her to initiate the conversation today. 'What happened to the painting of the cranes?' she asked.

A large brush painting of a flock of cranes resting beside a pond had adorned the wall beside Fei Long's desk, yet the space was conspicuously empty today. Fei Long looked up at the blank spot as if unaware until that moment.

'I'm having it replaced,' he replied curtly before returning to whatever he was composing. 'I'm very busy today,' he reprimanded before she could speak again.

So no change. At least, not for the better. She'd been wondering all morning if her girlish imagination was making too much out of nothing. For hours, she'd waited anxiously, only to come here and face the harsh truth.

Silently, she went to the writing table and seated herself. A scroll had been placed beside a blank length of paper. Fei Long had arranged it so they wouldn't need to speak at all. Clearly she was to practise copying the characters. She prepared the ink against the inkstone, taking comfort in the ritual when there was little comfort to be had.

It was hard not to be disappointed.

She took the brush from its case, settled into the proper posture and dipped the tip of the brush into the ink, drawing lazy circles to keep her spirits up. A quick glance at Fei Long showed him unchanged, head bent, writing with furious intention. His eyebrows slashed downward in a frown.

With a soft exhale, she positioned her brush and started to write as well, though at a much slower, deliberate pace than Fei Long. With each character, she tried to discern if it was one she knew. She had memorised nearly a hundred of them. It always pleased her when she recognised parts of a simpler character combined to make more complicated ones.

Today the composition seemed to be about rice and farms. Just a report of some sort that Fei Long had pulled from the elder Lord Chang's papers. She preferred it when it was a passage from a story or a poem.

Yan Ling frowned as she smudged the top of the next line. Her stroke had been too heavy and it ruined the beauty of the whole piece. And so early in the task, too. She hated that. Even reports about rice and millet could still look pretty, in their own way. There was nothing to do but continue.

At the end of the page, she set the brush down in its holder. Her hand was stiff from gripping the brush too hard again.

She shook it to try to loosen her fingers, using her left hand to massage the knuckles. At the same moment, she heard Fei Long get up from his chair.

Her eyes flickered to him. She couldn't help it.

He was packing some items into a leather satchel: a wooden case, some papers. It wasn't even an hour into their afternoon, yet he was preparing to leave.

'Should…should I go?' she asked uncertainly.

He was standing over his desk and staring at the tidy surface as if in a trance. When he turned, it took a moment for him to focus on her. She was far, far from his thoughts.

'No. Stay.'

He came to her and her pulse quickened, but he was only there to look over her work.

'Better,' he pronounced.

She nodded. All she could see was the smear of ink on the ruined second column. She wondered if he really even cared and why it mattered that her characters had to be perfect anyway. Of course, Fei Long was meticulous. He always cared that things were in order. That everything and everyone was in their proper place.

'Here.' His voice softened by the tiniest of notes. 'I'll show you how to write your name.'

She shifted her chair over to accommodate him and he moved in beside her. With measured grace, he took hold of the brush, dipped it into the ink and started to write on the edge of the practice paper.

Two characters emerged in Fei Long's bold script, one on top of the other. There was no hesitation in his strokes. It was as if her entire name flowed out as one spoken verse, each lift of the brush a mere pause between words.

'Yan Ling,' he said when it was done.

Her name looked so much more elegant and complex than the girl it represented. 'Thank you,' she murmured.

He set the brush down, but remained beside her. Was he any

closer than usual? Was his voice just a touch warmer when he addressed her? She couldn't know. She would never be able to know for certain.

'Now you,' he said.

She tried to mimic his technique in her own deliberate manner. Fei Long waited patiently for her to finish with his head bent close to watch her work. This was his subtle, silent apology. No words. Just a small bit of gentleness to counter his earlier harshness.

'Good,' he said once she was done. He straightened abruptly. 'Keep practising.'

She fought very hard not to watch him leave.

Old Man Liang was overseeing the porters out front as they loaded the cart. The steward didn't meet Fei Long's eye. Instead, he watched over the proceedings as if he were directing a funeral. The crates were lifted and lowered with sombre ritual like caskets into a grave.

'Lord Chang's spirit would be sad to see this,' Liang said. It was the same protest he'd given when Fei Long had told him of the decision.

The loyal steward was afraid of upsetting his master even in death. Liang had been more concerned about keeping the elder Lord Chang ignorant and happy than being direct about the state of the household finances. To give bad news was an offence. The last thing Liang wanted his master to do was lose face, so he hid everything, trying to resolve the issues himself, with disastrous results. The two men were old fools together.

Last came the long wooden box that contained the wall painting of the cranes. The birds had been in that study for all his life. Fei Long had counted them as a boy—there were seventeen. His father had stood over his shoulder, directing his studies, under the watch of the winged creatures.

It wasn't merely the loss of their family heirlooms that Fei Long mourned. They were forced to sink to the level of traders, bartering with the various antiques and artworks that his father had collected. There was no other way to pay the creditors quickly.

'Be careful, Old Liang.'

Liang stroked his beard once, then nodded silently. The porters helped the steward climb up into the passenger's seat of the wagon and the driver headed off. The items were going to an art dealer who lived near the East Market—a man who promised to be discreet.

Fei Long waited until the wagon reached the end of the street before turning in the opposite direction. As delicate as the steward's task was, his own required even more secrecy. He insisted on going alone, but brought his sword.

The location was to the south of the entertainment district, in a less reputable area populated by hovels and gambling dens. Along the boundary of the poorer neighbourhood, several extravagant residences had risen up, fed by wealth earned off the dice tables and brothels.

A knot formed in Fei Long's stomach as he travelled to where the streets grew narrow and dank. The buildings were packed together with no space in between. Privacy was for the wealthy. He was looking for a man named Zōu, or the Bull, as they knew him in these parts.

Fei Long stopped before a garishly painted mansion, glaring in green and gold. The architects had copied popular imperial architecture, with dragons curling along the rooftops and an ornate set of doors set with brass rings. Two rough-looking characters stood guard at the front entrance. No doubt Zōu considered his home a palace in the slum, and he, its reigning sovereign.

'Chang Fei Long is here to see Lord Zōu,' he said to the guardsmen.

'What's your business?' The taller, rougher of the pair looked him up and down. His gaze paused at the hilt of Fei Long's weapon.

'Payment.'

The knot in Fei Long's gut only tightened as he was let in. Zōu owned several gambling dens and pleasure houses, according to Old Man Liang. For the last three years, Zōu had also owned his father.

Fei Long was brought into the parlour where a middle-aged man reclined indolently on a sedan chair. Zōu was dressed in a robe of gold brocade and turquoise, as ostentatious as his home. It took quite a few bolts of cloth to clothe him as well. His nickname must have come from the squared shape of his shoulders, which seemed to hulk over his neck, much like a bull's. His face was broad as well. A big man in appearance and manner.

'The precious son,' he said with great amusement.

'Lord Zōu.' It took some effort for Fei Long to bow to him.

That seemed to amuse Zōu even more. 'Come sit.'

The Bull was no nobleman, but it was etiquette to treat one's enemy with respect, at least upon first engaging. A young woman with brightly painted lips brought them wine as Fei Long took a seat.

'I won't be long,' Fei Long said, declining the wine. He pulled the wooden case out of his satchel and placed it on the table between them.

'What, no finesse? You must have a drink. This is the start of our association, after all.'

He didn't want to be associated with this slum lord any more than he had to be. Fei Long knew that the city guards and magistrates turned a blind eye on such illicit activities, but men like Zōu were a disease.

'Let us be plain with each other.' Fei Long slid the wooden case across the table. 'Here is your payment for the month and I want to discuss terms for resolving the entirety of my father's debt.'

'Terms?' Zōu barked out a laugh. 'I rather like the current terms as they are.'

Of all the creditors, his father's debt to Zōu was the greatest and the most unfathomable. Fei Long found out that Old Man Liang had been making monthly payments for over a year, yet the debt had not decreased.

'How much does my father owe you in total, my lord?' He forced the honorific out through gritted teeth. 'This debt *will* be settled.'

At that, Zōu's smile dissipated to be replaced with a cold, shrewd look. 'Your father is dead,' he sneered. 'This is money *you* now owe me, *my lord*.'

'And I intend to pay our debt, but you will no longer bleed us each month. Tell me how much.'

Zōu shook his head patronisingly. 'Fei Long, my friend. You would do well to learn to be more like your father. He was a spirited fellow. The room always glowed brighter when he arrived. We regret his loss.'

'The number,' Fei Long demanded.

Zōu didn't blink. 'Two million cash.'

Hot anger speared through him. 'You lie.'

'Two million,' Zōu repeated calmly, 'since you've shown yourself to be so inflexible.'

'There is no way my father could owe you that much.'

'What do you wish to see, my young lord? Proof? Your father was always a cheerful, charismatic fellow. We'd drink, trade jokes. "Bull," he'd say. "Just between friends, I don't have your money today." "No problem," I'd say. Never a problem. I have marker after marker, stamped with your father's seal. I have marker after marker that he signed when he couldn't pay for those first markers. The Bull is a businessman, not a cheat.'

Fei Long's stomach turned. This is what Liang had been afraid to tell him.

'There must be—' he shoved the words out '—some deal we can arrange.'

'There is no deal. The Chang family owes and it must pay. You see, your father was a remarkable man. As a gambler, he was always a failure, but he had such powerful friends behind him. There was always more money to be found somewhere. Why, I hear you had several expensive gifts delivered to your beloved sister from the Emperor himself.' Zōu nodded smugly. 'I think I like the arrangement we had. Why change such a beautiful partnership?'

Fei Long clenched his fists so tight they shook. His father had let himself be trapped by this demon. He couldn't let it go on. He wouldn't.

'This is something we'll no doubt need to discuss.' He regarded the slum lord evenly. To show his anger would be a weakness. 'For now, I'll take one of those markers.'

Zōu's smile dropped. 'Whatever do you mean?'

'My father owed you money and I've paid part of his debt. Return the marker.'

'You don't understand, young Lord Chang. This monthly payment is merely interest.'

'I do understand. Money lenders are not allowed to collect excessive penalties. Abusive usury is quite illegal. I'll have the marker now...or should I consider what other illegal activities you practise?'

They locked gazes. The den lord's eyes beaded within his rounded face.

'You did mention how my father had some very powerful friends,' Fei Long said lightly.

Zōu's mouth twisted. 'Orchid! Bring the box.'

The Bull continued to scowl at him while his painted concubine brought over a lacquered box inlaid with mother of pearl. He opened it and, without looking, fished out a wooden marker and tossed it across the table.

'I'll see you again next month, Chang Fei Long.'

Chapter Twelve

Summer was coming to Changan and so was the light, easy gaiety that came with it. The trees along the main avenues yielded a bounty of peaches and plums. The morning sun roused the household into activity early and by the afternoon all of the windows and doors of the house were thrown open to let the breeze flow through.

It was the sort of day that made it hard to concentrate indoors. Fei Long found himself rising to look out the window into the courtyard, or scan the bookshelves. Anything to stop from thinking about numbers. Fei Long had come to hate the clicking of Old Man Liang's abacus. He listened to the desolate sound of the counting beads every morning while the steward went through the accounts.

He was still staring out the window when the door opened. He turned to find Yan Ling standing beside the desk and he willed himself to relax. Their hours together were a sanctuary of peace. He could shove all the collection notices to the back of the drawer and take refuge in the comforting formality of their lessons.

'You always do that, my lord.' Yan Ling smiled at him pleasantly.

'Do what?'

'Inspect me as if you're looking for flaws.'

He was taken aback. He didn't realise his scrutiny had been noticed. 'It must be habit from commanding soldiers.'

It was hard not to take her in, now that she had spoken of it. The season had brought a glow to her. She was wearing a light blue dress with half-sleeves today. Her forearms were exposed and he thought about reprimanding her about it, but he stopped himself when he realised there was nothing improper about the style. Only he would be distracted by such an innocent display of pale, smooth skin.

It wasn't only Yan Ling's appearance that had changed. She had become more reserved over the last week, less likely to engage him in spontaneous conversation or questions. The change caught him off guard.

'You're doing very well,' he pronounced.

'A compliment,' she replied with wonder.

'In your studies,' he amended, though not certain why he felt the need to.

She angled her face away so he only caught the trailing end of a smile. 'I have the best of instructors.'

Her speech was losing the country accent of the provinces. She even moved differently, held her head higher. When she walked into a room, he could no longer see any remnants of the tea girl he'd first met. Occasionally, he would see her doubled over in laughter with Dao or Bai Shen and the sight always sent an inexplicable ache through him. She never laughed that way in his presence.

Yan Ling was exceeding all his expectations—and he hated it.

Yet the more she sensed his displeasure, the harder she tried. He'd stopped criticising her.

'What is that?' she asked, looking at the wooden case laid across his desk.

He'd left it unopened after its arrival that morning. He should have stored it away completely.

'It's a map.' He reached down to unfasten the pins that secured the lid. There was no use holding off any longer. 'This came from the Foreign Ministry.'

He lifted the scroll from its case and Yan Ling came around to help him, taking hold of the wooden dowel at the centre. They pulled the edges of the heavy paper apart until the map spanned the entire surface of the desk.

The curve of her neck hid against the blackness of her hair as it fell over her shoulder. He was stricken with the urge to stroke his fingers over the smooth skin and explore the elusive shape of her; an urge he quickly banished.

'A gift,' he said, moving closer as her eyes roamed over the painted mountains and rivers. 'From the Emperor himself.'

She stared at it in wonder. 'This is our empire.'

'And what lies beyond.'

'Beyond,' she echoed. Her fingers curled over the edge of his desk.

The borders of the empire to the north were drawn out as a majestic wall, though he knew that the Great Wall of the First Emperor only spanned several stretches of it. Beyond that final boundary lay the neighbouring tribal kingdoms of the north.

He pointed to the city near the western region of the empire and then paused. Yan Ling liked to take a moment to try to absorb new knowledge.

'This is Changan,' he continued steadily. 'Where we are. The character for "peace" is one you should recognise.' After a moment, he moved upwards to the far north-western corner of the map. 'This is the land of Khitan.'

She let out a soft breath. 'It's so far.'

'Not so much.' He measured out the distance with his hand, walking across the map from thumb to little finger several times. 'I'd estimate a two-month journey, perhaps three. That's why the caravan is scheduled to leave mid-summer. You'll be in Khitan before the winter wind sweeps through the plains.'

Yan Ling ran her hand absently along the embellishments along the bottom edge. 'It's very beautiful,' she said, though it wasn't admiration in her tone.

Indeed, the map could have been displayed as a work of art, but he'd been unable to bring himself to mount it despite the bare section of the wall left by the absence of the cranes. He couldn't bear the reminder of the vast grassland frontier of Khitan.

The desolation in her voice pierced him, but he had handled it with feigned confidence. Yan Ling had shown nothing but complete dedication and it was his duty to remain unwavering as well.

'You'll make the voyage with an appointed court ambassador as well as an escort of attendants and guards. Every need will be attended to.'

'Servants at my beck and call,' she replied dutifully. 'Who would imagine such a thing?'

'You'll be treated as a princess for the rest of your life.' He had no choice but to push on. 'It is normal to feel homesickness when going so far away. The feeling will pass.'

'I don't feel any homesickness for the village where I came from.'

She met his eyes and her gaze was so clear it cut him like glass. He could feel every breath labouring through his lungs, but she turned away first.

'We always knew this was where I was meant to go,' she conceded softly. 'Changan isn't my home anyway.'

'Right. Very good thoughts.' He should thank heaven that Yan Ling was so practical. She'd risen from nothing and this was an unfathomable opportunity for her.

'Tell me more about Khitan,' she said.

He rolled up the scroll and returned it to its case. 'Khitan is ruled by a tribal confederation,' he began. 'The people live as nomads along the grassland steppes with several permanent settlements, but their capital isn't very different from our cities.'

'Who am I to marry, then?'

It took courage to ask that question as calmly as she did. He would be just as strong in return. He couldn't falter now.

'The current khagan petitioned the imperial court for a peace marriage as the previous leader had done. By showing his alliance with our empire, he strengthens his own position among the other tribes.'

She paused, as if taking a moment to absorb everything he'd told her. 'Do you know,' she said finally, forcing a smile to her lips that made his soul ache, 'once I'm a princess, I'll outrank you.'

'Yes,' he said hollowly. 'I suppose that's true.'

'When you first told me about the alliance marriages and these false princesses, I thought you must be trying to trick me.'

She wandered away and he was left stranded, trailing after her with his gaze. Was it only an illusion, or did she stand taller? Her newfound grace put a barrier between them.

'I thought you were so stiff and fussy at first,' she said, amused at his expense.

Strange how he barely remembered their journey other than a few disjointed fragments. His mind had been occupied and his unexpected travelling companion had been only another burden. Yet here he was, hanging on Yan Ling's every word.

He ventured towards her. 'And what do you think now?'

It was beyond improper. He had no right asking such a damning question.

'Well, now I know it to be true.'

Her eyes glittered brightly at him and the incline of her head revealed what might have been the hint of a smile. When had she learned to be coy? Or maybe it wasn't learning at all, merely an innate knowledge that all women possessed.

Maybe all this learning was pointless. A Khitan chieftain

had no need for a well-bred lady. Why had he been so determined to change her? Fei Long retreated to his desk and closed the case with more force than he intended.

Yan Ling regarded him with disappointment that the conversation was over. He was no fool. The boldness and danger of such evocative conversation was tempting, more intoxicating than wine. His heart was pumping fast from merely a few innocent words.

'Everything you told me will come to pass, won't it?' she asked.

He gripped the map case. 'Yes.'

'I should thank you, then, for your generosity.' Her voice faltered and she finally looked away, embarrassed.

'Don't say that,' he ground out.

His stomach clenched. Her show of gratitude highlighted the ugliness of their deception. The household was surviving off an allowance from the imperial court: Yan Ling's bride price. Fei Long went to her so suddenly that she swung around to face him. In Yan Ling's eyes he saw trust and hope.

'You don't need to thank me for anything,' he said gently. 'I should be thanking you.'

'Because we're in this together,' she said uncertainly.

He nodded, breathing deep. 'Together.'

He wanted to confess everything to her right then, but it would have been for no one's benefit but his own. He'd considered spilling his worries to Yan Ling more than once while she studied quietly across from him, but it wasn't her burden to bear.

They never spoke of such personal matters in their family, even amongst themselves. It was taboo. That was why he had been shocked when his father's death had revealed the disastrous state of the household finances. Debt on top of debt, and it wasn't merely the amounts that were troubling.

Yan Ling went to the writing table to prepare for the day's lesson while he watched her for as long as he dared. Then he returned to his desk and stared at the deeds to several holdings until his blood cooled. He would have to sell the plots of farmland. It was a sensible transaction, and wouldn't raise any scandalous rumours. Fei Long would seek out respectable buyers. Nothing that would make the family lose face.

Only when Yan Ling bowed her head to concentrate on her writing did he allow the pain to escape. Just a moment of weakness before his mask was back in place. This was what was best for Yan Ling. She was going to a position of honour and privilege. It was what was best for all of them.

The lessons continued over the next week and even Yan Ling had to admit things were becoming easier. All the little details that had seemed impossible to remember at first began to fall into place naturally. She never felt quite the proper lady, but it wasn't as if she were being presented before the divine Emperor. All she had to do was convince the Khitan court.

That morning, she strolled through the courtyard beside Bai Shen, practising her posture and the hundred little things he always schooled her on. She couldn't get complacent, Fei Long reminded her. It seemed he watched her more intently now. She would catch him scrutinising her, the notices and letters on his desk forgotten. It was her signal to sit up straighter and focus harder.

'Why are you always doing that with your hands?' Bai Shen stopped mid-step to scrutinise her posture.

Yan Ling held her hands at her midsection, fingers clasped one hand over the other, elbows extended. 'This is how the court ladies are always standing in paintings,' she argued.

Since the night of Bai Shen's performance, Fei Long had relaxed the restriction on her leaving the house. She'd made short excursions with Dao into the city parks and marketplace. One of her favourite activities was looking at paintings.

'But it looks so docile.' Bai Shen's frown deepened until she unclasped her hands.

'I think it looks elegant,' she said, pouting.

He responded with a snort.

Bai Shen had covered different expressions and how to communicate an array of subtle emotions through just the angle and intensity of her eyes. She shot him a poisoned look. She was quite good at this one. She'd practised in her mirror.

'You need to observe how the courtesans in the pleasure pavilions entertain,' he said.

'As if Fei Long would allow such a thing.'

She had asked Fei Long if they could return to the Pear Blossom Gardens for another show, but his answer had been an outright refusal. She'd sulked. His denial could only be a reflection of her poor behaviour that night.

Her chin lifted. 'And I wouldn't seek instruction from women of ill repute.'

'How innocent you are.' Bai Shen's taunting was usually good-natured, but this morning he was intent on challenging her every word. 'Gentlemen don't go to such places for sex.'

She blushed at his candid use of the word. 'Then what do they go for?'

'To be enchanted. Every movement is a sensual act. An accomplished courtesan can drive a man mad with lust with the sight of a bared wrist.'

She sniffed. 'As if a man would notice such details.'

'So now you're an expert on men.'

Everyone seemed irritable lately. Fei Long had become more pensive and gloomy and today Bai Shen had traded his usual cheer for a short temper. She wondered if he was suffering from another hangover.

'Men may not notice, but they still understand,' Bai Shen lectured. 'Not in their heads, but deeper. It's a hidden language.'

'Show me, then.' Apparently she still didn't know how to enchant and entice. Fei Long certainly ignored her. Maybe she was getting irritable too.

'This is called the lotus hand.' He held out his hand, thumb and second finger touching lightly. The other fingers remained slightly curved with the little finger extended.

'Lotus,' she repeated, curving her fingers into the same position. Oddly, her hands did seem more elegant.

Chi wu. He demonstrated between each gesture. 'Butterfly.'

She shook out her hands, feeling foolish for prancing about. She was starting to suspect that some of the exercises Bai Shen presented were for his own amusement.

'Does Fei Long go to these courtesans?' she asked.

'Ah…' Bai Shen raised a knowing eyebrow.

'Put your eyebrow down. I was just talking of this and that.'

Fei Long had been leaving during the evenings, often times alone, and she was left to wonder where he went. She'd never considered it might be for companionship. The thought of him surrounded by these mysterious and beautiful women, waving their seductively bared wrists at him, made her scowl.

'Well, if you're wondering…' Bai Shen folded his hands behind his back, continuing their stroll casually '…Fei Long doesn't have a taste for delicate evening flowers. He seems to prefer awkward country tea girls.'

'Stop teasing me.' Her mood darkened, yet she followed after him, hanging on every word. 'And I don't care who he prefers. Why would I? I have a most exalted wedding in my future.'

He cast a sceptical glance over his shoulder, then turned to face her. 'You can't lie to me, pretty lady. I can see how you're blushing just thinking of him.'

'I'm not blushing.'

'He's behind you,' he said pleasantly.

'Now who's lying?'

A dangerous look flickered across Bai Shen's face. Before she could react, he grabbed her and trapped her against him.

She shoved at his shoulders. 'Bai—'

Her protest was cut short as he pressed his mouth over hers. The shock of the kiss stole the fight from her for only a second. She braced her hands against his chest, trying to twist away, but he only held her tighter.

Suddenly, his grip loosened. Bai Shen was torn violently away from her and she staggered from the force of it. Fei Long appeared as a dark blur with his hand clenched around the collar of Bai Shen's robe. His other hand closed into a fist.

'Wait—' She couldn't find her voice in time.

Fei Long struck him square across the face and Bai Shen staggered to the ground.

'Bastard.' Fei Long moved to stand over him, his eyes hooded and black with rage.

Never had the differences between the two men been more evident. Fei Long stood like a citadel, broad-shouldered and imposing. Bai Shen was slight and wiry by comparison. He raised himself onto one knee.

Blood flowed from his lip and Bai Shen's eyes narrowed. For the barest second, a look of rage crossed his face. 'Have you gone mad? How am I going to look pretty for the performance tonight?' He pressed a hand to his split lip and tried to play off the incident, but it was too late.

'Get out,' Fei Long commanded. 'If you ever set foot in this house again, I'll kill you.'

It was a quiet, deadly promise. Yan Ling's heart pounded as Bai Shen picked himself off the floor. What had happened? Fei Long had lost his mind. Both of them had.

She tried to push forwards. 'He didn't mean anything.'

Fei Long ignored her as he waited for Bai Shen to leave. The actor brushed the dust from his robe.

'You see?' he said to her. His lips curled into a mock smile, but his eyes remained distant.

Only after Bai Shen disappeared out the front gate did Fei Long face her.

'I meant what I said,' he warned her, as if she were in allegiance with Bai Shen. 'He will not come by here again.'

He crossed the courtyard and disappeared into the interior of the house, while she was left beneath the glare of the sun, bewildered. She could still feel the imprint of Bai Shen's hands against her back. Her mouth still throbbed from his assault. And that was exactly what it had been. The actor had never shown any hint of interest in her, she was certain of it.

She ran after Fei Long, weaving her way through the inner corridor of the east wing. It was a part of the house she'd only been to once in her wanderings. The door at the end of the hall had been flung open. She went to it and found Fei Long at the centre of the room with his back to her, shoulders tense.

'Bai Shen didn't mean any harm, my lord,' she said, nearly out of breath.

'Yan Ling.' Fei Long turned slowly. 'This is my private chamber.'

The fire was gone from his expression. He'd replaced it with an impassive mask.

'Please. You know Bai Shen. He was only playing.'

'Playing?' His voice hardened. 'That's all the world is to the two of you. One endless game.'

'The two of us—' she sputtered, affronted. 'How can you blame me for any of this?'

She kept seeing Bai Shen on the ground, his face bloodied, with Fei Long towering over him, yet it was if she was the one who'd been stricken. Something had broken between all of them. She didn't know what or how and she was so very confused.

Fei Long regarded her coldly, but his jaw was clenched. The vein in his neck pulsed and she could see the rise and fall of his chest. He was holding himself back with control strained so tightly that it was ready to snap. All her hours with him, in close quarters in quiet reflection, told her this.

'Bai Shen was only trying to make you—'

'Angry,' he finished for her.

She was going to say jealous, but she fell silent, realising how humiliating and revealing that thought was.

'I am angry.' His tone remained flat. 'You're under my care, my protection. As is everyone in this household. I won't allow anyone to be mistreated like that.'

'But he's your friend.'

'Not any more.'

Whatever Bai Shen had intended, he'd gone too far. Fei Long was closing himself off. The walls of his ire rose around him.

'Why are you doing this?' she whispered.

She wanted the uneasy peace between them back—all those unspoken thoughts and hopes, as frustrating as they were.

His stone-cold voice pierced through her. 'Go outside and close the door. You're not to be in here.'

Fei Long waited for the door to shut and separate him from the rest of the world. From Yan Ling. He continued to wait long enough for her to walk the short length of the corridor. She'd go back to the gardens or retire to her room. Wherever she went, it would never be far enough. He would still think of her and seek her out to the furthest reaches of his senses.

The grasslands of Khitan were not far enough.

If he'd had his sword, he would have killed that fool Bai Shen. The actor was always looking for an excuse to goad him, but by all the demons in hell, this wasn't a game to Fei Long. Seeing Yan Ling in another man's arms had been the most vicious of taunts, because Fei Long knew what was inevitable. In less than two months, she would be taken from him to be delivered as a peace offering.

Fei Long sat on his bed at the far end of the room and sank his head in his hands. Yan Ling slept in a similar one. He'd been in her chamber not two weeks ago. He knew how her skin glimmered beneath the moonlight. Knew where she slept only a short distance away from his chamber.

That bastard had been kissing her. *Kissing* her. Yan Ling didn't deserve to be treated like that.

He dug his fingers into his scalp until there was edifying pain. All those afternoons they'd spent together. Alone. Unattended. He'd had thoughts, but thoughts only. He had always remained respectful toward her as their stations demanded. H would never take such liberties. Yan Ling trusted him and sh had worked so hard to better herself.

The room grew hot, nearly stifling as the day reached noor time. He lay back on the bed and closed his eyes. There wa too much for him to do, but he wasn't yet ready to leave thi confinement.

There would be no afternoon lesson today. He couldn't bea being so close to Yan Ling. He didn't know why he'd lashe out at her as well. His anger had no beginning and no end.

There might not be a lesson tomorrow either.

Chapter Thirteen

Fei Long declared that there would be no lesson for the last few days and Yan Ling was too intimidated to question him about it after he'd coldly put her in her place. Bai Shen didn't come by for the rest of the week either. She was hoping he would return to set everything right. The two men were almost like brothers—brothers who traded insults and fought and were opposite in every way—but brothers none the less.

If the scoundrel had just returned with a humble apology and a few witty remarks the next day, all might have been forgiven. Instead Bai Shen stayed away and Fei Long continued to shut doors between them. Without her morning or afternoon lessons, it fell upon Dao and Yan Ling to come up with their own routine.

Dao had no complaints. She'd ushered Yan Ling to the market, holding a parasol over her like a dutiful attendant.

'We don't have to be so formal,' Yan Ling protested. It was important for them to maintain appearances, but it still felt unnatural being coddled so.

'You don't want to take up any sun and get dark,' Dao insisted.

She wondered if Dao had been such a nag to Pearl. The
were trailed by the burly Huibin, one of the fetch-and-carr
attendants who helped with the market purchases and wei
wherever he was needed. They moved to the shade beneat
the row of trees at the edge of the lane. The heat only fade
slightly in the wane of the afternoon. She wore a simple rob
today, though she would have considered the peach-coloure
cotton an unimaginable luxury not a month ago. The fabr
was light and more suitable for prolonged activity like the lor
stroll to the market.

'Dao, do you have anyone?' she asked.

'Anyone?'

They were crowded close to one another so the shade of th
bamboo parasol covered both of them.

'Like a young handsome someone, you mean.' Dao laughe

There were two different Daos. In front of Fei Long, th
master of the house, Dao was timid, respectful and chose he
words with utter care. When the two of them were alone, Da
threw words about like a fisherman scattering rice.

Yan Ling lowered her voice. 'Yes, so?'

Speaking about such a personal issue out in public mad
her nervous, but the crowded city seemed a more secure plac
for secret yearnings than the Chang family home.

'Who would I possibly be fond of? Old Man Liang ha
hardly any teeth.'

Yan Ling stifled a laugh.

Dao went on. 'Those boys in the kitchen and the stables
Or that mule Huibin over there? Worthless.'

Yan Ling cringed and didn't dare look back to see if th
manservant had overheard. 'Huibin's not so bad,' she whis
pered.

Dao sniffed. 'You're right. He's the best of them. So, no,
haven't anyone.'

Yan Ling knew that the household adored Dao—adored he
for her cleverness and feared her for her sharp tongue.

'I was just trying to imagine what it must be like,' Yan Ling said wistfully.

'It must be the weather.' Dao sighed.

'What?'

'When the spring turns to summer in this city, it does this to everyone. One becomes moody. Starts writing poems.'

Yan Ling smirked. 'I don't believe I've written any poems lately.'

She gave Dao a playful shove as they turned the corner. She could see the towering gate of the central market at the end of the street.

'Well, you must not have a special yearning for someone either,' Dao said.

Her heart skipped faster at just the empty thought, even before she filled it in with a name. With a face. 'There's no one.'

'Otherwise you would have never agreed to come with Lord Chang to the city.'

'Or agree to be married to a barbarian,' she added absently.

'It truly is a beautiful opportunity for you. A dream.'

'Yes.' Her voice trailed away. 'Truly.'

The buzz of the East Market had reached them. They passed beneath the arch of the gates into a sprawl of shops and warehouses. Traffic flowed lazily today, indolent in the sun and slow sticky-syrup time of the afternoon.

The main market was comprised of a grid of two north–south lanes intersecting two east–west lanes. Yan Ling counted four times that she had visited the East Market, yet she hadn't explored even half of the merchants. Dao would usually grab her hand and drag her along impatiently, bypass the sightseeing to go directly to her favourite spots. In contrast, Yan Ling wanted to see everything. She would spend hours going from one stand to another if left on her own.

Along with the permanent buildings, there were stalls set up within empty lots and draped with canopies to block the sun. Street pedlars also roamed the lanes, hauling a cart of sweet pastries here, a basket of salted eggs there. Every speck of the market was dedicated to commerce.

A display of painted jars at one stand caught Yan Ling's eye. The small break in her stride was all it took for the grey-haired woman to waddle towards them.

'Come in, come in, my beautiful ladies!' The grandmother figure beckoned them closer with a wave. 'We have perfumes, powders, paint of all colours.'

The shop was a wooden enclosure draped with a blue-cloth canopy overhead. Dao lowered the parasol as Yan Ling stepped inside. A collection of small jars and porcelain containers had been arranged on the counter. She ran her fingertip over the blue-glaze pattern on a round dish that fitted in the palm of her hand. It was so pretty for something so insignificant.

An elderly man, presumably the owner, sat in the corner of the shop, fanning himself. He apparently left the selling to his wife.

'For your lips,' the old woman cooed. She opened the lid to reveal the cinnabar tint inside. 'Look here. Such a beautiful colour. So vibrant, perfect for a young lady.'

The clever woman went on to coo about how lovely and flawless her skin looked. The flattery was an obvious and overused ploy, yet it worked. Perhaps she was starved for compliments lately.

'I saw lower prices at the shop near the south wall,' Yan said casually.

She continued to look over the display while she battled over the goods with the old woman. It was an elaborate language: a mix of insult, coaxing, denials and promises. An art form where you fought just as hard for a single copper as you fought for a hundred. Finally this was something she knew, something she was good at.

'I'll give you a good price,' the woman cooed. 'Choose two, I'll give you a better price.'

They settled quickly with only a few rounds back and forth and Yan Ling and Dao emerged from the shop with the cosmetics wrapped in a parcel of paper. Dao opened the parasol and they both ducked under it, heads close, laughing.

'That old woman was tough,' Dao said.

'Everything was so shamelessly overpriced,' Yan Ling remarked. 'But I suppose it is the capital.'

They had bought the cinnabar tint and a bottle of perfume as well as face powder and nail enamel. Their shoulders brushed lightly as they scanned across the stands, seeking out the usual purchases: embroidery thread, a few medicinal herbs for Old Man Liang. The market was a welcome distraction. It had been a long time since Yan Ling had been able to think of anything besides Fei Long.

Until that very moment. Now he was back in her thoughts.

'There you go again,' Dao said. 'Sighing long and loud.'

Yan Ling hadn't realised she made a sound. 'I was just thinking of how much I'll miss you when I go,' she lied.

'Silly girl,' Dao scolded, touched. 'But you're going off to marry a prince. A mysterious and exotic prince.'

'I don't think he's a prince,' Yan Ling argued. 'Just a tribal leader of some kind.'

'We were just debating between the stable and the kitchen boy, remember?'

They laughed together. By then, it was time to return. Her feet had begun to ache and they still had a long walk back through the residential quarters. The two of them left the market with Huibin following doggedly behind. Halfway home, the crash of cymbals and drums broke through the afternoon haze.

'Isn't it late for a wedding?' Yan Ling remarked.

'Must have been an auspicious hour.'

They paused at one end of the street to watch as the wedding procession approached a residence. The groom was dressed in a blue robe with a broad red sash draped over his shoulders and tied in front. A train of attendants bearing gifts followed behind him along with an empty sedan lifted by four porters.

Dao sniffed enviously. 'I've always dreamed of being married.'

'Why can't you marry?'

'What, with no family to make the match? No prospects? A fat, old magistrate once asked the elder Lord Chang for permission to make me his concubine, but the lord refused, thank the Goddess of Mercy.'

Dao's explanation shouldn't have come as such a surprise. Yan Ling's prospects had been even worse when she had been at the teahouse. That was why her master and mistress were so eager to be rid of her. They had no hopes of marrying her off and she'd only be trouble when one of the local boys got her pregnant.

It had been easy to leave her village behind. She didn't have anyone she wanted to hold on to. No one to go to the market with. No one who would carry her to bed and cover her with a blanket so tenderly. Even if he acted as if it never happened the next day.

When had she started to expect so much more?

The procession reached the bride's house, which was marked by red draping over the door. The family came out to greet the groom. Everyone was dressed in their finest for the happy occasion. Finally the party disappeared into the house while the sedan waited outside. There would be tea and gifts and ceremony within before the bride emerged, ready to be taken to her new home.

Dao sighed and took hold of her arm affectionately as they walked back. 'You really are fortunate, you know.'

'Yes, very fortunate,' she echoed hollowly.

'Close your eyes.'

Her nose twitched as Dao dusted the pale powder over her face.

'Stop making such faces. You'll cause wrinkles.'

Yan Ling had spent that morning bathing and then washing her hair. It was now held in an elaborate design with combs and pins that Dao had spent over two hours twisting into place. After that, Dao had sat her down and pulled out an array of creams, paints and powders.

The powder brush teased over the tip of her nose and she sneezed. 'It tickles,' she protested.

'Be still for one moment, will you?'

Yan Ling finally thought of the room as her own, though she still wasn't accustomed to having so much space to herself. She always felt more comfortable when Dao was there with her. She opened her eyes to see Dao mixing a paste with a dark blue-green tint on a shallow dish. It was much like grinding ink. Dao used a thinner brush with a fine point this time.

'This dye is made from sea shells. Very expensive. Close your eyes again.'

'Have you done this before?' Yan Ling asked.

Dao snorted. 'Many times! Don't worry. I'll make you as pretty as a spring flower.'

'You sound like the old woman from the market.'

The tip of the brush traced delicately along her eyelid. There was something soothing and decadent about being pampered.

'Do you know why I was so angry yesterday morning?' Dao said. 'That green vase in the front parlour was gone.'

'The large one that's as tall as I am?'

She nodded. 'I was certain that someone had broken it, but was afraid to say anything. I interrogated everyone about it and no one knew anything.'

'That's odd.'

Yan Ling opened her eyes as the brush lifted. Dao looked at her carefully, turning her head this way and that. Her dimple deepened as she pressed her lips together. Then she nodded in approval.

'And then this morning, I found something else missing. An ivory figure of the Weaver Girl.'

This sounded alarming. 'Are you certain?'

'It was my mother's favourite. Of course I noticed it was gone.'

The revelation was a shock. Fei Long would be furious if he found that one of the servants was stealing from him, but all the servants seemed so forthright and loyal.

'I can mention it to Fei Long today,' Yan Ling offered.

'Fei Long?'

She blushed. 'Lord Chang.'

'Hmm.'

Yan Ling narrowed her eyes in warning and Dao fluttered her lashes in response. The girl could be precocious when she wanted to be.

'We shouldn't trouble the lord with such insignificant matters,' Dao said dismissively, lifting her brush again. 'I'll discuss it with Old Man Liang first.'

'You don't need to be afraid of speaking to him.' Yan Ling closed her eyes as the tip of the brush outlined her eyelid. 'Lord Chang is quite reasonable.'

'It's not fear. This is out of respect.'

Had the servants been so distant from the elder Lord Chang? Yan Ling marvelled over the divide between Fei Long and the household servants. She'd always been aware of her place in the teahouse, but everyone, even her master and mistress, had been of humble birth. Perhaps this had put them on more common ground. She resolved to bring up the missing items with Fei Long.

'I had a thought about what you were saying yesterday,' Yan Ling ventured.

'What was that?' Dao chose another brush and dipped it into the vermilion tint.

'Wait, that's too dark.'

Dao muttered something about her being too timid and leaned in to outline Yan Ling's lips. The fine brush glided carefully over her mouth, sending a tingle down her spine.

She supposed she could always take one look in the mirror and wipe it away.

She couldn't go to Fei Long so blatantly painted and perfumed, though she wished she was brave enough to do it. He'd take one look at her and be stricken. He'd see her with new eyes. And then...

And then she had no idea what next. What could he give her other than a single look of desire? One look and nothing else.

But she wanted so much to have that one look.

She turned her attention back to Dao. 'You were talking about marriage. Perhaps Lord Chang could help you. He can stand as your guardian and accept proposals for you.'

'Shush! I need to get your mouth just right.' Dao's expression hardened as she bent close. 'There are no proposals for me, Yan.'

'Of course there will be. You're so pretty. Men would fight over you for those dimples alone.'

'I can draw some in for you, if you like them so much,' Dao teased.

'What about Bai Shen? He's very handsome.'

'Li Bai Shen? He's beautiful and no one knows it better than Li Bai Shen himself. But you are an absolute failure at matchmaking.' Dao sat back with a satisfied look and set her brush aside. 'There.'

Yan Ling peered into the mirror at her new face. 'I look so different.'

She recalled Lady Min's reaction when she'd taken her first look at a woman who was her and wasn't her at the same time. Lady Min had removed all feminine artifices, going so far as to cut off her beautiful hair. Yan Ling had come to take on all that Min had left behind.

Could she really be the lady in the mirror? Staring at her shaped eyebrows and painted lips made the enormity of her task come to light. One sitting before Inspector Tong was nothing compared to the months, the years ahead.

'I won't be able to fool everyone,' she said quietly. 'Not for ever.'

Dao attempted to reassure her. 'The Khitans have never seen a Tang princess. Who's to tell you how to do this or that?'

Yan Ling peered into the mirror again, trying not to compare herself to the little tea girl in her mind. The woman who looked back was elegant and confident. Her secrets were her own. Perhaps they would add to her allure.

Everything that used to feel so hard only weeks ago wasn't so difficult any more. She could talk correctly and managed to move with some grace. She even remembered not to slouch when she sat.

The tea girl was nothing but a thin shadow in the corner. She'd never had a proper mirror in the back room of the teahouse. All she'd seen of her old self were occasional glimpses in passing, dim reflections in pools of water. Yan Ling had never known what she'd looked like to others. That girl didn't exist any more. Maybe she had never truly existed at all.

'Right. You're right,' she told Dao, stronger the second time. She grabbed the powder and brushes excitedly. 'Now let me try on you.'

Yan Ling paused before the door to the study. She pressed her lips together, resisting the urge to run her tongue over them. She could feel the waxy gloss of the vermilion tint and taste the clove oil in the balm. Dao had re-applied the colour right before her afternoon lessons.

Why did it feel as if it had been an entire age since she'd last been here? She exhaled slowly, collecting herself. All she had to do was concentrate all her energy on appearing natural. And relaxed, too. Gently, she tapped on the door before letting herself in.

Fei Long was at his great cherrywood desk. As always, he was at the end of reading some important note or finishing a last stroke on a letter before shifting his attention to her. His expression was thoughtful and distant, but soon he would look up. For a few heartbeats, his attention would only be on her. She used to hate it so.

He finished scanning the page before closing the book. When his black eyes settled on her, Yan Ling's stomach fluttered and her pulse jumped. She clasped her hands before her, but then remembered that this made her look too docile. She unclasped them and dropped them to her sides.

'How are you today, my lord?' Her greeting came out a little thin.

His gaze swept briefly over her face. The frown line between his eyes sharpened.

'What is this?' he asked slowly.

Her face burned so hot that she doubted she needed the rouge on her cheekbones. His eyes narrowed in on her and she wanted to shrink away. The door was right there at her back. He appeared somewhat displeased...but Fei Long often looked that way when really he was just deep in thought.

'We purchased some make-up at the East Market yesterday. Dao put it on me,' she added weakly.

And now she was like a little child, blaming someone else.

His lip curled. 'You look ridiculous.'

Her heart squeezed tight. Then it plummeted, like a crushed and ruined butterfly.

'Well, we were just trying it out to see,' she muttered.

In so few words, he had scattered all of her confidence, all of her hopes. Her chest hitched and an alarming pressure gathered at the bridge of her nose. Yan Ling sat down at the writing desk and fumbled for the handkerchief tucked in her sleeve. Keeping her face angled away, she swiped at the offending tint.

There was no pleasing Fei Long. Not looking at him, she scrubbed at the tint until her lips were raw. She wanted it off, all of it. The powders, the perfume and all pretence that she could be a lady worth any notice.

'Yan Ling.'

He rose from his desk to move towards her. She stared down at the handkerchief as her vision blurred. It was smudged with red.

She stood in a panic, keeping herself turned. 'I have to go.'

'Yan Ling.'

His voice was louder this time. Closer. She tried to slip past. Wouldn't look even when his hands closed around her shoulders.

In the next moment, she caught a glimpse of Fei Long's face, of his dark and tortured eyes. A muscle tensed along his jaw before he lowered his head.

Her breath rushed from her at the first touch of his mouth. His hand lifted to slide over the back of her neck while his kiss soothed over lips still sensitive from the rough scouring she'd given them. Yan Ling trembled, confused. A lost sound escaped from her.

With that, Fei Long broke the kiss. His fingers lingered on the side of her neck while he looked at her, an unspeakable question in his eyes. He was breathing hard.

Her thoughts came too fast. This was more than just the press of lips together. Fei Long's touch burned away all memory of Bai Shen's kiss. There was no mistaking this. Fei Long desired her. He desired her the way she desired him.

His lips parted as if to speak, but he said nothing. He started to pull away, but she couldn't let that happen. Not after she'd yearned for him for so long.

She came to him, tilting her head up. Her heart thudded with so much force she shook with it. She wanted so much to glance away. To hide. Fei Long was so masculine and so beautiful that it frightened her.

He took her chin in his hand. The pad of his thumb caressed her cheek and her chest seized.

'Yan Ling.' The third time he'd said her name, and each time so different. This was the one that pierced her. His voice burrowed so deep that she ached inside.

She dug hers fingers into the hard muscle of his arms as his head lowered. He tipped her chin gently to receive the kiss and a breathless hunger took over as he claimed her with his mouth. Harder this time. He used his tongue to taste her and she gasped—excited, frightened. With his hands against the small of her back, he pressed his body hard against her, making her knees go soft. Whatever came next, she wanted it.

Suddenly, his hands tightened over her hips. He held her so fiercely it was nearly painful. She could feel the heat of his skin and the taut coil of muscle and sinew through his robe. A shudder ran through him.

He pulled away roughly then, holding her at arm's length when he couldn't get enough of her only moments earlier. His chest heaved as he stared at her as if he didn't know what had just happened. But she knew, in every part of her, to the very tips of her fingers and toes.

'Forgive me,' he breathed.

It was the first time he'd apologised since she'd met him. For the one thing she'd wanted more than anything else for him to do.

With surprising calmness, Fei Long went to the door. Before she understood what was happening, he'd left her. Yan Ling remained alone in the study with her heart caught in her throat. The heat of his embrace slowly ebbed from her skin until she was left cold.

Chapter Fourteen

He had to put an end to this.

Fei Long retreated to his chamber where he soaked a wash-cloth and ran it over his face. The cooling effect of the water was only temporary. He had to leave the house. Perhaps ride out to the parks outside the city.

Because Yan Ling tasted like cloves and honey and he had to get away. He doused himself with more water.

Avoidance hadn't resolved anything. Being away from her only left him wanting, which led to the disaster in the study. He could control these feelings. He *had* to control them.

These urges were entirely inappropriate. He was master of the house, not a creature of impulse and passion. What he needed was a strict plan of action. He left his chamber and found Dao at the front of the house, dusting the furniture and antiques.

The girl straightened and bowed, surprised to see him. 'Lord Chang.'

'Have Miss Yan Ling join me for dinner tonight.'

'I'll tell her, my lord.' She regarded him while a band of heat circled his neck like a noose. Was that disapproval and speculation lurking behind her dormant expression? He must be imagining things.

He turned to go, but then remembered. He hated the appearance of uncertainty as he faced her again. 'One more thing. She's most likely in my study. If you'll tell her…tell her that there is nothing else for today. She's free to go.'

Dao nodded and he left her staring after him, her eyes wide with curiosity. He went to Old Man Liang next. The steward was preparing to take several documents to the municipal office as well as to collect payment on the farmland sale. Fei Long informed the steward that he would take over those tasks.

'Y-yes, my lord.' Old Man Liang looked wounded as he handed over the papers. He stroked his grey beard in thoughtful silence.

Somehow Fei Long was managing to offend everyone today. Ever since he'd returned to the capital from his military post, there had been an uneasy balance within the house. The servants went about their duties while he maintained peace and order on the surface, but behind it all, he was holding together the ragged edges of an open wound, frantically stitching it closed with one hand.

They had some semblance of harmony, didn't they? At least for a brief moment. Though Pearl and Lady Min were gone, everyone had seemed content. Even Yan Ling had seemed happy. As Fei Long walked through the courtyard, it was as if a storm had washed over the mansion. The harsh wind had scoured away the thin veneer of paint from the surface, revealing the rot and decay beneath.

The servants all looked upon him with nervous anticipation in their eyes. He saw hope there, but he also saw fear. They never complained and always did their duties, but they were waiting for the inevitable. If he couldn't resolve the debt, everyone would be left destitute. Loyal people who had spent generations in service to the Chang family.

If he hadn't sworn off spirits long ago, he might have considered a drink.

He wasn't as adept as his father at hiding their troubles. All he could do was face them head on. He headed out to the stables to fetch his horse himself, leaving another shocked attendant at his breach of procedure.

This fire inside him would fade, Fei Long insisted as he rode from the house. There were more important matters to attend to. Much more important than his own desire for a woman he had already decided he couldn't have.

By the time he returned for dinner, Fei Long had his strategy mapped out. He'd rehearsed what he would say. Yan Ling was a practical, intelligent woman. She would agree with him.

Warm, welcoming smells greeted him as he re-entered the courtyard, a further sign that peace and order had been restored. The dining room was set up with lanterns. The panel doors facing the courtyard had been propped open and the curtains tied back to provide a view out into the courtyard.

When the family had all been together, they would share their meals every night: Father, Lady Min, Pearl and himself. Many, many years ago, Mother had been there as well. Lately he had been taking his meals in his study or with Old Man Liang in the front parlour. The dining room was practically a mausoleum.

He only had time to lock the payments away in the back rooms before returning. At the dining-room entrance, Dao intercepted him, stepping smoothly into his path with her head bowed humbly.

'Do you need assistance, my lord?'

'Not at this time.'

He tried to continue forwards, but she slipped around him again, resuming the same humble position.

'Dao—' he began, in a warning tone. She was becoming

bolder since Yan Ling's arrival. Her demeanour almost bordered on impudence.

'Assistance with your robe, my lord? And I can have a wash basin brought to you, if you so wish.' Her eyes flickered over him and the sheen of dust from the road seemed to magnify into a mud bath.

He exhaled impatiently. When he dined alone or with an old steward with age spots, he didn't need to worry about such things. However, Yan Ling would likely come to dinner impeccably dressed and groomed, down to the very last eyelash. A lady in manner and appearance. Wasn't that the purpose of her education and training?

Fei Long conceded defeat and retreated to his chamber to wash his face and change into a fresh robe. He returned to the dining room just as Yan Ling appeared, or more likely she had been waiting for his arrival to co-ordinate her entrance.

'My lord.'

'Miss Yan Ling.'

Always the same greeting, but his heart pumped harder this time.

Her outer robe was a thin, lace-like material and patterned with silver butterflies. The silk sheath she wore inside was a pale blue and the black of her hair caught the light. It was combed smooth and pinned on top, but otherwise allowed to fall free down her back. He could make out the shape of her shoulders through the gown. As she walked beside him, the fall of the silk hinted at the slender waist and gently rounded hips beneath.

Dao had been right to urge him to change. He would have looked like a peasant beside Yan Ling, their roles unacceptably reversed. Yan Ling had grown beautiful, he had to admit it—no, that wasn't right. It wasn't as if she'd transformed in the last month. He and his hapless crew consisting of the shameless actor and the clever servant girl couldn't take credit. He had simply wasted too much time not noticing.

They seated themselves across from each other at the table that was meant to hold at least three times their number. Yan Ling glanced briefly at him before staring down at the table. Her hand wandered nervously to her neck. Oppressive silence hung between them.

He cleared his throat. 'How long has it been since you came here?'

She looked up, startled. The drop of a feather could have startled her at that moment. 'Heavens…over a month, my lord.'

There was something different about her. A warmth that blossomed over her skin. And a nervous vulnerability that only made her more vibrant. More real. Which was not favourable for him. Not favourable at all.

When she was perfect and composed, he could distance himself, but tonight her cheeks were pink, her eyes alight. She looked exactly as she did right after he'd kissed her, as if it had just happened. As if he'd just let go of her only a heartbeat ago.

And he had. The kiss was still very much alive and unfaded for both of them.

Yan Ling looked down again, suddenly very, very interested in her bowl. He did the same. Yes, it was fascinating. There were blue patterns in it. He didn't give a damn about it or this dinner. Only Yan Ling.

'I've decided that we should discontinue our writing lessons,' he said.

'Oh.' She looked up, blinking in surprise. 'I suppose I can continue practising with Dao.'

'Dao?'

She looked uncertain, as if she'd offended him. 'I couldn't remember everything you taught me each day, so Dao would help.'

His chest rose. Something welled within him. Pride. He laughed, shaking his head in amazement.

'What is it?'

'Dao is quite clever, but it still took a long time for her to learn how to read,' he said. 'It takes many, many years.'

Her expression fell. 'Why would you try to teach me in so short a time then?'

'I wasn't teaching you how to write.'

She frowned.

'I was trying to instil patience and discipline.'

'Patience and discipline.' Her voice trailed away, not quite understanding.

'You did throw a pot of tea at me the first time we met,' he reminded her.

It was how his father had taught him discipline: thousands and thousands of writing drills. Perfect strokes and lines. Before you could learn to express yourself with the brush, you had to learn the rules and perfect them. Fei Long didn't realise at the time that discipline was the one thing his father was wholly unqualified to teach.

'Well, I—' She stopped herself.

'What is it?'

Her lips tightened, but then she took a deep breath. Her back straightened as if she were readying herself for battle.

'I liked our lessons.' Yan Ling raised her chin and held on to him with those captivatingly dark eyes of hers. 'I'll miss not having them, but maybe we should speak plainly about why you're really doing this.'

Despite her bold words, a hint of pain flickered across her face. It was magnified a hundred times in his own heart.

'Because it's the honourable thing to do,' he said steadily.

'Not honour.' Color rose to her cheekbones. 'Rules. Your *Three Obediences and Four Virtues*.'

'I am thinking of your welfare.'

He tried very hard not to think of the texture of her skin and how she had felt beneath his hands. Cool to the touch, but still warm beneath. There were other women. Plenty of them. He could have one that very evening, if he wanted.

Just having the thought while Yan Ling sat across from him sickened him. He really was a dog. Lower than a dog that you kicked just for the hell of it. He had to remember that.

'What happened today will never happen again.' His words fell heavy, as if he were a magistrate handing down a sentence. His own sentence. 'I can promise you that.'

'Can you?' she challenged softly.

'It will not happen again,' he said, forcing conviction into the words. 'It cannot.'

All the light drained from her. 'Yes,' she said. 'Yes, I know.' When she faced him, her eyes glistened, but she didn't turn away. 'You told me as much the very first night we were together, didn't you?'

'The first night—?'

'In that tiny roadside inn. Because of who you are.' Her voice faltered. 'And who I am.'

She dropped her shoulders back in the chair, retreating as far away as she could.

'You have a good memory,' he said stiffly.

A few painful moments passed. The attendants had all but disappeared though the dishes remained on the table. In the way of servants, they knew when to stay away. When Yan Ling met his eyes again, the light had come back into them, but it was a different fire there. One that sparked.

'This isn't about my welfare. You'll always be Chang Fei Long and I'll always be the humble tea girl. The silken robes, the lessons, they don't matter at all. You wanted me to fool everyone, but I could never convince you.'

Her words cut into him, one stab after another, too quick for him to defend. 'That isn't what I meant. We can't be together—'

'Because I'm beneath you.'

'*No.*'

The force behind his retort stunned her into silence. They could hear the crickets in the garden.

She pressed the back of her hand over her mouth as she tried to compose herself. He could hear the catch in her breath. Her face revealed a flood of emotions: yearning, disappointment, despair. The two of them were like twin mirrors set against one another. Yan Ling reflected everything that he kept hidden. He wanted so much to take away the pain.

'No,' he said, quieter. He could feel the spirit draining from him. 'That's not it at all. Don't you understand that I can't allow this to happen? My father—'

He stopped himself. He wanted to try to explain to her, but it was too personal. A private matter that should be buried with his father. Fei Long stood and looked out into the garden. Beyond the glow of the lanterns, there was nothing but dark and formless shapes.

'I think of you, Yan Ling, more than I should.' A wave of longing struck him. 'When I see your face at night, I don't see the tea girl or the elegant lady. I only see you.'

He could see her now, even though he couldn't face her.

'I think of you, too.'

Her soft confession nearly unravelled him. He had to get this all out and be done with it.

'If I acted on these feelings, if I…if I took what I wanted, it would be an abuse of authority. You're under my care. That was what I meant when I spoke of our positions. I won't treat you like that.' His mouth twisted. 'As if you're here for my pleasure.'

The whisper of silk told him Yan Ling had risen. She approached him while he counted each step with the thundering beat of his heart.

'You told me I wasn't your servant,' she said.

'You aren't, but that doesn't change who I am.'

He turned before she could reach him and took a step away. They had to keep their distance. Yan Ling came closer anyway.

'The only hours of the day when I'm truly awake…' her lower lip trembled '…are when I'm with you.'

He dug his nails into his palms. It was the same with him,

the very same. Yan Ling was his sanctuary, a butterfly trapped within cupped hands. But no one could ever keep a butterfly. He'd have to let her go.

'You have a future in Khitan as a princess. Here, there's nothing but ruin and sorrow.'

She was close enough to touch. He could smell her perfume.

'I'm not afraid, as long as we would be together,' she said.

'No.'

Her voice rose. 'If I'm not your servant, then I can choose.'

He was suddenly weary. 'I'm asking you not to. It would be pointless.'

The finality of it sank deep into him. He was tempted to tell her about the debt, the dishonour that hung over them, and how he sometimes wished he wasn't shackled with this duty. But the shame of it stopped his tongue. He'd vowed to shield her from all fear and uncertainty so he swallowed the secrets like a bitter poison.

'It's better for you this way,' he said, keeping his tone even.

Yan Ling pulled away. There was nothing left to do but watch her go.

She paused before stepping out into the courtyard. 'You speak of boundaries between us, my lord.'

His breath caught as he looked at her. She drew herself up and faced him without wavering and Fei Long realised that they hadn't taught her a thing. Yan Ling's poise and strength came from within.

'We're not master and servant, but you and I will never be equals,' she said with infinite sadness. 'These boundaries between us exist because you insist that they must. It is impossible for you to see any other way.'

Chapter Fifteen

Yan Ling opened the door to her chamber and slipped quietly inside. She wanted to close her eyes and be alone. She wanted to sleep and sleep so this could be over and the hurt would be done. There was no use fighting against the stars and the moon. Fei Long wouldn't be Fei Long without his rigid sense of responsibility.

She gasped when something moved within the dark of her room.

'It's me,' Dao whispered.

A single flicker of light appeared behind the painted screen. There was a shuffling sound as Dao came out from the sleeping area. She carried a single candle upon a holder, which she set upon the tea table.

'I'm so glad you're back.' Dao took hold of both of her hands, squeezing them tight.

'What's wrong?'

'Promise me. Promise you won't fall in love with him.'

Love.

She'd never dared to even think of it, but her pulse skipped at the mention of the word. 'I don't know what you're talking about.'

'Oh, don't pretend.' Dao glared at her, irritated, but still concerned. 'Fei Long and the way he looks at you.'

Yan Ling started to deny it again, but she would only be met with scorn. How many hidden glances had they exchanged? How many times had she pondered and ached for him? So many lost moments that amounted to nothing.

'There is nothing between us, Dao,' she said, resigned.

'Is that true? Really?'

'Yes. Nothing.'

She couldn't keep the bitterness from her voice. Dao released her hands and let out a breath. For a moment, Yan Ling considered that Dao might have been jealous, as fervent as her warning was, but the girl had never shown any special feeling for her master. No one could hide her emotions so well.

'Why are you so worried suddenly?'

'I know how these things always end.' Dao pulled Yan Ling onto the couch beside her. 'These noblemen. They're cultured and refined. They say all the right words to lure you into their beds, whispering promises of security and marriage. In the end, you'll have nothing but scandal and ruin.'

Doubt crept into her. Dao's warning seemed to echo Fei Long's words. There was something there—a pain buried deep.

'Dao, are you telling me…?' Could she have been so wrong about Fei Long? She was horrified, but she had to know. 'You… and Fei Long?'

'No!'

Relief flooded her.

'Not Fei Long.' Dao lowered her voice. 'The elder Lord Chang…and my mother.'

Yan Ling sat stunned.

Dao turned away, blinking rapidly. 'Fei Long doesn't know. No one knows.'

'You mean Lord Chang never recognised you as his daughter?'

Dao shook her head. 'He allowed us to remain in his home,

which was generous. Do you know how many servant girls are forced out by jealous wives when they're discovered to be pregnant?'

Yan Ling had no memory of her parents. She didn't know if they had abandoned her deliberately or had come upon some misfortune. Dao had known her father, yet she had grown up with the shame of his denial. Even Fei Long tended to overlook her.

'I'm so sorry,' Yan Ling said, her heart in every word.

Dao sniffed once. 'That is all past. It doesn't matter, but I can't bear to see this happen to you. You must know how fortunate you are.'

Yan Ling kept on hearing these words. This was best. She was fortunate. Her future was bright. Everyone believed so but her.

'Fei Long wouldn't shame me like that,' she argued. 'He's been nothing but honourable.'

Too honourable, except for the one moment of precious scandal when he'd kissed her as if he'd die if he didn't have her. They'd both been wrong together and it had been *magnificent*.

'Oh, Yan. It won't be a sinister seduction like some lurid play. Lord Chang will be handsome and charming. He'll woo you.'

If Dao only knew how much she had longed for exactly that, but Dao was right. It was only an illusion. She could be nothing more than an affair. Fei Long had told her as much. His own father had had a proper wife and a concubine, but that hadn't been enough. Why, Fei Long was practically a monk for refusing her, protecting her from his desires as well as her own.

'It won't happen,' Yan Ling assured.

'Don't forget that, all right?' Dao chewed on her lower lip as she waited anxiously.

Yan Ling would go to Khitan as they'd planned. Fei Long didn't want her. It didn't matter now where she went, did it?

This was always what he had wanted. He'd made her promise from the beginning to see the plan through to the end.

'I promise.' Yan Ling tried to imagine herself fleeing far enough away for the ache inside to fade. 'I won't forget.'

A day went by in agony.

And then another.

There were no more lessons to occupy her afternoons. Yan Ling had haunted the front part of the house and dawdled in the parlour. One of the chairs at the end of the sitting room had a view to Fei Long's study, so she had sat there to struggle through a book of poems even though the light was poor and she could only understand a few of the words.

She had caught only Fei Long's dark silhouette as he went through the door. Of course she had hoped he would look into the sitting area and see her intent on her book. He'd pause and then come to her simply out of courtesy—or because he was irresistibly, uncontrollably drawn to her.

He had done none of those things.

She could still hear his harsh tone as Fei Long declared there could be nothing between them. Her heart would shrivel all over again, but then the kiss. The kiss! The fragments of her memories refused to fit together.

It was a silly game and she had known she was tormenting herself, but she had wanted it to hurt, if pain was the only feeling she was permitted to have. She had become hopelessly tragic.

By the next day, Yan Ling's stomach was in knots from the moment she woke. By the time she sat before her dressing table, the knots had transformed into a swarm of butterflies. Would Fei Long ever speak to her again? The uneasy, burdened silence between them had been preferable to this. At least she could see him and hear his voice.

'I need to do something,' she moaned as Dao pulled a comb through her hair.

'Don't you have wedding gifts to sew?' Dao suggested pointedly, her eyes growing sharp in the mirror's reflection.

Yan Ling decided she'd liked Dao more before her bolder nature emerged.

The two of them separated as Dao went to see to her duties at the front of the house. Yan Ling went about collecting the sewing basket and embroidery thread with a good deal of ill humour, even if no one was there to hear her slam the drawers in the storage closet. She didn't need Dao's protection or not-so-subtle reminders when Fei Long wouldn't even look at her any more.

Traditional wedding gifts were items of clothing a bride would present to the groom's family to show her skill with a needle. She wondered if the true *heqin* princesses deigned to embroider the shoes and robes themselves, or did they have their army of handmaidens do so?

The bolts of cloth had been stacked onto the shelf above her reach. She positioned the footstool and searched through the sewing basket for a pair of scissors. Needlework would be good for her. It was time-consuming, meticulous work and a perfectly acceptable excuse for sitting in her lookout spot in the parlour.

She balanced herself on the stool and reached up to unravel a length of black cloth from the bolt. All she needed was a square of it for the embroidered design.

'You should get someone to help you,' a deep voice spoke from behind her.

She started, but a firm hand pressed against the small of her back to steady her. Fei Long. Heat flooded through her from the point of that one touch.

'Scissors, Yan?' he admonished.

'I was just—'

'You could fall and hurt yourself.'

His broad fingers closed over hers to remove the iron shears and set them on a lower shelf. Her heartbeat raced and she was afraid to turn around as he guided her down from the step. Only Dao had ever called her Yan, but the effect was so, so much different when Fei Long did it. She couldn't control the quickness of her breathing when she finally did turn to face him.

Fei Long didn't meet her eyes. Instead he reached past her, stretching overhead to retrieve the bolt of cloth himself. He was close enough that the edge of his sleeve brushed against her.

'There,' he said, depositing the cloth in her arms.

His manner had retreated back to formality, but he was still there. Watching her. She imagined… No, she *wasn't* imagining. There was a touch of colour to his face that she'd only seen once before.

When he'd kissed her.

'Is there anything else you need?' His breath hitched slightly beneath the brusque tone.

Her eyes darted to the shelves, searching for something else to ask him for. As if she could rationally keep him there by fetching things.

'Dao told me I should be preparing wedding gifts,' she began. 'I thought I would embroider something. You had mentioned that many officials of the Khitan court have adopted Han clothing. Perhaps a pair of shoes?'

His eyes glazed over as she babbled on. Fei Long had no interest in these womanly concerns, but she flushed happily from having him so near after he'd avoided her for so long. The space of the closet shrunk to enfold them and she never wanted to leave.

'Whatever you think is best,' he said.

'Did you sleep well?' she blurted out as Fei Long started to dismiss himself. All those lessons on etiquette and clever conversation—worthless!

'Well enough,' he replied stiffly.

He didn't appear to have slept well at all. The dark circles beneath his eyes gave them a sunken look.

Pining, her heart insisted. Thinking of me. *Me.*

Silly, torturous thoughts again.

He gave her a small nod of appreciation. 'Thank you for your concern.'

'Are you quite busy today?'

There wasn't really much more she could do to delay him. They were stowed away in a storage closet and the door was open. Soon Fei Long's rigid sensibilities would take over and she dreaded the moment. Until then, he had come in there on his own to be with her, hadn't he?

'I have some business to attend to, but...' He paused, as if considering those boundaries he spoke so dearly of. 'I think the outcome will be good.'

Fei Long never spoke of his business affairs in anything more than a passing comment. He certainly never spoke of his hopes.

'I'm sure you will find success,' she assured dutifully, but she meant it deep in her heart. It was so hard to speak to one another like this. Whispering across so many walls and hoping that some meaning carried through.

'Thank you,' he said again, while he looked upon her with a controlled expression that she could read to be anything: thoughtful, doting or indifferent.

He backed out of the closet and stood aside as she slipped out past him. The rest of their conversation was nothing more than a few murmured farewells. Just sounds with no meaning, but her heart still clung to each word.

Out in the parlour, she cut out a small portion of cloth and set it into the embroidery frame. Fei Long retreated into his study while she sat and tried to work out what she should create, while at the same time trying not to think of the impending wedding or her nameless, faceless husband-to-be.

She would do a tiger. There was an exquisite painting of one in an art shop in the East Market that she had fallen in love with. In her mind, the colours would be striking: orange-and-gold pelt against dramatic black stripes. The tiger in the painting had looked ready to leap off the scroll. Grace and power curled through every stroke, from the glint in its eye to the tip of its curved tail.

After holding the image for a moment in her mind's eye, she threaded the needle and began in earnest. She was too impatient to sketch out the tiger and the needlework accomplished the task of keeping her hands busy, though her mind wandered quickly to Fei Long as she stored away every touch and look and the indolent warmth of being near him in that little closet.

At the end of the hour she looked down to find that the last ten stitches were miserably jagged. She'd have to cut them out and redo them. Her tiger was looking a little skimpy as well. It wasn't nearly as glorious as she'd imagined. The only sewing she'd ever done was mending her own clothes. Perhaps a tiger was a bit ambitious.

There was a brief rest for the midday meal, which Fei Long conspicuously took in his study. A tray of food went in and an empty one was carried out. Yan Ling stabbed her thumb while watching the attendant open and close the door.

Many hours later, the study door opened again. She paused from sewing to see Fei Long leaving with a large wooden case under his arm. He didn't see her this time...or didn't want to see her. She watched, unacknowledged, until he disappeared out into the courtyard.

It was late. Very, very late.

Dinner had been hours ago. Afterwards, she'd taken her position in the parlour again, listening for sounds in the courtyard to indicate someone had arrived. Her skinny tiger with the crooked tail was nearly done and she was beginning to fret. Actually, she had begun to fret hours ago. She went to seek out Dao, who had just retired to her room.

'He must be out at a teahouse or something,' Dao said irritably.

'Are you certain?'

'No, I'm not *certain*. But it's not my place to wonder where Lord Chang is at every hour.'

Like you've been doing, came the unspoken reprimand.

Dao glared at her, but Yan Ling was too worried to be intimidated. Fei Long never told anyone where he went, but he usually wasn't gone so late.

Perhaps he had decided to go to one of the entertainment pavilions of the North Hamlet that night. He had seemed hopeful about his business deal. Maybe it had gone well and he was now celebrating in a cloud of wine and courtesans. Jealousy tore at her with scarlet-manicured nails, but her anxiety far outweighed any thoughts of other women.

'I'm worried,' she told Dao.

Dao narrowed her eyes, but relented and came over to wait with Yan Ling in her room. They passed the time by setting up a *xiangqi* board, but Dao captured so many of her pieces so quickly that Yan Ling knew she wasn't presenting much of a challenge.

Another hour passed and Yan Ling couldn't sit still any more. 'Something's wrong,' she insisted.

'Nothing is wrong.' But even Dao sounded a little uncertain.

'We can ask Old Man Liang.'

'No. He's asleep by now.'

'But he might know where Fei Long has gone.'

Dao gave her the eye, both for using Fei Long's given name and for suggesting they disturb Liang with her trivial worries. The steward was the eldest member of the household and was afforded a special place of respect because of it.

Yan Ling won the argument, mainly because she rushed out of the room before Dao could stop her and Dao wasn't undignified enough to wrestle her to the ground in the hallway. Old Man Liang had a private chamber in the back of the house and Yan Ling slowed to a tiptoe as they neared his door.

Dao crowded in behind her. 'You're being foolish,' she reprimanded in a hushed voice.

Yan Ling tapped very lightly and respectfully on Old Man Liang's door. It opened without pause. The steward was still fully dressed and a cascade of lantern light glowed from behind him. He had been awake as well.

She was no longer worried. She was outright afraid.

'My lady.' He stroked his beard fretfully.

'Old Liang, do you know where Lord Chang could be?'

The wrinkles about his eyes deepened. 'I can't say.'

Her heart raced with growing panic. 'Can't say? What's happened?'

Yan Ling didn't know if he was worrying her, or if it was she who was agitating him, but the old man clasped his hands together. 'Why would you think something has happened?' he asked.

'Liang,' she began sharply, mustering enough authority to border on disrespect. 'Tell me.'

'Lord Chang wanted to be discreet, but he's been gone for so long!'

The steward's dilemma had frozen him into inaction. Fei Long wanted secrecy and Old Liang was loyal and tight-lipped above all else. In his eyes, the threat of losing face was worse than the threat of physical harm.

'Where has he gone?' Yan Ling asked.

'Yes, tell us!' Dao joined in as well.

'He went to the lower canal district.'

She turned to Dao. 'We'll go look for him.'

Dao paled. 'That's a bad area, Yan. We can't go there alone at night. The ward gates are closed.'

'It's likely nothing,' Old Man Liang insisted. 'Lord Chang must be late coming home, that's all. He's gone out for a night of leisure.' He scratched at his beard nervously while he spoke.

It was obvious everyone was frightened, but no one seemed to know what to do or how to find Fei Long. It wasn't the way of servants to question their master's activities. Yan Ling considered the city guards, but they had no real cause to issue a report. It wasn't late at all for the North Hamlet and the surrounding areas.

She told Dao to fetch Huibin while she coaxed an address from Old Man Liang.

By the time Dao met her back in her chamber, she knew exactly who could help.

'Huibin is gone for the night,' Dao replied, irritated. 'Some new sweetheart.'

'Perhaps it's better if we go alone,' Yan Ling said. 'Less people to account for to the guardsmen.'

'Guardsmen?'

The two of them hurried to Fei Long's study. Dread had crept into her bones. Something awful had happened to keep Fei Long away, she was sure of it, but she had to stay calm.

'You need to write a special pass,' she told Dao.

Yan Ling set the lamp onto the desk and opened the drawers. Her hands shook as she rifled through the contents. The official seal had to be in here somewhere. She'd seen Fei Long use it countless times on documents and letters.

'But it's illegal to forge a pass,' Dao protested.

'The guards at the gate barely paid attention when I went through last time.'

Fei Long had been with her then and he had been the one to present the pass. The guards might be suspicious of two women travelling alone at night, but she couldn't worry about that now. They would need to be convincing.

'Write that we're in urgent need of a physician,' Yan Ling directed.

She encountered a stack of papers with some writing on it. There was something odd about the characters, but she didn't have time to investigate. She swept them aside and found a small wooden case nestled at the bottom of the drawer.

Dao prepared the ink and started writing. She slid the paper over once she was done. 'When have you been out at night?'

'It was only once.'

She had never ended up telling Dao about the evening at the theatre. It was too precious a memory for idle gossip.

Yan Ling lifted the jade chop from its holder and pressed the carved end into the dish of red ink. She pressed it firmly on the bottom of the letter, leaving a red impression of the Chang family seal.

'Does that look official enough?'

Dao frowned. 'I suppose.'

'Let's go then.'

They took a lantern with them and headed out of the mansion. Yan Ling hoped she could remember the way. Her palms started sweating as the ward gate appeared before them. The arch towered ominously overhead. The sight of it made her heart thump.

She wiped her hands over her skirt. 'Look natural,' she told Dao.

The younger woman nodded silently. It was acceptable for them to be nervous. They were in a frantic search for a physician.

Yan Ling handed over the pass to the guard and kept her posture straight, meeting his eyes without wavering. She was a high-born lady. There was no reason for him to question her. After an interminable pause, during which he must have read the pass a hundred times, the guard finally returned the paper and waved them through.

She let out a great sigh once they were clear of the checkpoint. 'We need to find the Pear Blossom Gardens.'

The North Hamlet was easy to locate as everyone seemed to be heading there. The two of them huddled close through the crowded avenue of taverns and gilded pavilions.

'I never realized what scandalous outings you were having,' Dao accused.

'It was hardly scandalous. Lord Chang took me to see one of Li Bai Shen's plays.'

Dao snorted. 'Entirely scandalous.' She sounded more than a little bit jealous.

There was no show at the gardens, but the park was full of people enjoying a night-time stroll or milling by the lake. Yan Ling cut through the wooded area to the entrance at the far end. Thankfully the alleyways at the back looked familiar to her. She found the gate marked with the theatre troupe's plaque and pulled Dao into the courtyard, towards the room in the corner.

Bai Shen would know what to do. He was knowledgeable about these parts and the district Old Man Liang had mentioned was supposedly only a short distance from there. Not a week had passed since his dispute with Fei Long. Even if Bai Shen was still angry, the two men were good friends. He had to help them.

A light flickered through the paper windows. Yan Ling knocked loudly. When there was no answer, she pushed the door open to find Li Bai Shen face down on the square table at the centre of the room.

'Heaven and earth, is he dead?' Dao exclaimed.

Yan Ling glared at her for being so morbid. Fortunately, Bai Shen stirred and made a moaning noise that sounded like a set of wheezing pipes. What was he doing passed out so early?

Though dishevelled, he was dressed in the finest forest-green robe with gold accents along the collar and sleeves. His long black hair fell loose over his face. He tried to shake it away as he spoke.

'Huh?' he muttered thickly.

'Wake up! Fei Long needs your help.'

He lifted his head gradually, as if it weighed a hundred *tan*. 'Fei Long?'

Dao came around to the other side of the table to inspect the jugs of wine strewn there, turning them upside down to reveal not a drop left. 'He's been at this a while.'

'Bring the wash basin,' Yan Ling suggested.

She grabbed Bai Shen by the shoulders to help him into sitting position. He was a disaster.

He blinked up at her. 'What's wrong with Fei Long?'

At that moment, Dao rushed over with the basin and upended it over his head. Yan Ling yelped and jumped back as water splashed everywhere.

'Fox demon!' he boomed, shooting to his feet. 'What in heaven is wrong with you, woman?'

'I just meant for you to splash some onto his face,' Yan Ling protested.

Dao sputtered, affronted. 'I didn't know!'

Bai Shen swiped the water out of his eyes. 'What's wrong with Fei Long?' he repeated, a bit more lively this time.

'He went out hours ago and hasn't returned.' Yan Ling showed him the address that Old Man Liang had given her. 'I think he went to pay a debt.'

Bai Shen raked a hand through his damp hair and blew out a breath. 'The gambling dens. This must be Boss Zōu's place.'

She didn't know who Boss Zōu was, but her stomach turned at the way he spoke the name. Her fears were further confirmed when Bai Shen grabbed a sword hooked onto the wall. He pulled his hair back into a topknot and pinned it.

'Let's go.'

It was the most serious expression she'd ever seen on the actor's face.

Chapter Sixteen

All evidence of his earlier stupor faded as Bai Shen walked the night streets. Yan Ling wondered whether this confidence was merely an act, but it didn't matter. She and Dao crowded close to him, borrowing from his courage as he pushed on through darkened alleys and deserted lanes.

'Fei Long didn't tell me he was mixed up with the Bull,' he said.

'He didn't tell anyone.' Yan Ling looked over her shoulder. She kept on imagining something jumping out at them from the shadows. 'Why are there no guard patrols in this area?'

'They remain scarce on purpose so they can deny any knowledge of the gambling and the black markets. Good business for everyone.'

Dao clutched a lantern with one hand and held on to Yan Ling with the other. 'It must be the elder Lord Chang's debt. Everyone knew he couldn't resist a wager.'

Fei Long had kept this burden to himself. Yan Ling hoped his father's spirit wouldn't be angry that they were speaking ill of him. They would need both the Goddess of Mercy and the Chang family ancestors to protect Fei Long.

'You two better hide back here while I go up to the Bull's headquarters,' Bai Shen said.

'Why?'

'They say he likes to acquire pretty young concubines.' The grave look he gave them made Yan Ling shudder. 'We don't want to give him any ideas about potential exchanges.'

She didn't like the idea of hiding out in the alley, but she didn't want to meet this crime lord either. 'What if he's killed Fei Long?' she asked, her throat closing up. 'What if he takes you, too?'

'He wouldn't do anything like that. Zōu is a businessman and it's in his interest to keep the peace. Fei Long isn't some drunken gambler Zōu can sink a knife into without anyone noticing.'

The blood drained from Yan Ling's face at the harsh picture Bai Shen painted. Her fingers went to ice.

'Damn that mouth of yours!' Dao scolded.

'We'll find him,' Bai Shen amended sheepishly.

They ducked into the side street to find a place to wait it out. As they turned the corner, a sudden movement between the buildings caught Yan Ling's eye. Two men stood over a third who lay on the ground. The dull glint of metal in one man's hand slammed her heart against her ribcage.

With a battle cry, Bai Shen unsheathed his sword and rushed forwards while the two of them were left scrambling after him. The men in the alleyway tensed and swung around just as Bai Shen broke into a screaming charge.

Suddenly he launched himself from the ground, twisted in mid-air to execute a flip and landed with the sure-footed grace of a cat. He braised his sword dramatically and the men scrambled away.

'What was that?' Yan Lin demanded, incredulous at his theatrics.

'This is only a prop sword,' Bai Shen replied, waving the blade.

She moved cautiously toward the man sprawled on the ground, then started running when she recognised the robe. Fei Long moved his head weakly as she came near. The side of his face was dark with bruises. All the breath rushed out of her as she fell to her knees beside him.

'Fei Long.' Yan Ling choked back her tears, afraid to touch or move him. All she could do was place her fingertips gently against the side of his cheek so he'd know he was no longer alone.

Bai Shen and Dao came up behind her. Bai Shen went to kneel opposite her.

'The death of me,' he muttered. 'Fei Long, can you move?'

Bai Shen gently probed along his ribs. Fei Long winced, curling into himself in pain.

Looking at Fei Long's battered body made Yan Ling sick to her soul. 'Can we take him out of here?'

'He's not spitting blood, but I can't tell if his ribs are broken.'

'Fei Long.' She leaned close and took hold of his hand. His fingers tightened weakly around hers. 'We're going to move you very slowly.'

With Bai Shen on one side and her on the other, they raised Fei Long gradually to a sitting position. He groaned with the effort. He was heavy, unable to help or resist. It was as if the man inside the body had been reduced to a pitiful mass of bone and flesh.

'I found his sword.' Dao came up to them with the weapon in her hands.

'He gave them a good fight,' Bai Shen said fiercely.

What did that matter? Fei Long was hurt, beaten and abandoned in these streets. But the anger seemed to vitalise Bai Shen. Anger was the only way to react and not fall into despair.

Fei Long's lips worked silently and she had to lean in close.

'Zōu,' he said.

The wheeze in his breath frightened her. He was only able

to open one eye to peer at them. The other one was swollen shut. Crying would not help. She would not cry.

'We have to get him home,' she said.

Bai Shen nodded, his expression tense. 'Stand him up.'

She had to hook Fei Long's arm over her shoulder to lift him. Bai Shen took his other arm and they raised him as carefully as they could. Fei Long sucked in a breath as she put her arm around his waist, but didn't cry out. It was just like Fei Long to swallow his pain in silence, but there was no hiding what those animals had done to him.

Once Fei Long was on his feet, they started walking him slowly towards the street. Dao picked up the prop sword and they made their way back to the less seedy parts of the district. Fei Long's chin dropped against his chest and his weight sagged against her. His feet dragged along at their urging. He would have collapsed the moment they let go.

As they entered the thoroughfare of the entertainment district, more than a few spectators stopped to stare at the odd procession.

'Too much to drink,' Bai Shen declared.

Fei Long appeared even worse in the light. His face was bleeding and he barely looked like the man she knew. His eyes were shut and she couldn't tell if he'd passed out.

At the ward gate, Yan Ling scrambled to think of a story to tell the guard, but Bai Shen was ready. He fished a silver coin from his belt.

'The lord would appreciate being returned to his bed as soon as possible,' he said. '*And* if his wife didn't find out.'

To his credit, the guardsman did check Fei Long to make sure he was breathing. Dao thoughtfully angled the lantern away during the inspection. The guard then looked over the quality of their clothes and seemed to accept the story. The coin was the most convincing part. It disappeared into his palm with a quick wink of silver.

* * *

When they reached the mansion, Dao ran ahead to open the gates while Yan Ling and Bai Shen led Fei Long inside. The walls enclosed them like the embrace of an old friend, but there was no relief yet. Fei Long still wasn't moving.

'Old Liang, we need a physician,' she said when the steward met them in the hallway to Fei Long's chamber. Then to Bai Shen, 'Go with him, please.'

Bai Shen was wily and knew all the tricks. He took Fei Long the remaining distance to the bedchamber and laid him as gently as possible on the bed. Then he hurried off with the steward to fetch a physician.

'I'll bring some water,' Dao volunteered, rushing away.

Yan Ling understood the sentiment. Everyone wanted something to do, even if it was something insignificant, to keep the overwhelming helplessness from sweeping in.

'Yan...Ling.' Each word came out in a laboured puff of breath.

Fei Long stirred as she rushed to his side. 'You're home.' She brushed her fingers tenderly over his face, keeping her touch as light as possible. 'Bai Shen is going to get a doctor. Do you need anything?'

It was important for her to keep on talking, though she didn't know why. After a long pause, Fei Long opened his eyes. He swallowed with difficulty and his voice came out as a faint rasp. She leaned in to hear.

'Your hands feel cool,' he murmured before closing his eyes again.

The knot in her chest tugged loose and pain poured into her until she didn't know if she could hurt any worse. Yan Ling laid her head down, her cheek against his. She was able to hold back her sob, but couldn't keep the tears from spilling.

Bai Shen and Old Man Liang returned with the physician who they'd roused out of bed at this late hour. Everyone waited anxiously in the parlour during his examination and Dao made tea that sat in the pot, growing tepid. At one point, the physician called for assistance and Bai Shen went to his aid.

After an hour, the physician left with a promise to return in a few days. They surrounded Bai Shen once he emerged.

'Broken ribs on his left side,' he reported. 'He needs to rest in bed for several weeks and move as little as possible. This will help the pain.' He handed a small parcel wrapped in paper to Dao. 'There's enough for tonight. The physician said you can get more from the herbalist tomorrow.' Then he gave a short bow to no one in particular. 'The show is over. Li Bai Shen will take his leave now.'

Bai Shen looked worn through and through. His feeble attempt at good humour only highlighted the ordeal.

Yan Ling stopped him as he was about to step out into the courtyard. 'Why don't you stay? It's so late and you can get some sleep here.'

He flashed her a half-smile. 'You remember what Fei Long said.'

At first she was confused. Then she realised he was referring to when he'd kissed her to make Fei Long jealous. It seemed like a memory from a previous life.

'That can hardly matter now,' she insisted.

Bai Shen's smile widened, but his eyes remained morose. A faint discolouring still showed on his jaw. 'That man takes every word he says very seriously.'

'Thank you,' she said as he turned to go.

'Fei Long is strong. He'll be all right, my pretty lady.' He added the last part to tell her to smile and she tried, but only out of obligation.

Bai Shen disappeared through the gate.

A little while later, Dao returned from the kitchen with the medicinal brew. Yan Ling moved to take it, but Dao stopped her.

'I'll do it,' Dao said, gently but firmly. She fixed a meaningful look on Yan Ling that was full of challenge.

As if a few moments alone in his chamber would make any difference. Yan Ling could rip out the seedlings of emotion that sprouted at the surface, but what she felt for Fei Long had taken root much deeper.

Every movement hurt. Breathing hurt. So Fei Long lay in bed and tried to move and breathe as little as possible, though he wanted nothing more than to grab his sword and storm into Zōu's stronghold.

He knew exactly which strike had broken his ribs. Four men had surrounded him in the street and crowded him into the alleyway. His sword had been wrestled from his hands and his fists couldn't hold them off for long. A blow to his face had staggered him to his knees. Then a kick to his left side knocked the wind from him. The fight drained away in a streak of black, radiating pain. After that, the blows had kept coming.

All this took on some form and structure as he laid there thinking and re-thinking through the last hours. At the time, there had been nothing but the rage of the attack and a haze of pain.

Someone came to spoon a bitter brew into his mouth. At first he thought it was Yan Ling, but it was only Dao. He tried to refuse. The thought of eating or drinking turned his stomach, but she was insistent. Eventually he was able to sleep as long as he remained flat on his back. Even the slightest shift brought back the pain in his side, like the stab of a dull knife.

He didn't know what time it was when he woke enough to call for assistance. There was light seeping in from outside and he could hear faint sounds of activity from the other parts of the house. He had survived the night and morning had come. His entire body throbbed and he couldn't even sit up on his own. An attendant came quickly to help him up and he bit back the indignity of it.

'Bring Miss Yan Ling here,' he instructed.

He leaned against the alcove wall, curling his fists tight and counting the minutes. He tried to convince himself he could will back the pain and push it to the back of his mind, but it didn't work.

'You're not supposed to be up,' Yan Ling snapped the moment she set foot in the room.

She set aside the tray in her hands and spent the next agonising minutes lowering him back onto the bed. Fei Long gritted his teeth against the jagged, piercing sensation at his side. By the time he was lying down again, he was out of breath and gasping shallowly. All this for a few inches of effort.

Yan Ling propped his head up slightly with the padded head rest and lifted a small bowl from the tray. He recognised the acrid, earthen smell.

'Drink,' she ordered, putting a spoonful to his lips.

It tasted like dirt and tree bark. He forced the brew down, before trying to speak. 'This isn't why I asked you to come.'

'Again,' she demanded.

She was relentless, spooning him the rest of the herbal tea with no conversation in between. Her expression remained hard and determined when he would have killed for a kind look from her. And he would have died rather than ask for it.

'And now the soup,' she said.

'Not now.'

'You haven't eaten. The kitchen made this for you.'

He shook his head vehemently despite the ache it caused.

Then she became coaxing. 'Please try.'

'No, Yan Ling.'

With a long sigh, she set the soup aside. 'Later, then.'

She sat on the edge of his bed, hands folded in her lap. Her gaze became distant and he closed his eyes not to have to see what had been so starkly revealed.

Yan Ling cared for him.

She cared for him so much that she fought not to show it, because he'd told her it was unacceptable.

'It's not so bad,' he said. Every word was an effort.

'You're lying,' she pronounced.

The physician had wrapped and bound his torso to restrict the movement and aid the healing. It added to his feeling of helplessness. He had to collect his strength for the next request.

'If you could go into my study and bring the ledger book…' He paused, gathering and catching his breath. 'And a leather satchel with important papers. You've seen me with it.'

Only when she had left did he open his eyes. When he'd lain beaten in that alleyway, he was certain that death was close. The attackers would come back to cut his throat and there was nothing he could do about it. The sound of Yan Ling's voice had called him back from the abyss.

Did she need any more proof than his broken body to show that he wasn't able to provide for her? He was about to give her that proof.

By the time she returned, the pain had receded to a dull throb, but it was still there, clinging and prodding at his muscles. The edge of it dulled enough for him to unclench his fists. He hoped the drug would leave his mind clear enough to do what needed to be done.

Yan Ling set the book and box of paper next to him and lowered herself at the edge of the bed beside his knees. He hated that he had to do this lying down, like an invalid.

'Open the ledger,' he said. 'Inside is the list of debts our family has incurred over the past years.'

'You mean your father?'

'Our family,' he insisted. 'There's also—' He took a breath. If he spoke slowly and tonelessly, he could go longer. 'There's also a list of earnings from different sales.'

'The cranes,' she said, realising. 'And the vases and ivory carvings.'

He nodded. 'And some of our lands as well. I've been able to satisfy most of the creditors, but Zōu didn't just want the money. I collected enough to cover my father's debt to him. It nearly emptied all we had.'

Yan Ling scanned the ledger, her lips moving as she added the columns. She might not be able to read all the notations, but she would understand the figures.

'Two million? Oh, Fei Long—'

'I never got to Zōu,' he said, cutting off her reply. Her pity would destroy him. 'They stopped me in the streets and stole the money. I'm certain it was his men.'

'You have to go to the head of the ward, then.'

'The head of the North Hamlet is in the pocket of the slum lords.'

She closed the book, her mouth set in anger. 'Then go higher. What about Minister Cao?'

'I can't go to Cao. Don't you see? It would ruin us.' He struggled to sit up, but Yan Ling moved to him, pressing firmly against his shoulders to remind him not to move.

'Stop, Fei Long. You're getting too excited.'

She was so close. Her gently curved mouth was right above him, out of reach.

'Minister Cao has staked his reputation to help us already,' he said, resigned. 'I can't go to Cao and insult him with this mess.'

'Then what will you do?' She frowned, not understanding, but with no choice but to accept.

'There is only one thing left.' He slumped back as all the energy drained from him. 'I will have to sell the house.'

'No,' she gasped.

It was the same cold surrender he'd felt when he'd let Pearl go. He had to cut away a part of himself to do it. He tried to seal off the wound as quickly as possible. There was no drug for this sort of pain.

'Moneylenders like Zōu seek out men that they can exploit.

They don't want just money, they want to enslave and control their prey. Then they can bleed them for ever. I've seen this happen before during my days as a student.'

Many of the favoured sons of wealthy families fell into the cycle of banquets and drinking and women. They bolstered their reputations through the parties they hosted. Sometimes they met with powerful friends, but many met with ruin, borrowing unspeakable amounts of cash that their families were required to pay. Fei Long could have easily fallen into the same trap.

He supposed his father found both alliances and temptation. This was why Zōu was delighted to hold his debt.

'I won't allow Zōu to bleed us dry. Better to make a decision now—while I can still have some control.' He ground his teeth together and a bitter taste filled his mouth. 'I'll work to find the servants placements in other households. They're loyal, good people. And you—by the end of the summer, you'll be headed to Khitan.'

Yan Ling looked away while he spoke. He followed the line of her neck and throat with his eyes, the same view she'd so often tempted him with, sweeping her hair back while she was writing. Of all the losses, he would regret losing Yan Ling the most. It was his one, selfish allowance.

'I'll most likely keep Old Man Liang with me, wherever we end up. He's always served my father well, but he's old and set in his ways. I need you to make sure he carries out my orders to sell the house. Dao is forceful enough, but she might get sentimental.'

Her gaze swung back to him. 'You insult me, Fei Long.'

A low fire burned in her eyes. She rose from the bed, setting aside the book. Her spine stiffened with anger.

'You don't think I have any sentiment for this house? I haven't been here long, but I have no other home. This has been the happiest time of my life.'

She turned on him, fierce and beautiful. In that moment,

he would have never believed the little mouse of a tea girl ever existed.

'I apologise,' he said quietly. 'I didn't know.'

'You and Pearl were born here. All your memories of your mother and father. I've never had these things, yet even I know how important they are.'

She swept away the papers and tucked them out of view.

'You are in no condition to make such decisions right now.' She sniffled, but tried to hide it by grabbing the bowl from the tray. She sat beside him and thrust a spoonful of cold soup to his lips without kindness. 'Get well first before giving such rash orders.'

He tilted his head to take the soup and swallowed obediently, barely tasting it. 'Yan Ling,' he began, as she turned to dip the spoon.

'Stop talking.' She fed him again before swiping the back of her hand harshly over her eyes. 'Really, Fei Long. Stop talking.'

Chapter Seventeen

Fei Long spent a week in bed, tended to by servants who took care of feeding and bathing him. Yan Ling stopped by to check on him at least once a day, but refrained from staying long enough to get angry with him. He obliged her by no longer talking about selling the house.

She was right. To give Zōu their family home would be surrender. He was not ready to bow down to a lowly crime boss. The new plan he was forming, however, would make Yan Ling even angrier.

After the first week, he was allowed to sit up, as long as he didn't move much. The Foreign Ministry had sent along writings about Khitan. Yan Ling would sit and listen while he read them to her. It seemed their daily lessons had been resurrected in this form.

'Do you want to continue?' he asked during one of her visits.

She was sitting near his feet with her back resting against the wall of the alcove. The position was intimate, scandalously so, but he liked having her there too much to protest. She was such a welcome sight after staring at the walls for hours on end. His convalescence had worn tiny holes in the barriers between them where light could peek through, but the barriers were still there.

He looked up after describing several Khitan customs to see Yan Ling with her feet pulled up on the bed.

She rocked back and forth absently, almost child-like. 'I was just thinking. Please continue.'

'Khitan women dress in jackets and skirts with leggings beneath to allow them to ride,' he read from a report written by the imperial envoys to Khitan. 'Many are trained in horse riding as well as how to use the bow and arrow.'

'Maybe I should learn how to ride a horse.'

He set down the report. 'There isn't enough time.'

'You're right.' She nodded, her expression veiled with sadness. 'I suppose there will be plenty of time to learn once I arrive there. I'll have to learn everything again: the language, how to stand and sit.'

As if all of their lessons were for nothing after all. 'You'll have an escort with an interpreter and some of the chieftains have learned our language.'

'It won't be so bad then at all,' she murmured.

Fei Long wasn't convinced and it was obvious that Yan Ling wasn't either. The sharp pain in his chest had nothing to do with his injuries. The ache came deep from within his soul. When he asked her if she wanted to continue, it wasn't only about the reading. He'd always assumed she wanted to go to Khitan, but he'd been blind to anything but his own purpose.

He could go with her.

The thought came as sudden as a windstorm. *Heqin* brides travelled along with an extensive escort. He could offer his services to the Emperor. His military position as squad commander had likely been given to another by now, though not yet officially terminated.

It was impossible, of course. They would have to constantly pose as brother and sister and it was harder for two people to keep up a ruse than one. More importantly, Fei Long didn't know if he could trust himself not to abduct her once they cleared the boundaries of the empire. He'd wear a mask and sweep her onto his horse to ride fiercely across the grassland steppes. The fantasy was not unsatisfying.

'Fei Long?'

'Hmm?'

'Let's talk about something besides Khitan.' She had tucked her knees close to her chest, suddenly appearing very small.

'Of course. Anything you wish,' he replied.

For a moment, they had nothing. He was struggling to find a new topic of conversation when Yan Ling spoke.

'Why didn't you take the civil exams?' she asked. 'Didn't the elder Lord Chang wish for you to carry on the family tradition?'

'Well, there were other—' He tried again. 'It would have been an honour to…'

Yan Ling was watching him so expectantly. No one had really questioned him about his choice. Certainly there were those who wondered why he would pass up the potential for a coveted position within the Six Ministries to pursue a military career in obscurity outside the capital. His father had had no objections. He had jovially accepted his son's path, just as he'd accepted everything that came his way, for better or worse.

'I might have gone on to take the civil exams, but I didn't qualify.'

'Oh, Fei Long. Do you always have to be so humble?' she chided.

'No, I didn't qualify.' He leaned back against the alcove, trying to find a more comfortable position. 'To be an imperial candidate, you must pass the qualifying exams. Do you know scholars from the provinces would study for nearly all their lives to be able to qualify and come to Changan?'

'But you were a candidate for a year. You told me so.'

She stretched out on the bed so her slippered foot rested

just beside his knee. They weren't even touching, but it stirred him mercilessly.

'We were wealthy,' he explained. 'We lived in the capital. My family name was well-known and I was a favoured son with well-paid tutors and impeccable calligraphy.'

Yan Ling giggled and he wasn't sure what he'd said to elicit it, but he was glad he had.

'Like any student of means, I studied the classics during the day and attended drinking parties in the entertainment district at night. A man could make a name for himself hosting parties alone. Everyone would come: scholars, poets, courtesans, entertainers.'

'Entertainers like the *magnificent* Li Bai Shen?' she teased.

He narrowed a glance at her, but it was in good humour. 'Indeed. This was when we began our illustrious association. I stayed out all night before taking the qualifying exams, which were a mere formality, I thought. Of course I was given passing marks and became a candidate for the imperial exams.'

'But…'

'But I began noticing things. Students who were much more astute, much more industrious than I, were struggling. Students who spoke with provincial accents and had names that were unknown. They never frequented the drinking houses and pleasure quarters. I wasn't so careless in my youth that I didn't start to wonder. Perhaps I merely qualified because of who my father was.'

'Your family legacy isn't something to be ashamed of,' Yan Ling protested.

'It wasn't shame.' He would never deny his family. 'I just… wondered.'

At some point, Fei Long considered that he had more in common with Li Bai Shen and his troupe of actors than the scholars who were supposed to be his peers. He was there among the imperial candidates because he looked the part and played the role so well.

'I wasn't entirely without merit,' he assured. 'I had studied the classics and I possessed a few other skills. I was competent on horseback. I could hit a target with a bow and arrow.'

Yan Ling's smile warmed him. 'You wanted to find your own path.'

Something about that sounded so dissident. It hinted disturbingly of rebellion.

'Sometimes a natural path simply reveals itself,' Fei Long countered.

Spending time with Yan Ling always relaxed him. He could speak freely without the lure of wine or music. He needed these hours with her. Not only to pass the time, but to centre himself. Having her close filled him with a purpose and lightened the weight pressing on his chest. In these small moments of peace, he could almost see another way. His own path, but it wouldn't quite reveal itself no matter how hard he searched.

Yan Ling was working on her embroidery beneath the shade of the patio. Dao sat beside her with a basket of the household mending. The day was too hot to stay indoors, but too glaring to sit outside beneath the sun.

A raised voice came from within the house which set them running.

'My ladies, quickly!' Old Man Liang called from the hallway.

At first Yan Ling feared that something had happened to Fei Long, but she went to his chamber to find him out of bed and dressed in a dark robe.

'My lord, you shouldn't be up.'

He raised a hand to quiet her. Moving with great care and deliberation, he straightened his robe and tied back his hair.

'I'm going to see Zōu,' he said.

'Are you mad? He'll kill you this time.'

'He won't.' Fei Long shook his head too calmly. 'No one

left to pay if I'm dead. The only way to deal with a man like Zōu is directly.'

Fei Long had been recovering gradually over the last weeks and was finally able to speak and breathe without effort, but she knew he wasn't ready for this.

'Why now?' she demanded.

'Zōu summoned me. His letter came this morning.'

While his back was turned, Yan Ling waved frantically to Dao who stood near the doorway. She hoped the servant girl would interpret the sign to mean 'do something useful to prevent him from leaving'. Either way, Dao nodded and darted away.

'What was that?' Fei Long regarded her suspiciously.

'Oh, nothing. It's very hot in here.' She fanned herself. 'If Zōu sent for you, haven't you considered it must be a trap?'

'The whole setup is already a trap. He doesn't need another one.' He sat on the bed to pull on his shoes. 'Do you know he dared to remind me that my payment was late? Zōu said he would be generous enough to allow some extra time—for additional interest. That man is without shame.'

Her heart ached as she watched Fei Long's laboured movements. She considered helping him, but that would be counter to her argument.

'What's your plan, then?' she asked.

'I've been thinking of this for a while. I'll go to him directly and honestly. I will impress upon him that I will not continue these payments and we'll negotiate an honourable deal.'

'That's it?'

He scowled at her doubtful tone. 'I can be an effective negotiator.'

Despite his stubbornness, it was so good to see him out of bed and moving about. She just wished it wasn't for the purpose of going out and getting his bones broken again. As Fei Long headed for his sword, she dashed to the wall ahead of him and snatched it off the shelf.

'Yan—' he warned.

'Wait until you're better,' she implored.

His dark eyebrows slashed ominously downwards. 'There are limits to how much impertinence I'll tolerate.'

'What use is a sword for you? You're slower than I am.'

He stalked toward her. 'Is that a challenge?'

She was caught in a dilemma. Losing face, private or public, was critical to Fei Long. Now that she had challenged him, he wouldn't back down. If she ran and he chased her, she might cause him to re-injure himself. If she didn't do anything, he was going to go ahead with his crazy plan.

At the last moment, she decided to duck towards the door, but Fei Long swept in to intercept her. He caged her easily, his arm braced against the wall, nearly pinning her with his body. Her pulse quickened.

'See?' he said softly. His face angled close to hers. 'All better.'

The bruises had started to fade. Fei Long seemed himself once again: strong, formidable, hard-headed. Yan Ling wanted to believe he was recovered, but she caught the tension along his jaw. Sweat collected on his brow.

She reached out to him. 'You're in pain.'

'It will pass.' He spoke quietly, but with a tone of impenetrable command. 'I know how this is done, Yan. The longer we wait, the more Zōu will believe he's bested me. His tyranny will build and build, just as it did with my father.'

Fei Long had been fighting his convalescence for weeks. She knew that the unfinished business with Zōu had plagued him the entire time, yet she kept thinking of him lying crumpled in that forsaken alleyway.

'Huibin and the stable boy are coming with me,' he assured her.

She would prefer an entire patrol of city guards, but Fei Long insisted this was a private matter.

'At least take some of your medicine,' she urged.

His lips pressed tight as he nodded. 'That might be a good idea.'

* * *

Yan Ling was still clutching his sword as she went to the kitchen to brew the herbal mixture, as if she feared that he would escape on the sly if she relinquished it. She returned with an entire bowl of the vile tea and stood by while he drained every drop. They exchanged sword for empty bowl.

'Be careful,' she ordered.

If anything happened to him, he was certain she would charge into Zōu's den herself. She followed him to the front gate where the two attendants were waiting. Out front, Fei Long encountered another guardian.

'I was in the area,' Bai Shen said casually. 'Buying radishes at the East Market.'

'Radishes?'

He slung his sword over his shoulder. 'I love radishes.'

Fei Long would remember never to underestimate the resourcefulness of women. 'Why were you skulking outside?'

'Well, I recall that the next time I set foot inside that house someone was going to kill me.' Bai Shen fell into step beside him. 'I might have risked it since you're still an invalid, but I decided to spare you losing two fights in one month.'

'At least get a real sword.'

The sword in Bai Shen's hands was ornamented with glass jewels. The blade was meant to dramatically catch the light while on stage rather than do any real damage.

'I intend to run long before it comes to any fighting.' Bai Shen sheathed his prop sword into the scabbard at his belt.

Not that any of the others were equipped for a fight either. The stable boy had a knife in his belt that he used for cutting rope and Huibin's size alone posed as a decent warning, but they were there for appearances only. In the words of Sun Tzu, excellence consisted of breaking the enemy's resistance without fighting.

The four of them continued on towards the North Hamlet and beyond to the seedy border of the gambling dens. There seemed to be a few more people wandering the streets that day. Fei Long recognised the pedlar hauling the basket to the corner as a member of Bai Shen's troupe.

'I asked a few of the fellows to come around,' Bai Shen said. Then, after a pause, 'What were you thinking going alone into that wolf's den? Have you offended so many people that you think you have no friends left?'

'This is my problem.'

Bai Shen snorted. 'That head of yours, Chang Fei Long, it's hard as rock. I don't understand what goes through it.'

Fei Long once thought to abandon his old comrades when he had left his reckless, spendthrift days behind him, but he hadn't considered the virtues of friendship and loyalty.

'I owe you a debt,' he admitted soberly.

'Forget about debt and duty for a moment, fool. There are more important things in life.' For once, Bai Shen cast aside his usual humour and bravado.

'The sun rises in the west today. Li Bai Shen is lecturing me,' Fei Long said.

'Snow falls in the summer. Chang Fei Long is making a joke.'

They were nearly at Zōu's mansion.

'I thought for sure you would have woken up by now,' Bai Shen said.

'What are you saying?'

'You know what I mean. You know *who* I mean. Look at the two of you circling like lovesick youngsters. It's not hard to decide what to do, Fei Long. It's not hard at all.'

Despite his irreverence, Bai Shen had shown himself to be a true friend. It was the only reason Fei Long allowed such a personal line of questioning.

'You only see what's on the surface,' Fei Long warned.

'I know what I see.'

The guards at the gate recognised him and before long they found themselves standing before the Bull in his sitting room.

Zōu tapped his thick fingers together and regarded the bruises still visible on Fei Long's face. 'Why, Lord Chang. Have you gotten into some sort of unfortunate accident?'

Anger was a sign of weakness. Fei Long kept his under control. 'Unfortunate indeed.'

'I knew something must have happened when I didn't receive your payment. From what I've heard, Lord Chang's son is nothing if not forthright and honest. A man among men.'

So the crime lord was choosing to draw out the predicament for his enjoyment. Fei Long knew then that he hadn't merely been robbed so that Zōu could keep him under his thumb. Zōu had done it because Fei Long had dared to stand up to him.

'You've got about all the money you're going to drain from the Chang family,' he said plainly.

'Ahh...then how will you repay your debt, being such a straightforward and honest man?' Zōu surmised.

'You must have something in mind.'

The crime lord's narrowed gaze sparked with greed. 'I like your style, Chang Fei Long, though it could use some refinement. Coming here like this so stubbornly after being beaten nearly to death takes spirit.'

Complimentary and taunting at the same time. Fei Long refused to respond. Instead he waited for Zōu's proposal impassively.

'I need someone relentless like you,' Zōu continued with glee. 'Someone to collect on a few debts from borrowers who are not as straight and honest. I'll give you a percentage of each payment you extract until your debt is gone.'

'No.'

Zōu raised his eyebrows. 'You really have no negotiation ability. No subtlety at all.'

'If I'm to dishonour myself as your underling, I might as well lose face completely. I'd rather fall to my knees and beg assistance from those powerful friends of my father's you mentioned.'

'Ah…corner a dog in a dead-end alley and he'll turn and bite.' The crime lord eyed him for a long time, stroking his thick beard thoughtfully. 'I have another thought. How's your arm?'

'My arm is fine.' It wasn't his arm that bothered Fei Long as much as the pain in his ribs when he moved too quickly.

'You know, I lost a lot of money on you several years ago,' Zōu said. 'Rumour has it there's a new prodigy in the field. A master bowman who can't be defeated. All the odds are in his favour. I could stand to make a lot of money if my champion managed to defeat this young upstart. I hope those *unidentified* alley dogs didn't hurt you too badly.'

Stand as the crime lord's champion? Gambling was officially illegal in the city, but the magistrates tended to turn an blind eye, especially when it came to popular events such as archery. It would be a tricky situation to navigate.

'When?' Fei Long asked.

'Two weeks.'

It was too soon. The pain in his side would be worsened by the strain of the bow. 'And if I lose?'

Zōu shrugged. 'Then you keep on paying until I recover what you owe me, one way or another. You may have powerful friends, but I have desperate, more deplorable acquaintances.'

'You'll keep your word?'

'Yes, of course,' Zōu waved at him dismissively. 'You're rather a pain to deal with, Lord Chang. And not nearly as entertaining as your father. Win this and I'll have ten times the amount you owe me.'

Lose and he would be truly out of options.

Chapter Eighteen

He expected to find Yan Ling waiting anxiously for him in the courtyard when he returned. Perhaps not expected as much as hoped. It was unseemly to speak too personally with the servants of the household. It only served to embarrass them. Yet Yan Ling wasn't a servant. He could share his thoughts with her, plan out ideas. She was something else entirely to him. Fei Long didn't know quite what that was.

As soon as he had returned after accepting Zōu's challenge, he wanted to tell her. She'd scold him and tell him he was mad, but he'd convince her and, in convincing Yan Ling, he might convince himself.

Fei Ling dismissed Huibin and the stable boy once they were inside the gates. Bai Shen took his leave with great drama, *humbly* refusing to set foot inside the walls, clearly going through extra effort to extract an apology.

With his escort dispersed, Fei Long set about looking for Yan Ling. He found her seated in the parlour. The sight of the uninvited guest across from her turned his stomach.

Inspector Tong.

He could only see Yan Ling in profile, but she appeared

pale as she nodded slowly. A desolate expression clouded her
eyes—one he hoped to never see again.

'Inspector Tong, what an unexpected surprise,' he declared
loudly from the entranceway, ignoring protocol. 'How are you?'

Tong looked at him as if he was an errant mosquito, buzz-
ing too loudly. Fei Long needed to get Yan Ling away from
that man.

'I was just now speaking to your sister about some new de-
velopments.'

She looked up at him, her eyes large in her face. 'The date
of the voyage has been changed. I'm to leave in two weeks.'

Tong stared with great interest at the bruising along the side
of his face. Let the minister speculate all he wanted.

'What is the meaning of this?' Fei Long demanded. 'Auspicious dates have been set. The journey was to begin mid-
summer.'

'We've heard news that the Uyghur delegation is also sending a bride.'

'That is an offence to our family.'

'Now you must listen here, Lord Chang. This is diplomacy.
The ambassador from Khitan has ensured us that the khagan's intention is to take your sister as his principal wife. We
just want to make sure that is still the case. We'll demand the
wedding be performed as soon as she arrives. The Emperor
is arranging for the fastest horses with several changing stations to ensure the fastest journey possible. Two weeks is the
fastest we can prepare.'

'Perhaps it is best that I go now.' Yan Ling spoke to no one
in particular, but each word rang in Fei Long's ears. 'Staying
longer would only prolong the sorrow of leaving.'

'I am very pleased that Lady Chang recognises her duty—
more so than her brother.'

'It is my humble duty to serve,' she said.

Her expression was empty, flat. All the hope had drained out
of it and looking at her left Fei Long gutted. Her hands were

folded obediently in her lap and she kept her head bowed. It was just too soon.

Too soon for what? He knew the journey was inevitable. That she would go away. Yan Ling had sworn to see this through to the end with him. He'd sworn to do his best to teach her. What would one month or two buy them anyway? Nothing but a little more time and a few more memories.

'I must thank the official for coming to tell us personally.' Fei Long was unable to evoke any sincerity.

Tong must have made sure he had the honour of delivering the bad news himself. Fei Long forced his tone to remain cordial as Inspector Tong gave a few more details and then took his leave with a bow.

Fei Long accompanied the official to the gate to ensure his dark presence was gone from the house. Yan Ling was still sitting in the same spot when he returned to the parlour.

'What does it matter—first wife, second wife, concubine?' she said, staring ahead. 'Still much more privileged than a lowly tea girl, right?'

She was asking for assurances, but he couldn't utter them. He couldn't lie.

'Yan, if you don't want to go—'

'What? Such nonsense. Of course I want to go.' She stood and paced away from him. 'I vowed I wouldn't disappoint you.'

That vow. The one he had no right to ask of her.

He rose. 'You don't have to do this.'

'Oh, the death of me,' she muttered.

'What is it?'

'The shoes.'

'Shoes?'

She clasped her hands together, her fingers twining in agitation.

'I won't have enough time to fix them,' she told him earnestly, as if the shoes were the most important thing in the world. 'I tried to embroider them. With tigers,' she explained while he stared at her. 'The left one is a little bit better than the right one, but they're laughable. Completely unacceptable.'

He was at a loss. Why were they speaking about shoes and gers? 'We can purchase new ones at the market.'

She nodded at his suggestion and took a calming breath, but it was no use. The storm clouds swept in. Her lips quivered before she crumbled. He went to her as fast as he could and folded his arms around her. She trembled against him, smelling like flowers and spring.

'Yan.' He pressed his lips against her hair and embraced her tighter. The effort made his wound ache, but the pain meant nothing if he could only hold her. 'You'll be all right. I'll take care of everything.'

He needed very much for those words to mean something.

Yan Ling raised her hand to his chest to push him away, but for a moment she surrendered, closing her eyes and resting her head against his shoulder. It wasn't long before she squirmed out of his grasp, but in that brief moment, she smelled right. She felt right.

In his arms.

'What happened with Zōu?' she asked, her voice choked.

'We spoke. You don't need to worry about him.'

'Right. No one need ever worry about anything.' She looked away to compose herself. 'Only you.'

They fell to silence. Bai Shen was right. He'd let this go on too long when he should have come to his senses long ago. Yan Ling didn't owe him this sacrifice. He'd done nothing to deserve it.

'I'll tell Minister Cao the truth—that Pearl ran away.'

'Don't you dare!' Her eyes flashed angrily as she swung round. 'You'll lose everything. All we've done, all we've worked for. Your family will be dishonoured. The entire household will be sent to the streets to beg.'

Her passion took him aback. 'This isn't your burden to bear.'

'Then why is it yours alone?' she demanded.

The words caught in his throat. He was stunned. He wa the eldest son. The only son. No one would ever question tha this was his responsibility and no one else's. 'You don't hav to do this…for me.'

'I'm not.' She bent her head. 'This is what I came here t do.' When she met his eyes, her gaze was clear. 'I'm just sa to go. Any girl would be. Call it weakness.'

'You're not weak, Yan Ling.'

He watched her as she pulled even further away from hin fighting to control her emotions. She wasn't very good at hi ing them. Not like him.

'Not weak at all,' he asserted, quietly, to no one but himsel

Yan Ling retreated to the solitude of her room, claiming tha she had a headache. She shut all the windows so it was dar and cool. Then she curled into a tight ball in the alcove of he bed and did nothing. No studying, no embroidery.

She counted days in her head. Inspector Tong would tak away the few she had left. No gradual farewell. No time t hoard memories. Her departure would be a cold, quick inci sion, separating flesh from bone.

Dao came in on silent feet like a cat to bring tea and a plat of sweets for her. She set the tray down beside the bed an sat patiently, not saying a word. Waiting. After an hour or so she got up.

'Feel better, Yan,' she said before slipping just as quietl away.

Of course Yan Ling didn't want to go to Khitan. She wante to stay in this beautiful city with fruited trees and glowing lan terns. She wanted to waste her days going to the market an her nights attending plays with fantastic costumes, but ther was a price and she had always known it.

And what hardship was it really? She was going as a prin cess to a foreign land. She would be looked upon with the high est regard and waited on by servants. She would never sleep o hard, cold floor again beside the ashes of a cooling hearth. Had she become so spoiled that she wasn't grateful?

She didn't want any such wealth or luxury. She wanted to be with Fei Long, but no matter how tender he could be or how heated his glances, he would never allow it.

He'd been kind to her. He'd been generous. It was selfish to ask for more, especially when he sacrificed so much for those around him. So she'd do this one thing and she'd do it with as much grace as she could, even if she had to grit her teeth the entire time. She'd learned such sacrifice from Fei Long. It was the one thing he could appreciate and respect. Forbearance.

By the time Dao came back with dinner, Yan Ling had recovered enough to present a good face. They set the tray in the sitting area and shared melon soup and plates of cooked vegetables and seared pork.

'Do you know they eat mostly lamb in Khitan?' Yan Ling asked, by way of conversation.

'I've had lamb before,' Dao replied. 'It's not bad.'

They ate in silence for a bit, picking up morsels from the small plates into their rice bowls.

'Lord Chang has been very quiet all day,' Dao reported.

'He usually doesn't say much.'

'I heard from Huibin that he's accepted some sort of archery contest.'

'Oh.' She was only able to be uninterested for a few bites. Archery? How is that supposed to help anything?'

'This is how Lord Chang is expected to repay his debt. Zōu expects significant returns from the betting.'

'You know about the debt, then.'

Dao looked downwards, concentrating on her rice bowl. It was acknowledgement enough. Fei Long had been so intent on keeping everything private, but all the secrets were out now. The entire household was involved.

'It doesn't seem like him to hinge so much on a wager,'

Yan Ling said. 'And his wound hasn't fully healed yet. He ca
barely walk.'

She was exaggerating, of course. Fei Long was getting be
ter day by day, but she was still worried. The physician ha
left strict instructions for him to continue resting and not t
lift anything.

Dao didn't share her concerns. 'Have you seen him with
bow and arrow? Everyone knows Lord Chang can't be beaten
The Great Shoot that year was legendary.'

There was some mention of it at the drinking house afte
the play. 'He was quite good?'

'Oh, more than good!' Dao's eyes lit up as she told the tal
'There had been several friendly contests in the parks lead
ing up to the festival, and rumours were circulating that there
was a young master, not yet instated in the imperial army, wh
could not miss.'

Yan Ling leaned forwards, hungry for every word.

Dao continued, 'But young Lord Chang was so humble, h
never told anyone that he was the bowman everyone spoke o
Maybe he didn't even know!'

'That is just like him,' she agreed.

'On the day of the shoot, everyone took wagers on wh
this prodigy must be. Many of the favoured sons of the cit
came out to the field dressed in colorful costumes, braggin
up and down, while Lord Chang was a quiet tiger lying in th
shadows.'

She could picture Fei Long perfectly as Dao told the re
of the story. After the first few rounds, a rain of arrows ha
fallen and the ranks began to thin. The crowd began to whis
per that down at the end of the line was a young archer wh
had not only hit every target, but whose skill and techniqu
was as clean and fluid as a line of poetry. He wasted not on
movement, not one arrow.

Soon the spectators had drifted to crowd around the far en
of the field to watch him and even the Emperor beneath h

coloured awning had taken notice. By the end of the match, it was the imperial archery instructor himself against Fei Long. The two of them would take an arrow from their quivers, draw back and shoot in tandem. Arrow after arrow. Dead centre.

'When the last arrow came up, do you know what Lord Chang did?'

Yan Ling ground her teeth with anticipation. 'He couldn't have missed!'

'Fei Long aimed high into the air and shot it deep into the forest, missing on purpose. Then he bowed before the imperial archer, acknowledging the older man's much greater skill and experience. So the instructor laughed heartily and let his final arrow fly in very same manner. They say the two arrows were never found.'

That was Fei Long to the very essence. Allowing the respected master to save face rather than claiming the glory for himself.

'He must win this time,' Yan Ling said, bolstered by Dao's tale.

But in her heart, she knew Fei Long hadn't fully recovered. He would never admit it to anyone, least of all his enemies.

'This archery contest is set for the fifteenth of the month. It's a much more private affair than a Great Shoot,' Dao said.

'Ten days,' she said wistfully. 'I could be gone by then, Dao.'

Time was flowing too quickly. She'd already wasted half a day shut inside this room. Suddenly Yan Ling was besieged by things she yearned to do and see: the Wild Goose Pagoda in the southern part of the city and the Serpentine River Park. She wanted to visit them all and she wanted Fei Long to be the one beside her, but everything the Chang family owned could be taken away.

'You know Yan, everyone was always drawn to Fei Long. He wasn't as fun-loving and boisterous as the elder Lord Chang, but people liked him.'

Yan Ling remained quiet. She knew where this would go.

'When I saw Lord Chang so badly beaten...' Dao paused to pour more tea '...I was heartsick. Such a tragedy brings forth great feeling.'

'I'm not falling in love with him,' Yan Ling assured, with a trace of bitterness. Dao was still staring at her. 'I'm not.'

'Good, then.'

She refused to speak any more about it. Anything she said would only reveal how deep her feelings had become and those feelings were unacceptable.

From Dao's perspective, the arrangement with Khitan was to everyone's benefit. Yan Ling's little lie to Dao was nothing when compared against the greater good.

Chapter Nineteen

Fei Long received a letter the next morning from Li Bai Shen delivered by messenger. He pulled the paper from its sleeve and unfolded it. The first line took him by surprise.

My family married me, Bai Shen wrote passionately, *to the other side of heaven*.

That incorrigible bastard. Not a single word was Bai Shen's. He'd copied Princess Xijun's famous lament at being married off to a foreign land. The actor refused to set foot into the house, but he had no objections to asserting influence and stirring up trouble.

Fei Long scanned the rest of the verses about the loneliness of living in a strange country and the princess's sorrow-filled longing for her homeland. Li Bai Shen. Shameless.

As if he needed the blade of guilt to be driven any deeper. Yan Ling wasn't a privileged princess, prone to sentiment and melancholy. She was a strong, practical woman. She might mourn her departure at first, but soon she would acclimate to the steppes as quickly as she had adopted Changan and the daily routine of their household.

The women of the Khitan were said to be more independent.

They dressed in male clothing and took on the same responsibilities as men. Yan Ling might enjoy that. He remembered her swaggering back and forth in front of him, disguised as a male attendant.

He was wrong to pity her. Yan Ling would embrace the open freedom of the grasslands. She would survive. If he knew anything about her, she would thrive.

He pressed a hand to his side as pain shot through his ribs. The injury had been bothering him since the walk through the city the previous day. He called for the servants to brew more of the physician's tea. The bitter taste of it had become so familiar that he could swallow it down without blinking. At some point, the kitchen had started adding honey to it. He suspected it was by Yan Ling's instruction.

She was taking on other responsibilities as well, conferring with Old Man Liang and Dao about the tasks that needed to be done. There was no one to take over the household while he was recovering. As Pearl's retainer, Yan Ling became the figurehead.

It would take perhaps half an hour before the tea took effect. He drank the medicinal brew four times a day to dull the pain and detested how much he depended on it. With only ten days to prepare for the contest, he'd have to continue taking it.

Once dressed, he went to retrieve his bow himself from the storage cabinet. Tucking it close to his body, he retreated to his study—not hiding, but not keen on anyone seeing him. Alone and behind closed doors, he attached the bowstring.

He'd had little use for it since returning to the city, but the wood was oiled and well-tempered. He lifted the bow with his left hand and his fingers naturally found their placement along the grip.

Fei Long took the proper stance and hooked two fingers against the string, pulling back gradually. His body responded with a throbbing ache down his left side, but it subsided. He pulled back further, then a little further.

Pain shot through his torso and the bowstring snapped back as he recoiled. He pressed a hand to his side until the throbbing eased.

Breathing deep, he tried it again, slowly this time, just to test his boundaries. Again, the streak of pain stopped him. He could only pull at a fraction of his strength. This was... not good. He didn't yet know what sort of contest it would be. The archery trials for the imperial exam had included shooting from standing position as well as in the saddle. He wouldn't be able to endure the strain of both riding the horse and aiming for his target. He could push through pain, but how many times and for how long?

The herbal brew started taking effect, whittling down the jagged edge of the pain, but it also fogged his mind. It didn't matter when he was resting in bed all day, but for the contest he would need to focus.

He'd go to the herbalist for another brew. He would also needed to start training so that he could work up to a full range of motion. There wasn't much time. Not enough time for anything.

Yan Ling would be leaving soon to become a far-married bride on the other side of heaven. He was losing her, but there was no way he could stop it while his own fate was hanging on a thread. He was one breath away from ruin. Who was to take away her salvation?

But if he could win.

If he could win, there was still the obligation to Minister Cao and the imperial court. There was the family honour and reputation. It was a cage of his own design, but there was no use thinking of those other obstacles until he won.

He raised the bow and took aim at an imaginary target. His mind and hands and eyes knew what to do. He could feel the sense memory flow into them—surer than anything else in the world. There were many things that he couldn't do, but he could hit a target.

Yan Ling stirred at the tapping sound on her window. At first she thought it might be a bird, but the sound continued, accompanied by a hushed voice calling her name. It was coming from the window that faced the courtyard. She rose to open it, squinting at the sunlight that streamed in through the crack.

'What are you doing here?' she mumbled.

It was Fei Long, crouching outside her window like some illicit village boy instead of the master of the house. She warmed at the amusing picture.

'Get dressed and come with me,' he said.

She rubbed a hand over her eyes. From the slant of the sun and the stillness throughout the house, she knew it was early.

'I'll get Dao to help me,' she said through a yawn.

'Just wear the clothes from the night at the Pear Blossom Gardens.'

He wanted her in disguise? She couldn't raise one eyebrow the way Bai Shen did, but she attempted it. Her effort most likely looked like a half-squint.

'Quickly,' he demanded.

She shut the window on him. What sort of caper was this, waking her so early in the morning and making most improper demands? It wasn't like Fei Long at all. How exciting!

The disguise had been tucked away in the corner of her wardrobe since the night at the theatre. A small, secret thrill went through her whenever she glanced at the boots. Fei Long had pulled them off her, his hand curled intimately over her calf. She pulled the robe and boots on hastily and tied her hair back.

Fei Long was waiting in the hallway. The quiver of arrows strapped to his back was the only explanation he offered as hey headed towards the stable. The attendant led the horse out to them just as they arrived, but the boy didn't make any remark at seeing her dressed in male clothing. He merely assisted Fei Long onto the saddle and handed him his bow, which Fei Long slung over his shoulder. She climbed onto the horse behind him with some assistance.

'How are you feeling?' she asked, placing her hands tenuously around his shoulders.

'I'm fine,' he said, irritated.

He snapped at her much the same way whenever she politely enquired about his recovery. She knew how Fei Long hated mentioning it, but he had moved stiffly when mounting the horse.

'I won't break,' he said over his shoulder before urging the horse forwards.

She grabbed on to him, her arms circling his narrow waist to hold on. It wasn't so much that he was angry as there was a lot on his mind. She'd become adept at interpreting Fei Long's moods, or at least her guess seemed to be wrong less often than for some others.

The archery contest was only three days away. Shortly after that, the imperial wedding procession was scheduled to leave for Khitan.

She wouldn't think of that now. Instead she laid her cheek against the space between Fei Long's shoulder blades and closed her eyes, letting the rhythm of the ride sooth her.

They moved through the ward gates and then travelled on the main avenues of the city to an area she hadn't visited before. A park spread out before them, as least four times the size of the Pear Blossom Gardens. Fei Long rode on to the grassy area and headed for a distant cluster of trees. The vibrant lushness of the green beckoned to her. When they finally dismounted, she let her feet sink into the dew-covered grass and inhaled the crisp scent of it. The city was a glorious place that she'd only barely begun to discover. As Fei Long went to tether the horse, Yan Ling noticed the row of straw targets propped up across the field of grass.

He came up beside her. 'I should practise at least once before the contest.'

She helped him unstrap the quiver, watching him carefully. His movements, though careful and deliberate, had improved from even a week earlier.

'What should I be doing?' she asked, holding on to the leather bindings of the quiver.

He presented a striking profile as he sighted the target in the distance. The bridge of his nose was high like an eagle's and his jaw was set with determination. He spent a few moments absorbing the energy of the shaded area before turning to her.

The corner of his mouth lifted as he replied, 'For now, just think good thoughts.'

He extracted a single arrow from the quiver. His eyes lingered on hers before facing the target. Again, he spent some time centring himself on the target in the distance before setting the arrow against the string. He righted himself in one smooth motion, taking aim with his back straight, head lifted. She could sense the awe of Dao's story in the confidence of his stance.

His arm pulled back and he let out his breath slowly, then held completely still as he released. The arrow sailed straight, but fell into the grass far short of the target.

That was just the first one, she told herself, though her stomach sank. She handed him another arrow and said nothing as he positioned himself to shoot again. The next one flew further, but still fell short. Yan Ling held her breath through each shot. The third one managed to embed itself within the lower corner of the target.

She didn't know if his performance was typical or not, but Fei Long was not pleased. He didn't show it with any impacient remarks or angry gestures. She only knew it in the steely set of his eyes. An unbearable tension settled over her, making her insides churn.

It was the sixth arrow that finally hit centre. Yan Ling was counting. She nearly let out a celebratory cry, but Fei Long was still not pleased. The next shot hit left of the mark. One more at centre, then the one after it flew wide. Her spirits rose and plummeted with each flight.

Fei Long lowered the bow after the last shot and held his hand out, flexing and curling his fingers.

'Your arm?' she asked. She knew he hated hearing her fuss, but what else was one to do?

'Just lack of use,' he said. It wasn't an excuse. Fei Long was trying to assess the problem. He shook his arm out and held his hand out for the next arrow. 'Let's continue.'

The next five shots showed some improvement, but remained inconsistent.

She went to fetch the arrows to give Fei Long a rest. After only four shots into the next set, he stiffened, pressing the heel of his palm to his side. Since this was Fei Long, it must have been hurting long before he showed any signs of weakness.

'You should rest,' she insisted when he reached for the next arrow.

She knew he hated when she told him to rest, as well, but she didn't care. This time, he didn't fight her. He lowered his bow and stood there, head down, thinking. She was genuinely worried now, not about the archery contest, but that Fei Long would push himself too hard.

'Will the target be that far in the competition?' she asked.

'I don't know what Zōu is planning.'

'Your body just needs to readjust. You're doing much better.'

She wasn't helping. She knew she wasn't helping when Fei Long pinned her with a cold look. The echo of her encouragement rang hollow in her head.

It was all Dao's fault. Dao had spoken of a legend, but what Yan Ling witnessed before her was a man struggling with his own limits. In three days, everyone else would be expecting the legend as well, including the crime boss.

Fei Long resumed his practice, attacking the target with a new determination. One in three arrows were hitting centre now, but a few of the misses were still flying wide. Was one in three good enough? She didn't think so.

Suddenly Fei Long bent over, clutching a hand to his ribs. His breath rushed out and his teeth clenched. She wanted to run to him, but she froze, unable to move or speak. It frightened her to see him like this.

He straightened and muttered a curse, kicking at the ground in frustration. The pain had cracked through the layer of calm shielding him.

Why had he brought her along? It must have been to avoid showing any weakness to the servants who depended on him. Saving face was so important to Fei Long.

Did he consider her an outsider whose opinion didn't matter? But a nobleman and a soldier wouldn't show such vulnerability to a stranger. Fei Long trusted her, in a way he trusted no one else. It was a rare gift, and it tore her apart to watch him, struggling to remain composed, when there was nothing she could do or say to help. Fei Long exhaled sharply and ran his hand over his face.

'I can use a lighter bow,' he said with a scowl. 'One that's easier to pull. The arrow won't fly as far, but the way things are going now…'

His voice trailed off and he turned to stare at the target again, his eyes narrowing as if looking upon an arch rival.

'Stop for a while and you can try again,' she suggested.

He opened his mouth to speak, but bit back the protest. His expression softened just a touch. 'Yes,' he relented. 'I can rest for a moment.'

Fei Long lowered himself down into the grass, legs out in front of him. He propped the bow across his knees and *tried* to look like he wasn't preoccupied with the target. She sat down across from him, sinking her fingers into the cool grass. The sun had risen to burn off the morning dew.

'Dao told me the story of the Great Shoot,' she said.

'She remembered?'

'She was thirteen years old at the time. Hardly an infant.'

Fei Long shrugged and set the bow beside him. 'I remembered her and Pearl as children at the time. My sister must have been eleven.'

'Dao said you were a giant to them, that you could do no wrong.'

He laughed at that, reaching up to rub at his shoulder. 'Like I said, children.'

Fei Long didn't realise how easily others looked up to him. She'd seen it among the servants of the household and even the actors in the Pear Blossom Garden. No matter how much he distanced himself, people were drawn to him. She was drawn to him as well, hopelessly so.

'Dao told me you were flawless that day.'

'She's mistaken.'

'You're being humble,' she admonished.

'Humility is a virtue.' He rotated his arm in small circles, wincing slightly.

'Here, let me help.'

Yan Ling forced herself to sound casual, but her throat went dry. She moved around behind him before her courage slipped away. Holding her breath, she placed her hands on his shoulders.

Fei Long lowered his arm and grew still, but didn't protest. She ran her hands over his back, curving over hard muscle and sinew. Her touch was gentle at first, tenuous. With each breath, her hands became more confident. She roamed over the span of his shoulders. His muscles were knotted into tight, unrelenting cords.

How many times had she wanted to do this while they were together in the study? Every time Fei Long had set down a letter to rub a hand over his temples, she'd imagined being bold enough to go to him.

'No wonder the arrows aren't hitting. You're so tense here.' She worked her thumbs in small circles near the base of his neck. Her pulse leapt as her fingertips grazed the back of his neck. Skin to skin. It was a wonder to be able to touch him.

'Maybe I make you nervous,' she teased.

'I don't get nervous.' His reply sounded strained.

She sank down further onto her knees and closer to him. She used the leverage to increase the pressure, rubbing at his neck and shoulders in earnest. A single breath filled him, then released slowly. She paused to absorb the shape and feel of him.

She swallowed to regain her voice. 'Better?'

He didn't say anything. His head tilted up and down as he nodded. A breeze blew by. A few figures appeared at the other end of the park, but she didn't care. They were alone together in the great city.

'Yan,' he said finally. 'Inspector Tong sent a message to the house yesterday.'

'I know.' Her hands slipped from him, lingering for just a second at the base of his neck. She stared at the contours of his shoulder blades through his robe.

'Not much longer now.'

'Don't you think about that,' she said harshly. Fei Long prohibited all talk about his recovery. She could refuse to talk about Khitan. 'Just focus on what needs to be done.'

'Hitting the target,' he murmured.

He picked up the bow and stood. She would have hoped to see the legend suddenly emerge, but it was more of the same. Fei Long still struggled to hit the centre, but there was a definite change. He didn't seem as displeased with himself. She didn't know if that was progress or not.

When the quiver was empty once again, she walked ahead to collect the arrows. As she returned, she saw Fei Long as a lone figure in the field of green. He had set the bow aside and stood completely still, not moving.

'Are we returning now?' she asked.

He turned to her slowly, his expression weighted and grim. She didn't know why, but her heart started pounding and her breath became short. She couldn't read anything in his demeanour. There was a storm cloud of warning about him and she could feel his gaze searing into her.

Fei Long nodded once. Yan Ling moved quickly to where the horse was tied. Something was coming and the weight of the inevitable hung over them. The warmth of the day transformed into an unbearable heat.

She slipped beneath the shade of the trees and bent to set the quiver down. As soon as she straightened, Fei Long was there. Her heart jumped from the shock of his nearness.

'I would give it all up,' he rasped.

She must have heard wrong. Her throat closed so tight she had to fight for the next breath.

'I would give it all up for you,' Fei Long said again, stronger this time. She staggered back a step as he came forwards. 'Yan Ling.'

He closed the distance between them. His hands came around her waist and his eyes darkened with an unfettered hunger she had never seen. Their bodies brushed as he pulled her close.

'What are you saying?' Her hands were trapped against his chest. She didn't know whether to flee or cling to him.

'You don't have to go to Khitan.'

She heard the words from his lips, then again in her mind,

but they wouldn't sink into her, no matter how many times he repeated them.

He lowered his head and she waited for the kiss to descend, but it didn't. Instead he touched his forehead to hers. For a few precious moments, he didn't do or say anything. She closed her eyes and listened to the cadence of his breathing.

Their nearness became a torment as she flushed with heat. Her fingers clutched at the front of his robe to pull him closer. Fei Long leaned in, his lips caressing restlessly over her cheek before seeking out her mouth. She opened her eyes to capture the moment.

The first touch took hold of her like the crash of a wave and her knees weakened. He parted her lips, willing her surrender with the sensual exploration of his tongue. She moaned softly as she returned the kiss that was quickly becoming so much more. He tore away her cap and dug his fingers into her hair while his mouth continued to take her.

It wasn't long before he was backing her deeper into the cover of the trees. Not long before his hands secured themselves against the small of her back and she was being guided down. Soon she was lying with her shoulders flush against the cool grass. The coarse blades tickled against the back of her neck and she could see fragments of blue sky between the branches above.

Fei Long leaned over her. His face, so familiar now, filled her vision. Masculine and beautiful in its harshness. He captured her mouth again, one hand cradled at the back of her neck to lift her to him. His other hand was braced against the ground beside her shoulder, securing her beneath the weight and pressure of his body. As if she'd ever want to escape.

When he broke the kiss he was breathing hard. She watched the path of his fingers, shivering as he delicately traced the line of her throat, then moved down to play along the boundary of cloth and skin.

She swallowed, suddenly aware of her disguise and the strange picture they must make. 'I look so funny right now.'

'I don't care what you wear.'

He parted her clothes, pushing aside the material with long, confident fingers. She held her breath as he curved his palm over her breast. His touch heated her skin. He watched her face as he stroked gently with the pad of his thumb. Her eyes closed as exquisite pleasure filled her. When he stroked again he was not so gentle—and her mind went white with sensation.

She exhaled in a small gasp, her back arching willingly. Her hips lifted until they brushed against his. In response, he pressed his full weight upon her. She could feel him. All of him.

His mouth sought her throat where he tasted her first with his tongue, then the sharp edge of his teeth. She shuddered as he devoured her. There was nothing reserved about Fei Long out here. He'd left his careful detachment in the confines of the study. This passion was for her, and her alone. She curved her arms around him and dug her nails into his back to urge him on.

He broke away to reach for her sash. His eyes grew black and distant as he tugged at it. The look was one of anguish. Her insides clenched. The ache of her desire transformed into a darker sort of pain.

'Like this?' she challenged softly. 'Here?'

His hand stilled on her waist, unable to answer, looking lost and confused. His chest heaved as he stared into her eyes. Desire flared as he came to her once again. He stroked his tongue into her mouth, claiming her. The fierceness of it both frightened her and set her toes curling. Her skin flushed and her vision darkened with sensation. She embraced him desperately, savouring this heated touch because she knew it couldn't last. She could taste the desolation in his kiss.

She pulled away and the shock of the loss made her weep inside.

'Come away with me,' he insisted.

Her eyes burned. Finally, everything she had yearned for, all the words he would never say, but she already knew her answer.

'No.'

'No?' He took hold of her hand and held it to his chest so she could feel his heartbeat pulsing against her. 'Yan.'

She had to be strong. 'We can't.'

'You and I can leave—'

'And give up everything? Your very soul?'

Yan Ling realised why she had been so frightened of the change in him. It was surrender she'd seen in his eyes and she couldn't bear it. Fei Long had only allowed himself to come to her from the edge of defeat.

'What of your family name?' she went on. 'And your home?'

His arms were still wrapped around her, but the warmth between them had drained away. 'Those things are already lost,' he said. 'I won't lose you as well.'

His hands fell away the moment she pushed at him.

'My lord.' The formal address was her shield. She distanced herself physically as well, crawling back away from him. 'You'll have us run away, then, like Pearl?'

His expression hardened—his shield. He couldn't answer her. Even if he were willing to forget everything he held sacred, she couldn't do it. They would be abandoning Dao and Old Man Liang. The entire household. Fei Long would be abandoning himself.

She knew what kind of man Chang Fei Long was. If he went with him, he would come to resent this decision. In time, he would resent her as well.

He let his hands fall by his sides. Desire still lingered in his eyes. Her own arms were hugged tight around herself, trying to keep her broken spirit from spilling out. For a few reckless heartbeats, she wanted to go with him anyway. If he asked her again, she didn't know if she could hold back, but Fei Long didn't ask.

He rose to his feet slowly, straightening his robe. She did the same, turning away from him. Neither of them spoke of it, but they decided to go home on foot with Fei Long leading the horse along by the reins. They didn't touch as they walked through the criss-cross of city streets.

At one of the main intersections, Yan Ling's pulse quickened as Fei Long reached for her, but it was only to pull a strand of grass from her hair.

Chapter Twenty

Dao stood beside the open wardrobe, pulling out robes and shawls and scarves in a rainbow of silk. All Yan Ling could do was sit on the bed and stare at the wooden trunk set between them. She was a lady again with embroidered slippers on her feet and jewelled pins in her hair.

'None of these belong to me,' Yan Ling protested. She had folded up an armful of robes, but no matter how much she packed away, Dao seemed to produce more.

'You have to look like a princess when you're in Khitan. Besides, there's no one here to wear them either.'

'You should have them.'

Dao made a dismissive sound, but then she reconsidered. 'Maybe this one,' she said, holding up a pink gown with a design of snow-white cherry blossoms.

'That one looks beautiful on you,' Yan Ling replied absently.

As far as Dao knew, the day had begun like any other. The interlude at the park had never happened. Fei Long had never asked her to give up everything and go with him. He hadn't kissed her in a way that made her eyes close and her toes curl.

It was hard to concentrate when all Yan Ling could think

of was that she'd made a mistake. Folding the garments was a mindless, routine diversion, but soon the clothes were gone, all packed away, and her mind was left open and wandering.

Dao went to the dressing table while Yan Ling went to gather all the practice papers from her lessons in the study. They were nonsense really, random passages that took on special significance now that the coveted lessons were over. She spotted the sheet where Fei Long had written out her name in a series of perfect tiny strokes. She could still hear the timbre of his voice while he had stood beside her that day.

'What is this?' Dao demanded.

Yan Ling jerked her head up to see Dao peering into her sewing box. Quickly, she folded the paper and tucked it into the pocket in her sleeve.

'Is this supposed to be a *tiger*?' Dao held up the pair of felt shoes.

Yan Ling had forgotten about her horrible embroidery work. 'No, that must be a picture of your father,' she replied sweetly.

Dao narrowed her eyes. Yan Ling batted hers.

'They were supposed to be wedding gifts for my barbarian husband. Tigers represent strength and good fortune.'

'You can't present these. Khitan will be insulted.'

'Do you think the slippers might spark a war?' Yan Ling asked without shame.

Dao did not look amused. Her peach-shaped face scrunched into a frown. 'Are you trying to make trouble, Yan?'

'I meant to buy new ones. You don't think Khitan will send me back for my lack of skill with a needle, do you?'

'Come on. Let's get to the market before the afternoon gong.'

Yan Ling pulled a purple shawl from the trunk and followed Dao to the door. 'I've been wanting to step outside. It feels so confining indoors today.'

'Why?' Dao shot her a glance over her shoulder. 'Wasn't your morning outing enough for you?'

Her heart skipped. So they hadn't been as discreet as she

had thought. 'Enough *you*. You would have been very proud of me this morning.'

If she could joke about the morning, then it must be bearable. If she could laugh, then it couldn't tear her heart out.

Fei Long was not in the courtyard. She didn't expect him to be, but as they went through the gate, she wondered what it would be like when she was taken far away. Would she irrationally search for him, seeking him out with all her senses? She had a feeling she would continue to do so, even once they were too far away to ever find one another.

Fei Long knew it was Yan Ling from the quickness of her step and the urgent, yet intimate way she tapped on the door. What he didn't know was why she had come, when he was certain she would spend the next few days avoiding him after what had happened that morning.

'Yes, come in.' His voice remained steady, his pulse did not.

She slipped inside, her silk skirts rustling against the edge of the door as she shut it behind her. 'Can we speak for a moment?'

'Always.'

He set his brush down and went to her. She looked up at him nervously and he was glad for it. He didn't know why she'd come, but he had certain hopes.

'My lord,' she began.

She had changed her mind. His heart thumped against his chest feverishly.

His throat went dry. 'Yes?'

They were standing beside the door, yet neither of them made a move to be seated. The pearl ornament in her hair distracted him more than it should have. Yan Ling had come to him combed, pinned and dressed in silk. She had looked prettier in the grass in a plain robe, with his arms around her.

She seemed flustered. 'They're talking about it all over the marketplace,' she said in a single breath.

'Talking about what? Did someone see us?' Fei Long realised he didn't care one bit if anyone had seen them.

'No, not *that*.' She skirted away from him, blushing furiously.

'What then?'

'The archery contest. They're gossiping all over the tea rooms and in the shops, too, about an unknown champion.'

He should have known. He paced a few steps away, rubbing a hand over his jaw. 'This is Zōu's doing.'

Zōu had promised his name would be kept secret. It was supposed to be a small gathering with private wagers. Clearly the Bull wanted to increase his take.

'It sounds like everyone will be there,' Yan Ling went on. 'There was talk of court officials coming as well—ministers and functionaries.'

They would all be there now that Zōu was publicising it. Though wagering was supposed to be illegal, archery contests were too popular to resist. Fei Long couldn't be seen consorting with a crime lord. It defeated the whole purpose of saving face.

'It's good that you came to tell me,' he said. 'I'll think of something.'

She nodded. Her fingers worked at the edge of her shawl nervously. He wished she didn't look like a rabbit waiting to flee.

'Is that all you came for?' he asked gently.

'Yes, that's all.' But she was still there. 'You seem better now…than before,' she ventured.

'You mean now I've regained my senses?'

'Yes.' She swallowed. 'You appear calmer.'

Yan Ling was anything but calm. The moment he approached, her breathing visibly quickened. Her lips parted and her skin flushed pink. He liked that.

'I'm thinking much clearer now,' he agreed.

The corners of her mouth fell. 'I'm happy to see it, my lord.'

She made no effort to hide her look of sorrow. Yan Ling

assumed that the walls of cold formality and self-denial were back between them. What she didn't realise was that walls that had fallen so hard could never be recovered.

When she ducked her head and murmured some excuse to leave, all it took was a slight shift of his position to halt her retreat. 'How many hours have we spent in here?'

'I don't know, my lord.' Her eyes were veiled as she regarded him. 'I didn't count.'

He'd kissed her only once in this study, but had thought of it many, many times. Yan Ling had all but seduced him, merely because he'd come close enough to smell her perfume. If he tried to take her in his arms now, she might succumb, but it wasn't what she truly wanted. It wasn't what he wanted either.

At least not all he wanted.

'Thank you for your concern,' he said.

He held the door open for her and watched her disappear out into the parlour before closing it. He could be cruel as well, as cruel as she had been in the park that morning. But Yan Ling's cruelty was the kind that had opened his eyes. He knew what he had to do.

Fei Long pressed a hand to his ribs to ease the throb building there. His mind and spirit were determined, if only he could will his body to obey.

Chapter Twenty-One

Why wasn't Fei Long practising? Yan Ling tracked his comings and goings for the next two days, becoming an incessant nuisance to the servants whenever she needed information. He had left the house once to go to the herbalist's shop and another time to drink tea alone at a quiet establishment in the corner of the East Market. Drinking tea by himself and brooding exactly like when she'd first met him.

Fei Long hadn't made another trip to the practice range. His bow hadn't left his room.

'He's given up,' she lamented to Bai Shen.

The handsome actor stood on one side of the front gate while she stayed on the other.

'There's nothing to worry about. You haven't seen Fei Long with a bow in his hands,' he bragged.

'You don't understand. I *have* seen Fei Long try to shoot. Do something, Bai Shen. Please.'

'What do you want me to do?'

'I don't know. Anything.'

She tried to talk to Fei Long directly, but Dao had become a diligent chaperon. The servant girl was quite skilled at redirection and obstruction. There was not one moment when Yan Ling was left alone with the master of the house.

On the morning of the contest, the entire household rose early from their beds. Yan Ling was relieved when Fei Long appeared in the courtyard. He wore solid black that day without adornment. His bow was slung over his shoulder.

She rushed to him. 'Good luck today. May every arrow hit its target.'

It took a moment for him to focus on her. 'Thank you, Yan.'

'I thought you were taking a lighter bow.'

Fei Long had brought the exact same one she'd seen him practise with that ill-fated morning. He glanced over his shoulder as if just realising it was there. 'I realised that would be admitting defeat.'

He sounded so grave and serious with the weight of the world on his shoulders and a thousand thoughts in his head. He was being stubborn, considering he tired too quickly with that bow, but she admired his courage. Pride bubbled within her, and then another, unnameable emotion took root.

Suddenly she couldn't breathe.

'I wish I could come and watch,' she said, barely keeping her voice from trembling with this new discovery. He was so determined and unwavering and she loved him for it. The thought settled into her chest and grew until there wasn't enough room inside her. She loved him.

'We don't know who will be there,' he said. 'And I don't want Zōu seeing you or Dao and getting any ideas.'

Fei Long always worried over the welfare of others before himself.

She placed a red scarf across his palm. Making sure Dao was nowhere in sight, she squeezed his hand once only. It ached to look at him with so much hope and fear in her heart. 'You'll do well today.'

He forced a smiled for her benefit. It was a painful thing to watch. She smiled back, equally pained. With a final nod, he straightened his shoulders and headed out to the competition.

As soon as he was gone, Dao came out from her room, wearing a plain grey tunic and trousers. She stopped to tuck her hair into the wool cap. 'Do I look like a stable boy?'

Yan Ling looked her over, head to toe. Her gaze stayed on the toe part. Dao followed her line of sight downwards.

'Oh.' Dao wiggled her feet within the pink embroidered slippers.

Bai Shen intercepted Fei Long at the end of the street and they ducked into a side alley. Without a word, Bai Shen took the quiver of arrows from him to lighten Fei Long's load and strapped it onto his back. The archery contest was located at the second-largest park in the city and was a short walk on foot. Fei Long had decided to leave before the Dragon Hour so he could get in position before the crowds gathered.

'Your opponent is some young hellion. They say he's a prodigy with a bow and arrow,' Bai Shen reported.

Much like they used to say about him.

'What else?'

'He's won several small wagers. In the last Great Shoot he made it to the final three rounds, but that's nothing. You've won the whole thing.'

'I never won,' Fei Long corrected. 'And past tournaments don't matter. Only today matters.'

'Right…here, drink this.' Bai Shen held out a flask. 'Same thing we drank five years ago before the tournament.'

Fei Long scowled. 'Actors and your superstitions.'

'Yan Ling said she was worried about you.'

'When did you speak to Yan Ling?'

'She told me to do something to help you.' Bai Shen gave the flask a few shakes. 'This might loosen the muscles up a bit.'

Fei Long kept on walking. 'This is a bad idea.'

He hadn't had wine in years and he certainly didn't want

to combine liquor with the herbal remedy he'd taken to dull the pain. Yet after a few paces, Fei Long stopped and held out his hand. Bai Shen pulled the cork and took a swig first before handing it over. Fei Long lifted the flask in a quick toast before tipping it over and spilling his portion onto the ground.

'Wait! That's good stuff.'

Fei Long handed the liquor back. The symbolic gesture would have to do.

They continued towards the park. He could already hear the hum of the crowd beyond the walls of the alleyway and they stopped just short of the end. Fei Long unwound the red scarf from his hand to tie it around the lower half from his face.

'Brilliant.' Bai Shen laughed. 'The crowd will love that. By the way, if you don't do something intelligent about Yan Ling once this is over, I've decided I'm going to steal her away from you.'

Fei Long glared. 'How is that information supposed to help me?'

'I just thought I should warn you. She's not usually the sort I fancy, but people can change.'

'Enough, Bai Shen.'

'We can't go exiling all our pretty women to foreign lands. It's a crime against the empire.'

'Enough.'

They'd reached the entrance into the street. Bai Shen exhaled, then alternatively flexed and relaxed his hands as if preparing for a theatre performance. Fei Long supposed this was much the same—a grand show for the masses.

They stepped into the intersection and faced the crowd gathered at the park entrance. News of their arrival travelled in a wave as soon as they saw the bow in his hands. A cheer went up and all eyes clamped onto him. Money and paper markers changed hands rapidly.

Fei Long looked straight ahead and kept on walking. Bai

Shen did his part to clear the way, his tenor voice carrying clear through the crowd. 'Move aside! Move aside!'

There were noblemen and merchants alike among the spectators. The city guards were gathered to keep the peace, but they were just as interested as everyone else in the match. The crowd was smaller, yet rowdier than it had been five years ago for the Great Shoot. That event had been sanctioned by the Emperor. This one was instigated by two gambling-den lords posing as self-made gentlemen.

Two canopies were set up on either side of the green. Zōu reclined beneath the one on the far end, attended by his concubines and bodyguards. The rival lord was settled opposite him under the shade of his own canopy, surrounded by his own escort.

Further down the line another tent had been set up. He recognised Minister Cao right away. Tong was with him, as well as several other ranking officials. Fei Long ducked away involuntarily, though his face was covered.

The other competitor arrived just behind him. Bai Shen was right. Here was a young man, pale-faced, with an intense energy in his eyes. For Fei Long, it was like looking at his own reflection. Not in appearance, but in spirit. He nodded once at the other bowman. The courtesy was not returned. His opponent was occupied with sizing him up.

Fei Long stared across the grass at his first sight of the field.

'The legendary Houyi,' Bai Shen said beneath his breath.

'And the Ten Suns,' Fei Long finished.

There were ten straw targets, painted in gold and set out at varying distances. The final target was elevated and stood at the far end of the park, only visible as a tiny globe representing the tenth and surviving Sun.

A public crier began reciting the rules. Ten arrows each. They'd shoot in two rounds, first at the five closest targets, then the five furthest. Fei Long would have rather done it the other way around. Take out the far targets while his body was still rested. They would only be allowed to shoot once at each target so there was no change for adjusting after a miss.

A toss of the die decided that Fei Long would shoot second. He watched his opponent walk into the field and take aim. His stance was strong, balanced. Fei Long didn't need to watch the arrow to know it would hit its mark. Five arrows flew in quick succession. Five arrows hit centre. The beauty of it had to be appreciated, even by someone who had never held a bow. There was undeniable harmony in perfection.

'There's still time to take a drink,' Bai Shen offered.

The wagering increased to a palpable level. Fei Long shook his head, barely hearing Bai Shen or the rest of the crowd. Were the odds for him or against him? It didn't matter.

He took the quiver back from Bai Shen and strapped it on. Then he took his time approaching the target line, listening to each individual beat of his heart, feeling the rush of blood pumping through him.

Archery was supposed to be a practice of skill and precision. Of focus and technique. Yet the most experienced archers also knew that minute details could cause arrow after arrow to veer astray. If your aim was off by a hair that day, there was nothing that could be done to fix it. There was something more than cold, clean technique to it, otherwise bowmen wouldn't need to pray to patron gods.

The sun was rising steadily, heating his back. Fei Long reached over his shoulder and took an arrow from his quiver. Carved from mulberry, it was light and balanced. He nocked it against the string and straightened, pulling his right arm back. The bowstring grew taut as it stretched, the tension and force gathering.

A hundred things had to be aligned for the arrow to hit its mark, but Fei Long knew them without thinking. He sighted the first target through the line of the bow, listened to his heart, slowed his breathing. The world receded around him. He exhaled steadily and released in the stillness between heartbeats.

* * *

Yan Ling dug her nails against the wooden rail. Beside her Dao held her breath.

Bai Shen had procured them a second-floor balcony in a drinking house that overlooked the park. A prime location considering the event that day. From where she stood, Fei Long was a black figure down below. She couldn't see his expression, but she could see the tension in his stance.

She prayed for him as he pulled back. He seemed to hold on for an uncommonly long time. The first archer had pulled back and released in one uninterrupted motion, without hesitation. She didn't know if it was hesitation that made Fei Long pause. He stood unmoving, arrow poised. Wouldn't he weaken the longer he remained that way?

When Fei Long released, a gasp escaped from her lips. She squinted at the target.

The arrow had hit home. One.

The next one flew shortly after. Then another and another. She couldn't follow them.

'Is he even aiming?' she cried.

'Yes!' Dao grabbed her shoulder and shook her happily. 'Five out of five. I told you so! Not an arrow wasted.'

She caught how Fei Long paused after the last arrow. He leaned slightly to one side before straightening and retreating from the line. In the practice session, he'd started struggling after only five arrows. She couldn't be sure, but these targets seemed further. Even the first five were a challenge.

The next round was beginning. Yan Ling held on to the rail to keep from falling as she leaned forwards to watch.

'He's good,' Fei Long said.

He stood side by side with Bai Shen as they watched his opponent shoot in the second round. The young man exuded confidence and his technique was impeccable.

'Not as good as you,' Bai Shen protested.

The archer's head twitched as if he'd heard Bai Shen, but he kept his eyes on the target. He'd hit the two suns on the far left side. There were two more arranged to the right. Each one was a good two hundred *bu* away. Just within the range of an infantry bowman. Fei Long could see the strain in his opponent's body as he pulled the string.

The young man was slightly smaller than he, so Fei Long had a strength advantage, but nominal only. Streaks of pain radiated from his side after only the first five shots.

The third arrow hit centre and the crowd cheered with excitement. More markers flew from hand to hand. People would be betting on each shot as well as the overall competition. His father had explained the intricacies of such wagering to him once. It was knowledge he hadn't found any use for.

His opponent took a moment to wipe sweat away from his brow. The fourth target was the furthest one yet. The young man pulled back as far as he could and released. The crowd groaned as the arrow flew wide.

'Disaster!' Bai Shen proclaimed.

Fei Long shushed him. 'Don't heckle.'

'He can't hear us.'

That was eight out of ten targets with the last one still to go. The final sun was an obscene length away; nearly an entire *li*. Fei Long tried to gauge the distance. Had he ever shot an arrow that far?

The rival archer was doing the same. He stood with his shoulder pointed to the tenth target for a long time. Finally, his expression hardened with resolve. He pulled the bow back so far that the wood strained against the string. At any moment something would snap: the string or the bow or the archer himself. He let go and the sigh of the release sounded like the blow of an axe. Fei Long's intention wrapped around the arrow as it soared, slicing through the air, flying true. Never mind that this was his opponent's shot. The technique of it deserved to hit centre.

The arrow fell just short. A sigh went through the crowd, followed by more chatter. Despite the miss, his opponent had done very well overall.

'Your turn—show him how it's done.'

Fei Long walked towards the line again, sinking deep within himself to conjure up the legendary match from five years ago. If only he could conjure up himself as he'd been that day. Fei Long had known the moment the shoot was over that he would never hit that well again. It had been one day in a thousand days. His mind had been clear, his body strong. The world was his for the taking.

Today his mind was anything but clear. He thought of Zōu and his smug look. The two million cash in debt hanging over his head. He thought of the family home where he and his sister were born. If he sold it and moved away, Pearl would never know where to find them. And he thought of Yan Ling.

More than once, she'd pulled him away from the brink of ruin because she was stubborn, where he was patient. She was impetuous, where he was forbearing. He believed everyone should fulfil his duty. She believed that everyone should go one better.

'Houyi!'

It took him a moment to realise that Bai Shen was yelling at him.

'They're going to disqualify you if you don't shoot.'

Fei Long lifted an arrow. He was just setting his eyes on the target, that was all.

He aimed and fired. Just like his opponent, he took the two targets on the right with ease. The wound had started to throb, pulsing at his side as a reminder of weakness. He sucked in a breath and pulled through the pain to claim the next target.

The fourth one was a challenge. He took his time centring it in his sight. His aim was steady. He timed his breathing, slowed his heartbeat. The moment he released, a sharp twinge made

him double over. The arrow flew foul, with no grace to speak
of as it loped into the grass.

The crowd groaned, jeered, swore. The bookies went mad.
New odds were frantically cast, all while Fei Long clutched
at his side and gulped in air. Off to the side, the Bull looked
like he was ready to snort with rage. If Fei Long had been in
a speaking mood, he would have told Zōu something about
karma.

Bai Shen came to kneel beside him. His eyebrows raised
sharply with concern as he put a hand on Fei Long's shoulder.
'Do you need to rest? I can try to delay them.'

'No.' Fei Long rose slowly. 'No, let's do this now.'

The pain would only get worse. He took his stance and faced
off against the tenth Sun. Bai Shen backed away and the crowd
hushed once again, all bets final.

Eight out of ten. He was at a draw, but for him that was the
same as a loss. The terms were that he needed to win.

He'd seen how the other archer had performed on this target.
His arrow had flown straight, propelled with all his strength,
but it had fallen short. Fei Long couldn't pull much harder, not
with his body in agony.

In the legend of Houyi, the tenth Sun was the one that remained. Zōu and his crony had placed the last target far enough
to taunt them. It wasn't meant to be attainable. Not with this
bow and his strength on this day, but he couldn't give up yet.

Fei Long sighted the target and pulled back as far as he
could, bending the bow until the wood creaked. Every muscle within him strained. His ribs screamed, but he could endure it for a single release. He had no other choice. If he shot
straight, absolutely straight, and the arrow was blessed by wind
and air—

He paused, lowering the bow and releasing the tension with
the arrow still in place. He'd shot this far before in infantry
drills, but it wasn't precision shooting. The purpose of the infantry was to let loose a rain of arrows.

All instinct left him in the wake of the pain. He tried to push the ache to the back of his mind, tried to draw forth the training and knowledge within him. The tenth Sun mocked him across the field as he reassessed the distance. The mask around his face became unbearably hot and stifling.

Fei Long straightened and sighted again. With a silent tribute to Houyi, he angled the bow upwards and let the arrow fly.

Chapter Twenty-Two

Fei Long tracked the path of the arrow as it soared across the park. He measured its speed and decline and somehow he knew. He turned his back on the target and started walking.

Bai Shen continued to stare down the field, transfixed.

'Come on.' Fei Long didn't pause as he passed him. He hooked the bow over his shoulder and lengthened his stride. The jubilant roar of the crowd confirmed what instinct had already told him.

The arrow had hit its mark.

'Let's go,' he called to Bai Shen, louder this time.

Zōu was up on his feet, grinning as if he'd held the bow himself. The Bull met his eyes and clapped his hands in acknowledgement. His debt was settled.

The crowd was coming alive behind him. He had to get out of there, away from the revellers and well-wishers while his identity was still hidden. At the edge of the park, he broke into a run. Bai Shen caught up to him.

'A truly humble man!' The actor laughed, keeping pace beside him. 'Not even staying to steep in the glory.'

They ran out into the streets and ducked into an alleyway. Fei Long's entire left side burned. He clenched his jaw and forced himself to breathe through it. The competition had pushed him to his limit.

'Fei Long!'

He knew that voice. He turned to see Yan Ling flying towards him.

'You were wonderful!'

He caught her in his arms and she squeezed him hard. Too hard. He winced, but held on to her, feeling her soft curves moulded against him. Nothing would make him let go.

'So wonderful,' she murmured, tugging the scarf away from his face.

Her eyes shone as she looked upon him, and he decided she was perfect just like that, safe in his arms, wearing that oversized robe that always failed to disguise her.

Bai Shen beamed. Dao scowled. And the chaotic noise coming from the street meant that the crowd from the park was spilling out onto the city.

'They want their champion,' Bai Shen warned. 'You baited them with that mask.'

The four of them set off, crossing and weaving through the busy streets like a pack of wayward demons. Bai Shen let out a whoop of triumph. A sense of lightness filled Fei Long, lifting him as his feet flew over the paved streets. The pain receded into the background. He hadn't felt this way since he'd been a boy, running with no destination through a city that never ended.

The weight of debt and ruin had finally been removed. There was only one thing left that kept him from soaring to the heavens. He slowed his pace so that Yan Ling was beside him. Her cap had fallen off and her hair flew behind her.

He hadn't allowed himself to dream about this until he won. And he'd just won.

Fei Long laughed. He was breathing hard and it would have been easier to run if he weren't laughing, but he couldn't help himself.

* * *

By the time they reached the mansion, they were all out of breath. Yan Ling and Dao disappeared through the gate and he could hear Yan proclaiming his victory to Old Man Liang. Fei Long started to enter as well, but Bai Shen halted at the threshold, still refusing to go inside.

'Come on, you scoundrel,' Fei Long said as he tried to catch his breath. 'That's not necessary any more.'

Bai Shen folded his arms stubbornly. 'You know what has to be done.'

Fei Long sighed, wiping a hand over his brow. 'I most humbly apologise to you, Li Bai Shen, for any unkind words or consequences I caused you to suffer.'

'Ah, very well said. Thank you, my lord.' Instead of coming in, Bai Shen grinned and turned to go, lifting his hand in farewell. He strode down the lane as if the day were his. 'Come see my next performance at the Pear Blossom Gardens and bring that charming attendant of yours. I'm playing the Monkey King.'

His voice faded with the distance. Fei Long watched him until Bai Shen disappeared around the corner.

Old Man Liang greeted him in the courtyard. 'Is it true, son?'

Fei Long nodded, a bit embarrassed by the overt pride in the steward's eyes.

'Ha, well done! Well done.' Liang patted his shoulder. 'Everyone went to see you,' he explained, seeing how Fei Long scanned the courtyard from corner to corner. 'Huibin said he was going to place a wager, but I told him you wouldn't like that.'

He only listened vaguely to the old man's report while he searched the courtyard for Yan Ling. The two women had disappeared completely into the recesses of the house. They'd probably gone inside to change out of their disguises. He loosened the scarf from around his neck and used it to dry his face. Perhaps he should wash up a bit as well before speaking to her.

He had to do it quickly. In mere days, the ambassador and an escort of court-appointed attendants would come to take Yan Ling away. The first part of the plan was to get her to agree to stay, the next part he had yet to figure out.

Doubt besieged him. She'd already refused him once before. Had the situation changed enough for her to reconsider?

He would have to face the wrath of the imperial court when there was no princess to send to Khitan. The family name would be scarred. Minister Cao, who had been their benefactor all these years, would shun them.

Fei Long was prepared to endure all of it. There were worse things than losing face. He'd decided this when Yan Ling had put him in his place back in the park. Saving face was only important for protecting the people he cared for. What use was honor, when he would live for ever in regret? If he let her go to Khitan, he would save face, but he would lose hope.

This was one time where couldn't fulfil his duty to the Emperor. He had no right to sacrifice Yan Ling. He'd never had the right. He'd only made every effort to convince himself that he did. She would be a princess, he'd told her. No longer a lowly tea girl with tables to clean and customers to please. And she'd believed him. Yan Ling had listened and absorbed every lesson he'd fed her. If that wasn't an abuse of privilege, he didn't know what was.

Could she accept him now, with all the hardship and uncertainty that lay ahead? More importantly, would he be worthy of her when his name and honour were gone?

Yan Ling waited in the garden of the local temple with Dao beside her. The arrangement was a tranquil one with a pond at the centre and a small grove of peach trees. Lady Min had chosen the location for the simple beauty of its garden.

'Don't lose focus,' Dao warned her. The girl had resumed

her role as a stern-faced chaperone as soon as they'd returned from the match.

'I am focused,' Yan Ling promised.

She focused on how Fei Long had looked when he'd wrapped his arms around her. For a brief moment, the boundaries between them had disappeared. He'd held her in daylight, without fear, as if she were precious. As if she belonged to him.

'I know I have to go soon,' Yan Ling said, agitated. 'Can't you let me dream just a little until then?'

'Dreams are dangerous. They make you forget what's real.'

Khitan wasn't real, Yan Ling insisted stubbornly. Changan was real. Fei Long was real. Even Dao with her disapproving scowl was more real than the Khitan barbarian she was supposed to marry.

'I'll miss you, Dao.'

Dao made an impatient noise, but she relented. 'I'll miss you, too.'

'Write me letters, all right? Make those imperial messengers ride all the way across the steppes to deliver them.'

'Of course.'

Fei Long had taught her so much and so had Dao. This her only way to repay them. Maybe it was being in the temple that made her so reflective.

Fei Long hadn't asked her to stay with him again, and even if he did, Dao was right. She would be a servant or a favoured concubine at best. She would have done so happily—until Fei Long took a wife. Then she would be relegated to the far corner of the house to be forgotten, her spirit crushed.

Better for everyone that she fulfilled her purpose in the peace marriage. Still, she hoped Fei Long would miss her for a long, long time. No, she didn't want him to find happiness elsewhere. She hoped to become a wound in his heart that wouldn't heal.

'Yan!' Dao reprimanded.

'What?'

'You looked so malicious right then. This is a Buddhist temple, you know.'

They hushed as a nun in plain grey robes, head shaven, stepped out into the garden. She shuffled toward them in her sandals, then stopped, pressing her hands together and bowing from the waist. 'Greetings, my ladies.'

Dao blinked twice, her eyes opening wide. 'Lady Min?'

Min bowed again, but this time her smile was unmistakable. 'I'm so happy you came. Miss Yan Ling, you're so pretty now!' the once lady, now nun, exclaimed. She hugged them both and led them to a mat set out before the statue of Guanyin. 'So what is this about an archery match? Tell me everything!'

Dao took over the tale, speaking in a hushed, yet excited tone. Lady Min listened with childlike interest, laughing aloud when Dao described the final shot that would certainly become legend. Several grim-faced nuns walked by on the garden path and regarded them sternly before continuing on.

'I'm too loud still, but I'm learning,' Min said.

Yan Ling was certain Dao had brought her to the temple to keep her away from the house and away from Fei Long, but now that she was here, she was glad. Lady Min had been the first friend she'd made in the city, though it had been a short acquaintance.

'At first I couldn't stop touching my head,' Min chattered on, as if starved for conversation. 'Once I asked for a mirror and everyone stared at me. I thought I would be sent home that very moment, but the abbess is very tolerant. She looks at me very tolerantly every time she sees me. I do sometimes look into that fish pond over there just to check my reflection,' she confessed.

They laughed together, hands held to their mouths to muffle the sound. Min looked content and Yan Ling was certain she still laughed every day. They said their farewells and Min again broke formalities to hug each of them. 'Come visit me again.'

'I'll actually be leaving soon.' Sadness hooked around her heart as she said it. 'To Khitan.'

'Oh! Oh, yes…like Pearl.'

Not like Pearl. Pearl had escaped with the man she loved. But Yan Ling was much more practical, as Fei Long had pointed out.

She should have run away with him that morning in the park, even if they had only made it to the ward gates before Fei Long came to his senses and insist they turn around. It would have been nice to be recklessly free for one small moment. She could remember that Fei Long had felt that impassioned once, with her.

Yan Ling squeezed the bridge of her nose to keep from tearing up. If Dao asked about her sorrowful look, she'd explain it away as the sadness of Lady Min's departure, though Yan Ling had hardly known the lady long enough to weep for her.

That night's dinner was a feast. They couldn't celebrate Fei Long's triumph with the rest of the city, but Old Man Liang purchased a roast pig from the butcher and the kitchen servants had been hard at work as soon as they returned. Everyone was drunk on their master's victory.

The entire household gathered in the banquet room for the meal. The panel doors were thrown open and additional tables and chairs were assembled in the courtyard so the feast could include everyone in the mansion. The tables were then loaded with plates of vegetables and platters of whole fried fish. Steamed buns were piled high to form a pyramid and you couldn't extend your arm without encountering a flask of wine. Everyone ate and talked and ate. It truly was a family in every way but blood.

Yan Ling tried to put on a good face. She took a morsel off every platter, but she could only pick listlessly at the meal. Fei Long sat at the head of the table and each man tried to get him to drink with them. Even the stable boy tried to ply him with wine, to everyone's amusement. As usual, Fei Long endured the taunts and enjoyed his tea.

Despite the laughter all around him, he barely broke a smile. He met her eyes once across the table and his look appeared weighted with thought, but she couldn't read anything deeper from it. Her keen ability to identify Fei Long's subtle moods failed her at this most critical time.

Midway through the meal, she gave up and stopped forcing herself to smile and laugh. It was impossible to speak to Fei Long alone. Everyone wanted his attention tonight. She'd heard the same story from ten different viewpoints about how Fei Long had won the match.

She sipped at a cup of wine and her face went hot, as she'd expected. Maybe she was hoping Fei Long would comment about it as he'd done after the play. Everything she did was a line, cast out into the ocean, trying to reach out to him from across the crowded room. All of her efforts failed.

Finally, she bid farewell to everyone. She was tired, she said. The day had been a long one. No one looked twice as she slipped away. Instead of returning to her chamber, Yan Ling went to the beloved study. It was dark inside and she moved about the room, lighting the lanterns. With all of them glowing, the study almost appeared the way she knew it—by the light of the afternoon sun as the day slowly waned.

She looked to the empty place where her writing desk once stood and her spirit shattered. The desk had been moved against the wall in the corner. She had been cast aside as well.

Yan Ling went behind Fei Long's desk and ran her hand along the intricate carvings along the back of his chair. There was a worn spot over the arm where his elbow rested. She sat down and touched her fingers to the smooth, bared wood.

Something had been bothering her for a while. The last time she'd been in Fei Long's study at night, it had been so dark she could barely see. They had needed to forge papers to get through the ward gates. When she had fumbled through Fei

Long's desk to search for the jade seal, she'd found something else as well. They had been so worried about Fei Long that night that she didn't have time to investigate.

She pulled the drawer open now, almost afraid of what she would find. More afraid of what she wouldn't find.

The stack of papers was near the top. They'd been shoved haplessly inside, which she wouldn't have expected of Fei Long. Holding her breath, she dug the papers out and laid them onto the desk. Her fingers shook as she separated the pages to spread them out.

It was the same two characters on each page.

'I must have been so obvious.'

She jumped and her hand flew to her throat. Fei Long stood there in the doorway, his gaze intent on her. Her pulse skipped dangerously.

'I was afraid everyone could sense my inner thoughts. The emotions shouted from inside me.' He came into the room and shut the door carefully behind him. 'The more I tried to hide it, the more I was convinced you could see how I felt in every look.'

Yan Ling stared down at the calligraphy. It was her name. Written over and over in so many different ways.

'There is a balance inherent in the art of writing, of *shū*.' His voice was quiet, stroking gently over her skin. 'Defined rules about how to write each character. Every stroke has its place and position.'

As he approached, she became aware how their usual situation had been reversed. She was the one who sat and waited as he came near. Yet he continued to instruct her.

'The discipline of it is learning how to express yourself within the confines of form and structure. The brush reveals every nuance, every internal emotion.' He met her eyes. 'If a few simple strokes could reveal so much, then how could anyone not sense the depth of feeling for you in every word I spoke, every movement that I made?'

Her tongue cleaved to the roof of her mouth. She struggled to find her voice. 'I didn't see. I hoped, but I didn't dare to dream.'

She looked to the papers again. He'd trained her in calligraphy to teach her patience and discipline while using the same techniques to try to control his own emotions. He'd buried them deep and only allowed then to show in one place.

In the forms, she could see the gathered memories of their days together. She could see the hundred different ways he thought of her. The flowing curves of wistfulness, the tight control of denial. It was all there. Anger, hope, longing. Desire.

'I think of you all the time.' She had to tell him how she felt now, even if nothing came of it. 'I'll always think of you. I'll never forget you, Fei Long.'

She would have kept on going, pouring out everything inside of her, but Fei Long had moved around the desk. He pulled her to her feet and cradled her face tenderly in both his hands.

'You're crying.' His thumb brushed over her cheek, wiping away a tear.

'I don't mean to.'

Yan Ling wished she could have been prettier then, not redfaced and swollen, but Fei Long lowered his mouth to hers. Her lips trembled so hard she couldn't return the kiss, but he didn't seem to mind. He kissed her again, moving gently over her mouth, his hand beneath her chin to raise her face to him.

If he had let her speak, Yan Ling would have told him so much more. She loved him. She'd always love him. So she tried to tell him in the way her body curved into him and the soft sigh of her breath mingling with his.

Her tears had stopped by the time he raised his head. His hands still framed her face. She let her eyes roam over his features to commit every stroke and curve to memory. All she could see was Fei Long: his piercing eyes dark with contemplation and the defined shape of his mouth, sensual in its own way. It was the only time she had allowed herself to take in the sight of him for as long as she wanted, not averting her eyes out of shyness or fear.

His expression shifted. Nothing more than a ripple of decision that settled in his eyes. His hands released her cheeks and he leaned ever so slightly towards her. The small of her back came up against the edge of the desk.

Her breathing quickened. 'Fei Long,' she whispered and it meant a hundred things. Most importantly, it meant yes.

He held her with his gaze as he lifted her onto the edge of the desk. Her feet lifted from the floor and for a moment she lost her balance, leaning back too far. Fei Long caught her. One arm moved around to brace itself just behind her and she raised her hands to his shoulders, her fingers digging into lean, hard muscle. She didn't know what came next, but she wanted it.

'Yan Ling.' The knot at his throat lifted and lowered.

His robe brushed against her knees as he pressed even closer, trapping her against the broad frame of his body. She wouldn't say anything this time. She was too afraid of breaking the moment in its most fragile state. Fei Long lowered his lips to the exposed skin of her throat, kissing her until her skin warmed and tingled. She tilted her head to bare her neck to him, offering him anything he wanted.

He lowered his hand and fisted it into the material of her skirt. In two efficient tugs, he lifted the silk enough to rest his hand against her bare thigh. But his intention was soon clear. Fei Long took her mouth again as he slipped his hand between her legs. He traced a finger delicately along the intimate fold of her flesh and she jumped. Her heart sped up uncontrollably. She could barely sit still, but Fei Long held her in place, anchored against him. His finger stroked upwards, then down with relentless patience, his fingertip just parting her. She moaned softly. He adjusted the angle of his hand beneath her skirt and pressed deeper so that his touch slicked directly over the hidden pearl of her sex.

Sensation shot up her spine and her body went weak. Her

lips parted helplessly in pleasure and he kissed her in her abandon, touching her intimately until she cried out. Her hands clutched at his robe and her legs parted of their own accord in a silent plea. All the while, Fei Long watched her intently.

She blinked up at him. His breathing had increased, but his expression remained hard and inscrutable. Her eyes glazed over as his fingers tormented her flesh. His touch was a constant now, teasing her relentlessly. If he stopped, she would die. If he didn't stop—she didn't know.

Her head fell back in surrender, but Fei Long was there to catch her. His other arm circled her now with his hand splayed against her back to keep her upright. She closed her eyes, shaking her head in denial, because the sheer torture of this was senseless. He commanded her with nothing but this single, unending caress and it became everything. Cruelly, inexplicably, everything.

She cried out as her body tightened. Fei Long crushed his mouth to her and she sobbed against his lips. Her inner muscles clenched and unclenched as she shook inside and out.

His touch became gentle on her now. Soothing. But even that was too much. She communicated to him with a small murmur of protest. All speech had left her, but he understood. He removed his hand and soothed her skirts back in place. Then he enclosed her in his arms and squeezed tight, exhaling in one long sigh as if he'd been holding his breath the entire time.

When she dared to open her eyes again, she saw the familiar study lit by the warm glow of the lanterns. But everything looked different. Her head was tucked beneath Fei Long's chin. Her cheek rested against his breastbone. His heartbeat thudded against her ear. His muscles remained coiled and tight.

Listlessly, she reached for his robe. There was no strength left in her body as she went through the motions of undressing him, but he wasn't co-operating. He stopped her hand with his own and she looked up at him questioningly. She didn't know much about coupling or the art of the bedchamber, but she recognised that Fei Long had introduced her to pleasure while denying his own satisfaction.

Before she could doubt herself, he kissed her again. Each kiss was different, she realised. The same simple construct with an infinite number of ways to render it. The papers on the desk rustled as he lowered her feet to the floor.

'Wait here,' he said.

He went to extinguish the lanterns and then came back to take her hand. They emerged from the study and Yan Ling could hear the servants carousing out in the courtyard and the banquet room at the opposite end of the house. Not much time had passed, though it felt like an entire lifetime to her.

Fei Long walked ahead, scanning each passage before leading her through. His hand was warm over hers while their fingers intertwined. As they turned the last corner, even as he pushed the door open, he didn't let go.

Inside his bedchamber, darkness enfolded her as soon as the door closed. The air rushed out of her when Fei Long snatched her up. Her legs were weak from what had happened in the study. Her skin was still flushed and sensitive.

'Light a lantern,' she said.

'But you're right here. I know how to find you.' She loved how intimate his voice sounded in the dark.

'Indulge me.' She was too shy to admit she wanted to see what he looked like.

He left while Yan Ling felt her way towards the far wall. Her hands found the woodwork of the alcove. She moved along it until she found the opening and sank down onto the bed.

Fei Long lit a single oil lamp and brought it to the bedside table. It cast an orb of light about him, leaving her on the outside watching him.

'I want you to ruin me,' she said as he came to the bed. 'Take everything. Render me unsuitable for anyone else.'

Her voice trembled. She'd never spoken such scandalous words, not even secretly in the privacy of her thoughts. The two of them had danced so carefully around one another for months. She didn't want any doubt at the end of the night. Fei Long couldn't hide behind his honour any longer. Let him seduce her and cast her aside—but she would have him make that choice rather than remain in denial of what they had between them.

His gaze was intent upon her. 'This isn't ruin, Yan.' He loosened his sash and peeled away the outer layer of his robe. In a few efficient movements, he opened his tunic and cast it aside as well, revealing the hardened planes of his chest. 'But I will take everything.'

He lowered himself beside her and reached for the pins in her hair. Her fingers brushed over his as she helped him. Then he slipped the silk from her shoulders, freeing her from the layers that hid her from him. Cool air washed over her skin as her arms were bared. He ran his mouth reverently over all that he had uncovered, kissing along the curve of her shoulder, touching his lips to her collarbone.

They sat facing each other, exploring. She touched him with hesitant fingers and ran her hands over the dense muscle of his arms. He sucked in a breath as she explored him, sliding down low over his abdomen. He was intensely beautiful. So strong. A faint, mottled shadow remained low on his left side.

'Are you well enough for...' She struggled for words. He hadn't taught her any suitable ones. 'For this?'

He regarded her incredulously and then laughed. The short, sharp bark of it cut through their gentle explorations. Fei Long untied the ribbons that held the embroidered swatch of cloth over her breasts. The undergarment fell away, shamelessly exposing her to his gaze.

Without warning, Fei Long bent and took her breast into his mouth, pushing her down onto the bed as he sucked with gentle insistence. She made a startled sound and her back arched. A new sort of pleasure took her. A dangerous sort, more unbidden and torturous than what he'd shown her in the study.

My Fair Concubine

His mouth was wet on her, and so hot. His tongue found her nipple and he circled it while her insides curled and clenched and she didn't know whether to free herself or hold on to him and never let go.

The moment the sensation overwhelmed her, he released the first breast to tease the other, making her body swell and tighten at once. The rapture of it lifted her hips into him. Fei Long groaned and pressed himself to her, fitting himself into the juncture of her thighs. She wasn't alone in this torment. Fei Long was there with her. They struggled together. The rigid outline of his erection pushed hard against her and she worked her hand between the crush of their bodies. Swallowing her nervousness, she eased her hand past the waist of his trousers and plunged downwards.

Fei Long tensed at her first touch. She explored the smooth hardness of him, so hot beneath the skin. She never imagined it being so. With a low sound in his throat, Fei Long closed his eyes and pressed his face into the crook of her neck. He ground himself mindlessly against her, filling her hand.

Then he pulled away and her hand slipped free. There was no trace of tenderness in him as he stood. His expression was heated steel as he removed his trousers. He untied his hair as well and for a moment stood naked over her.

She took him in, all of him. Her mouth was painfully dry and even swallowing didn't banish the knot in her throat. This was what she had wanted to know—the sight of Fei Long when there were no more boundaries between them. She took the vision deep into herself. It would always be there, no matter what the morning brought.

He moved with swift purpose, returning to the bed and lowering himself. Thick black hair framed his face. She only had time to anchor her fingers into it before he was parting her legs. In the next moment, he used his hands to position himself against her. One careful push and he entered her slowly, taking away all thought and speech and breath. He thrust again, deeper and fuller. His body breached hers with only a moment of pain and soon he was gliding into her.

Her body accepted him, recognising the sensations that had been unknown yet eagerly awaited. She was slick from being pleasured so thoroughly, but it wasn't complete until now. She didn't realise it until the plunge of his body into her made her heart race. Fei Long pinned her with his weight and filled her. The scent of him surrounded her.

She pressed her lips against his throat and tasted the salt of his skin. The thrust of his body took on an exhilarating urgency, a riotous intensity that she could feel through the height and breadth of her body. There was no time to think. Only feel.

He was taking everything, just as he promised. Just as she wanted.

She wrapped her legs around his hips and held on.

Chapter Twenty-Three

There was heat around him. Tight, silken flesh. Yan Ling.
Yan Ling.

Her body lifted and he closed his arms around her, using the
leverage to take her more fully. He couldn't get enough. His release built rapidly. Her body tightened unbearably around him
as if urging him on. He complied. He had no choice.

His muscles locked as he peaked. He bowed his head against
her neck in surrender and worship. His hands dug into the small
of her back to angle her hips for his final thrusts. It was greed
that made him seek every last drop of pleasure.

His body released into her and then Fei Long stilled, drained
of everything that had been building inside him for so long.
Only then did his senses come back to him.

Fei Long didn't know what to say. He relaxed his hold on
her, not realising until then how hard he'd gripped her in his
frenzy. Yan was a slight, slender woman and he'd forgotten in
the burn of desire. He'd used her so completely.

'Did I hurt you?' he asked, which was an unreasonable question to ask once all was done.

'No.'

The silence stretched on. Fei Long raised himself up so that he could see Yan Ling. Her hair was in disarray. Her eyes were lidded and sensual and her skin radiated with an inner light. Beautiful.

He touched two fingers to her cheek. 'Are you all right, Yan?'

She nodded, but winced slightly as he withdrew from her. Yan Ling was a maiden and he had completely forgotten himself, taking her roughly for his own pleasure. Shame gutted him.

'I'm sorry,' he said, his voice hoarse with remorse.

'Sorry?' Her tone became guarded.

'You're inexperienced and I was—' he fought for the right word '—impatient.'

Yan Ling stared at him. Suddenly her eyes grew wide and she burst into laughter. She shook with it and he could sense every tiny vibration with her lying beneath him. The clear, sweet sound warmed his soul.

'Impatient?' She wiped at the corner of her eyes, she was laughing so hard. 'I suppose all that calligraphy didn't help after all.'

'No,' he said, his chest swelling with fondness. 'Not at all.'

All those days, writing her name over and over like a love-sick scholar. Wasn't he quite the tragic hero?

He held her closer. Kissed her forehead, the bridge of her nose. Anywhere that he'd neglected her. She wrapped her arms around him and buried her face against his shoulder.

'I didn't mind,' she said softly, shyly. Which in itself was new. He'd never known Yan Ling to be particularly shy.

Fei Long eased her back to the bed and kissed her mouth tenderly. Took time now to explore the rise and curve of her breasts. Her figure was slight, but perfectly rounded. He ran his hands down her waist, her hips, seeing her once again for the first time.

It should have been their wedding night. A night of discovery. He treated it now as if it was, learning the smooth skin of her inner arm, the rougher texture of her hands. Not a lady's hands, but he loved them because they were hers and they told a story that was no one else's.

Yan Ling explored him as well, running her hands over his chest and down his arms and back. She stroked his side lightly, very lightly, asking him if it hurt. It didn't. All the pain had disappeared. Or rather it had become insignificant in the wake of something much greater.

Her touch grew bolder and his body heated. But it was a steady fire this time. He was able to give her the patience and discipline he strived for, letting her arousal build, entering her with care. Even as her heat surrounded him, he watched Yan Ling, striving to learn the nuances of her passion before the fire took him.

He held himself back long enough to feel her convulse and shudder. The pressure gathered in his lower back, nearly unbearable. He fought it back while her nails bit into his shoulders. The sound of her broken cries of pleasure finally pushed him over. He couldn't hold back any longer. The climax ravaged his body before it released him.

Then they were still. An absolute and rare peace like no other.

But the peace didn't last. Yan Ling kissed his shoulder once, then grew serious. 'What are we going to do, Fei Long?'

'Fall asleep.' He slid down beside her and pulled the blanket around both of them.

Her lips pressed tight as she bit back her protest. He was relieved. He'd already placed too much of a burden on Yan Ling and it had been wrong of him to do so. He'd find a solution—he didn't know what, but he would. She didn't need to worry about it.

Yan came to him, resting her head in the crook of his neck.

Her hand drew a lazy pattern over his chest. Eventually she began to drift. Her soft weight grew heavy in sleep. He stayed awake a while longer to watch her.

All Yan Ling needed to know was that he'd take care of her. She didn't need to sacrifice herself for his sake. From the beginning, he was the one who should have been prepared to give up everything.

Yan Ling opened her eyes. The chirp of birdsong outside told her morning was near, though it was still dark. For a moment she floated, still soaked in sleep, until memories of the night came back to her. She was in Fei Long's chamber. In Fei Long's bed.

She faced outwards from the alcove. The dimness washed the colour from everything, leaving the room in shapes and shadows. She could feel the cradle of Fei Long's body nestled securely behind her.

'Are you awake?' He ran a soothing hand from her arm up her shoulder.

She nodded, making a sound of acknowledgement even as she closed her eyes again. She didn't want to wake yet. It would mean she'd have to get up. She'd have to set foot outside this chamber and face what they were both afraid to admit. What they had couldn't exist outside these closed doors.

'Do you know how many times I agonised over this part of your neck or this one ear?' His mouth brushed over her neck before he took her earlobe between his lips, sucking gently. A shiver ran down her spine, making her breath catch and her toes curl restlessly. 'You would gather your hair with your hands and sweep it over your shoulder to keep it out of the way before you'd begin to write. And I'd watch you, barely able to breathe.'

She squirmed against him, pleased. 'I never knew.'

He ran his hand between her breasts and down over the flat of her stomach. His voice was low and sensual in her ear. 'The sight of your wrists would make me ache. You once brushed your bare forearm over mine while we were looking at a map.'

So many little moments. She remembered them, too. She'd held them close to her breast as secret memories that only she held dear. But she'd been mistaken.

Fei Long's hand had reached her leg. He ran the flat of his palm over her in a broad, soothing motion before gently parting her thighs.

'Are you still sore?'

His voice was heavy with desire and her pulse quickened. Her body grew damp even before he touched her. His fingers stroked lightly. She whimpered and arched her back into him. He drew out her desire, touching her until her body became liquid and heat beneath his fingertips.

'Can it be done this way?' she murmured in surprise as he positioned her with his hands so her back was to him and she felt the blunt tip of him intimately parting her.

She couldn't see his face. All she knew of him was through tension and touch. His hand cradled her breast and his body shifted against hers, his legs curving against the back of her thighs.

'Yes,' he said, low and enticing against her ear. He slid into her in a slow, consuming penetration that stole her breath. 'There must be a thousand ways to make love.'

He withdrew slightly before sliding back in. Small, slow movements. He took her with just the shifting of his hips. His hand dipped to slide over the small bud of her sex, adding more pleasure while all she could do was writhe against him. The position left her open and vulnerable, helpless to do anything but accept and feel.

She curved her hand back to sink her fingers into his hair. It was the only way to hold on to him as he filled her, flooding her with sensation. Her other hand closed over his as he caressed her breast.

'Yes,' he said again, this time harsher as he urged her on.

Her throat was completely dry and she gasped with each thrust of his hips. Though she barely moved, her heart raced. She could feel Fei Long surrounding her, securing her against his strong body as desire became desperation. Their skin was slick with sweat and heated beyond endurance. She breathed shallowly. His own breathing was laboured and rough.

She sobbed with every sharp tug of pleasure when he touched her just so, lightning quick above the apex of her sex, slow and grinding immediately below where his thick organ filled her.

'Yes,' he shuddered as he beseeched her. There were no words for what he wanted, but she wanted it too. 'Yan,' he pleaded.

Yan Ling pushed back against him as hard as she could as every muscle within her tightened. His muscled body formed a brace for her in her passion. She cried out, the sound strained within her throat. A vindicating and final rush of pleasure arched through her. An exquisite pain beyond thought.

He increased his penetration at the last edges of her climax, before the last wave had subsided. His hand tightened on her hip to pull her harder against him and he hooked his leg over her to increase his possession. He couldn't move as deeply in this position, but he didn't need to. She gasped at the force of his thrusts and the hunger behind it. Her body was swollen with sated pleasure, squeezing tight around him, urging him on to his completion. Only then could they both be free.

He groaned, deep, guttural sounds akin to pain. Her soft cries joined his. It *was* pain. The most desperate sort of yearning that could only be cleansed in one way. Soon his body shuddered and thrust deep. He held her rigid against him as he lost himself inside her.

These last throes were so beautiful to her in their animal

baseness. All thought and civility fled and there was no denying that they belonged to each other. Him to her. Her to him.

Finally she could breathe again. She tucked her arm beneath her, resting her head against it. Fei Long curved his arm around her with languid possession. With his other hand, he pulled her hair back from her neck and pressed a kiss to the exposed skin. The nearly unbearable heat between their bodies cooled rapidly to a perfect cocoon of warmth.

She chuckled softly, unable to contain her happiness.

'What?' Fei Long asked, his voice thick.

'Nothing.' She closed her eyes and snuggled against him.

'Tell me.' He gave her hip an impatient shake, perturbed even at this small denial.

'A storm of passion,' she murmured, burying her smile against the crook of her arm. 'You swore there would never be such a thing between us.'

'This isn't a storm of passion.'

'No?' She wriggled her bottom against him smugly.

'No.'

Fei Long just couldn't bear being wrong, could he?

'This is love,' he argued.

She stilled, minute tension travelling along her entire body. Fei Long grew quiet as well behind her. All she could hear was his steady breathing. The soft brush of it tickled the hairs at the back of her neck.

Fearfully, she turned in his arms. The morning dimness left him in shadow and she had to strain to see his face.

'This is love,' he repeated.

How could he say it so calmly when her insides danced in circles? Her heart roared. She started trembling. In contrast, Fei Long reached out a steady hand to brush her hair away from her eyes.

'We have to hide away,' she said. 'Together.'

He'd come with her, wouldn't he? He loved her.

He loved her.

'We're not going anywhere.'

'What about Khitan and the betrothal? The Foreign Ministry will come to take me.'

'They'll come to take my sister, but I'll tell them Pearl is gone and I couldn't stop her.'

She knew it wasn't as simple as he tried to make it sound. He was being Fei Long again, taking the entire burden on his own shoulders in silence.

'But Khitan is expecting a princess,' she argued. 'And after the assurances you've given Minster Cao and Inspector Tong—'

Fei Long remained stoic. 'I'm prepared for the consequences. Our family name—' At that, a pained look crossed his face, but he continued. 'Our family name will suffer. We may never regain honour before the eyes of the imperial court and all of Changan, but this is my burden to bear.'

'The imperial court could have you beaten for disobedience. They could denounce your family and strip you of everything.'

The enormity of it left a hollow feeling in the pit of her stomach. After his triumph that morning, she would have thought Fei Long would fight to keep what was his, honour be damned.

'I have to go,' she choked out. It made her sick to say it.

'I won't let you do this for me.'

'Not for you.' She couldn't look at him. Her body went numb. She needed to be somewhere else, to be someone else to do this. 'For Dao. For Old Man Liang and the stable boy. For this house.' And for Fei Long. For his ancestors as well. Could he ever understand? This had become her family as well. 'I won't let you give up everything you've fought for.'

He reached for her, resting his forehead against hers just as he'd done in the archery park, but there was something different in him this time.

'If I wasn't certain before, then I know it now. I know it

in my soul.' His voice grew thick with emotion. 'When you refused to run away with me, you all but denounced me as a coward.'

'That wasn't my intention—'

He silenced her by holding her tighter. 'You were right. And I realised there were two things I would face ruin for rather than giving up without a fight. Our family home is one. The other is you, Yan.'

'But you could lose everything,' she whispered.

'I'll face the foreign ministry and the imperial court with head high.'

He lowered his mouth to hers, pouring all his sincerity and intention into a single kiss. 'Stand beside me,' he said.

Fei Long was fearless, and she wanted to believe he could succeed.

'Yes,' she said when he lifted his head. 'Always.'

She'd seen Fei Long achieve the impossible, fighting through pain and despair to triumph. If he had enough hope to carry them, then so would she. She tilted her head to return his kiss. At that moment, the chamber door swung open.

'Exactly as I thought!' Dao charged into the room, a blue-grey blur, eyes blazing.

Yan Ling sat up and shrieked in surprise, while Fei Long had enough presence of mind to grab the blanket and wrap it around her. Of course that left him fully exposed. One glance at his nakedness and Dao's eyes widened in alarm. She turned sideways, blushing furiously.

'This is my private chamber,' Fei Long admonished.

'Have you no shame, my lord?' Dao stared at the wall, keeping her eyes averted while still pointing an accusing finger at him. 'Using your position to seduce a maiden.'

Apparently Fei Long had no shame. At least not about being unclothed. Yan Ling threw the other end of the blanket over him so that they could huddle together beneath it with her holding one edge and he the other.

It was the first time Yan Ling had heard Dao speak so sharply to Fei Long. She wasn't spared either. Dao pinned an accusing glare on her next. 'And you! I thought you were more level-headed than this. I told you not to fall for Fei Long.'

'Dao, it's not like that.'

But it was. She had fallen for Fei Long. She'd fallen for him long before Dao or anyone could warn her away.

'Do you know how much I envied you? If I had a chance to become a princess, I would get on my knees and thank the Goddess of Mercy,' Dao railed. 'Instead you let yourself be sweet-talked by…by him! Giving up a good marriage to be some man's concubine.'

Fei Long bristled. 'Yan won't be anyone's concubine. I want her as my wife.'

'Truly?' Yan Ling asked.

'You must have known after all that—' He turned to Yan Ling, only to see that the question hadn't been addressed to him. She was looking at Dao.

'Truly?' she asked again. 'You…envied me?'

Some of the fire faded, but Dao remained fervent. 'I envied Pearl as well. I've barely been outside these few neighbourhoods, let alone the city. Why do you think I listened so ardently to all those stories about Khitan?'

Yan Ling looked speculatively at Dao, then to Fei Long. Then they both looked back at Dao. In contrast to her earlier scolding, she shrank before their mutual gaze.

'What…what is it?' she asked meekly.

Chapter Twenty-Four

The procession wove though the street like a dragon toward the front gate. At its head was a gilded palanquin carried by four porters. A parade of musicians with cymbals and horns struck up a festival tune and a long stream of additional attendants followed at the tail.

'Inspector Tong isn't among them,' Fei Long reported. He stood at the gate, representing the head of the household as well as acting as a lookout.

Yan Ling and Dao waited behind him in the privacy of the courtyard. Dao wore a fitted red jacket and skirt. The embroidered jacket was a mix of the fashion of Changan and the tribal clothing of the northern lands. Yan Ling stood beside her in a plain grey servant's robe with her hair plaited in a simple braid. Once again, Yan Ling was trying to disappear, but Fei Long would always seek her out. She captured his attention more so than Dao in her red silk and jewels.

The ladies embraced once, holding on to each other until the sound of the cymbals neared. When they let go, Yan Ling retreated along the courtyard wall toward the front parlour. Fei Long caught the quick motion as she wiped her eyes with her

eeve before disappearing. In contrast, Dao was clear-eyed
nd bright as she came to stand next to him.

'I wish you a hundred years of health and happiness,' he
aid. The corners of his mouth lifted as he added, 'Little Pearl.'

'Thank you, *Elder Brother*.' Her tone lowered reverently.
ao stood on her toes to kiss his cheek.

The brief contact lingered with him. A remainder of things
nsaid and long overlooked. They had grown up in the same
ousehold. Servant and master. He'd never questioned it be-
ause of the boundaries he held as sacred.

Dao took one last look around the familiar courtyard, then
lashed him a wide smile before pulling the red veil over her
ace.

The sedan stopped right before gates and as soon as the por-
rs set the poles down, the music also halted. Fei Long bowed
ormally to the palace official and gave his well-wishes for the
ourney while Dao stood absolutely still, face covered, beside
im. The veil would be removed as soon as she was secured
1 the wedding sedan, but for now that part of the ritual served
1eir purpose. When it was time to go, he held out his arm to
uide Dao to the transport and pulled aside the curtain for her
) step inside and be seated.

'Take care,' Fei Long said.

She nodded and he let the curtain fall back. To think it
ould have been that easy all along. Everyone was off to their
roper destiny, like pieces of a wooden puzzle, all falling into
1eir rightful place—

'Fei Long!'

Until an all-too-familiar voice called out. Minister Cao Wei
ad arrived in his private litter. The elder statesman came
heerfully up to him.

'Brilliant work the other day in the park, my son!' Minister
'ao gripped Fei Long's shoulder proudly.

Fei Long swallowed, but his throat remained parched. 'I'm
ot certain I understand, honoured sir.'

Cao cast him a sideways glance and chuckled. 'Always s humble.' The minister looked to the palanquin next. 'Ah, goo I came in time to say farewell to Pearl. An unusual circun stance detained me from coming to see you last time.'

Fei Long's jaw clenched. They couldn't be thwarted nov Not after all the elaborate ruses and schemes.

'Minsiter Cao,' he called out in desperation, 'we can't kee the Khitan delegation waiting.'

'What's a few moments? I'm certain the ambassadors won mind.'

Fei Long had never, never been adept at making excuse: Minister Cao reached the opening of the sedan and Fei Lon tried desperately to remember all of the schemes Li Bai She had spoken of. Since it wasn't reasonable to wrestle the mini ter in the street and steal his money, Fei Long could only watc in horror as the minister reached for the curtain.

'Your father was a dear friend of mine and I've known th two of you since you were children. Of course, I had to com today.'

Cao opened the curtain and stopped short, his brow wrir kling into a frown. Fei Long started to stutter out an explana tion, but Dao found her voice first.

'Uncle Cao. How kind of you to come and see me!'

The sides of the sedan blocked Dao from view, but her ton was cheerful. Unfortunately, she didn't sound anything lik Pearl and Cao would know it even with the veil.

'What is the meaning—?'

'I remember sitting in your lap and pulling your beard, m lord,' Dao went on, undaunted. 'How time goes by.'

Cao's frown remained fixed for a few moments more be fore he broke out into a grin. 'Ah, yes. Have a safe journey my dear Pearl.'

The minister let the curtain drop back in place and turne to Fei Long, who was prepared to have the imperial guard sent after him at any moment.

'You.' Minister Cao wagged a finger at him, smiling broadly. 'You might have the potential to be a good politician after all.'

'No, sir.'

The carriers took their positions and lifted the sedan up to turn to the palace. From there, the caravan would be meeting with an entourage of bodyguards and emissaries from Khitan and then Dao would be on her way as an imperial princess.

'I should accompany her Highness as she goes to meet the Khitan ambassadors,' Minister Cao offered. 'Make sure our girl is sent off safely.'

The procession departed in the same way it had come, in a haze of ceremony and trumpets. Yan Ling returned to stand beside him as the cymbals faded.

'You did know about Dao, didn't you?' she said.

'We…we don't speak of such things so openly,' he stammered.

But he'd always suspected. He supposed Minister Cao had known as well. Dao had lived her entire life keeping a secret that everyone had known, but no one openly accepted. His dear Little Sister.

'Now that your sister will be auspiciously wed, you should think of starting a family of your own,' Yan Ling suggested innocently.

'Perhaps I should consult a matchmaker.'

She snorted. 'If you see fit.'

He took her hand. Her fingers were cool and calming beneath the summer sun. 'I need a woman, you know. And only one woman will do.'

They looked at one another for a long, contented moment before heading back into the house together.

The neighbourhood gossips chirped louder than the cicadas that summer and indeed they had much to talk about. Chang Wei Long, the favoured son of a government official, fell in love with a humble servant girl. By the end of the summer, news of the wedding spread to every teahouse and tavern.

It was said that Fei Long wore a red scarf on the day of the wedding, much like the red scarf worn by a mysterious bowman in an illicit archery tournament a month earlier. He also wore a pair of felt shoes embroidered with tigers. As malnourished as said tigers were supposed to be, it was rumoured that Fei Long wore them proudly wherever he went. His new wife set about completing a new pair to exonerate herself.

For all her faults, the tea girl Yan Ling, now Chang Tai-tai or Madame Chang, was praised as the embodiment of industriousness and determination; truly a carp who had jumped through the dragon's gate.

The match must have been an auspicious one for the Chang family. A month after the wedding, the Emperor invited Fei Long to the palace at the north end of the city. Several targets were set up and Fei Long instructed the crown prince himself. An appointment as archery master of the city guard quickly followed.

Many, many months later, a letter came from Khitan. It was the last one before the winter season made the grasslands difficult to pass. The khagan noted the grace, charm and unnaturally sharp tongue that their Tang princess possessed.

It might be quite a while before the Khitans asked for another princess.

* * * * *

HISTORICAL

Where Love is Timeless™

HARLEQUIN® HISTORICAL

COMING NEXT MONTH
AVAILABLE JUNE 19, 2012

RENEGADE MOST WANTED
Carol Arens
(Western)

AN ESCAPADE AND AN ENGAGEMENT
Annie Burrows
(Regency)

THE LAIRD'S FORBIDDEN LADY
Ann Lethbridge
(Regency)

TEMPTED BY THE HIGHLAND WARRIOR
The MacKinloch Clan
Michelle Willingham
(Medieval)

REQUEST YOUR FREE BOOKS!

 HARLEQUIN® HISTORICAL:
Where love is timeless

2 FREE NOVELS PLUS 2 **FREE GIFTS!**

YES! Please send me 2 FREE Harlequin® Historical novels and my 2 FREE gifts (gifts are worth about $10). After receiving them, if I don't wish to receive any more books, I can return the shipping statement marked "cancel." If I don't cancel, I will receive 6 brand-new novels every month and be billed just $5.19 per book in the U.S. or $5.74 per book in Canada. That's a savings of at least 17% off the cover price! It's quite a bargain! Shipping and handling is just 50¢ per book in the U.S. and 75¢ per book in Canada.* I understand that accepting the 2 free books and gifts places me under no obligation to buy anything. I can always return a shipment and cancel at any time. Even if I never buy another book, the two free books and gifts are mine to keep forever.

246/349 HDN FEQQ

Name	(PLEASE PRINT)	
Address		Apt. #
City	State/Prov.	Zip/Postal Code

Signature (if under 18, a parent or guardian must sign)

Mail to the Reader Service:
IN U.S.A.: P.O. Box 1867, Buffalo, NY 14240-1867
IN CANADA: P.O. Box 609, Fort Erie, Ontario L2A 5X3

Not valid for current subscribers to Harlequin Historical books.

Want to try two free books from another line?
Call 1-800-873-8635 or visit www.ReaderService.com.

* Terms and prices subject to change without notice. Prices do not include applicable taxes. Sales tax applicable in N.Y. Canadian residents will be charged applicable taxes. Offer not valid in Quebec. This offer is limited to one order per household. All orders subject to credit approval. Credit or debit balances in a customer's account(s) may be offset by any other outstanding balance owed by or to the customer. Please allow 4 to 6 weeks for delivery. Offer available while quantities last.

Your Privacy—The Reader Service is committed to protecting your privacy. Our Privacy Policy is available online at www.ReaderService.com or upon request from the Reader Service.

We make a portion of our mailing list available to reputable third parties that offer products we believe may interest you. If you prefer that we not exchange your name with third parties, or if you wish to clarify or modify your communication preferences, please visit us at www.ReaderService.com/consumerchoice or write to us at Reader Service Preference Service, P.O. Box 9062, Buffalo, NY 14269. Include your complete name and address.

HHI1B

*Carol Arens, Harlequin® Historical's newest
Western author, brings you an exciting tale of a most
improper convenient marriage! Set against the backdrop
of the Wild West, with an utterly unforgettable rebel
cowboy, it's certainly not to be missed!*

Here's a sneak peek of
RENEGADE MOST WANTED

Emma flashed Matt Suede what she hoped was a seductive smile. She leaned into his hug and became distracted by the playful dusting of freckles frolicking over his nose and across his cheeks.

Matt bent his head, whispering in for a kiss.

Emma pressed two fingers to his lips, preventing what promised to be a fascinating experience.

"Matt, honey, you did promise me a proper wedding. I don't think we should keep the preacher waiting."

Matt's arm stiffened, his fingers cramped about her middle. There was a very good chance that he had quit breathing.

The marshal let out a deep-bellied laugh that startled poor Pearl and made her whiney. "Looks like you been caught after all, Suede."

"If you ain't The Ghost, you can't deny being the groom," someone snickered.

"Since you don't see a spook standing here, I believe you're looking at the groom." Matt Suede's voice croaked on the word *groom*.

"The problem is, I don't recall you having a steady girl, Suede," the marshal said. "Just to be sure you and the lady here aren't in cahoots, I think the boys and I will just go along to witness those holy vows."

HHEXP0712

A man slapped his thigh and let out a roaring hoot. "Singing Trigger Suede goes through with this marriage and we'll know he's telling the truth."

"You've got the wrong bank robber, boys. The next hour will see me hitched and tied."

Matt bent his mouth close to her ear. His breath warmed her cheek.

"You sure you want to do this, ma'am?" he whispered. The men standing nearby wouldn't hear him, since they stood close to the barn door, and the traffic traveling down Front Street drowned his words to anyone but her. "I'm better than that old drunk, but only a little."

Find out what happens next
in RENEGADE MOST WANTED in July
from Harlequin® Historical and look out for future books
by the evocative Carol Arens!

Love Inspired HISTORICAL

celebrating
15
YEARS

DOROTHY CLARK

brings you another story from

PINEWOOD
WEDDINGS

When Willa Wright's fiancé abandoned her three days
before the wedding, he ended all her hopes for romance.
Now she dedicates herself to teaching Pinewood's children,
including the new pastor's young wards. If she didn't know
better, Reverend Calvert's kindness could almost fool Willa
into caring again. Almost.

Wooing the Schoolmarm

Available July wherever books are sold.

www.LoveInspiredBooks.com

LIH82923

LP616